Risky Business

Hearts on Display

Book Three

Kimberly Keagan

HEARTS ON DISPLAY

Charles Walraven
(b. 1833)
Co-Founder, Denwall
Department Stores
m. **Laura Shaw**
(b. 1840)

.... **Robert "Bert"** (b. 1865)
Unexpected, Hearts on Display Book 2

.... **William "Will"** (b. 1867)
Perfect, Hearts on Display Book 1

.... **Edward "Ned"** (b. 1876)

.... **Caroline "Caro"** (b. 1879)

James Dennison
(b. 1843)
Co-Founder, Denwall
Department Stores
m. Sarah Fenwicke
(b. 1843 d. 1878)
m. **Myra Kuntz**
(b. 1845)

.... **Max** (b. 1867)

.... **Helena "Lena"** (b. 1869)

.... **Louise "Lou"** (b. 1871)

.... **Beatrice "Tris"** (b. 1876)

.... **Alexandra "Alix"** (b. 1878)

ONE

February 12, 1897
Philadelphia, Pennsylvania

One sister married, two to go.

Helena Dennison prayed they wouldn't be in any great hurry.

She sipped her coffee, hoping to coax life into her sleep-deprived body. Louise's wedding had gone off without a hitch, despite the threat of snow. God willing, married life for Lou—Papa insisted on nicknames for all his daughters—would be as blessed as the ceremony had been.

Now, Lou and Stuart were off on their honeymoon, but the rest of the family—Papa, Myra, Max, Beatrice, and Alexandra—were here, all recovering from a celebration that had lasted well past three in the morning.

Pale gold tinged the linen tablecloth and gleamed off the silver serving pieces as winter sunlight filtered through lace curtains. Papa rustled the newspaper, while their stepmother chirped on about the latest society gossip, and Tris reached for the jam.

Lena's fingers itched to snap a photograph, but, alas, her Kodak No. 2 was up in her bedroom. Besides, no one would appreciate her taking pictures of them after a late night of revelry.

Papa folded the paper and smiled at his wife of four years.

Myra, who appeared the most well-rested of the group and lovely in a mauve morning gown, dabbed at her lips with a napkin and returned the smile.

"One daughter married, Myra, my dear," Papa said. "Three to go."

Great minds thought alike—except Lena firmly excluded herself from any such list. She wanted to see all of her siblings married, or at least all her sisters, before she ever thought of settling down herself. And by the time that happened, she'd be very long in the tooth. Truth be told, there was something to be said for being independent. Or so she'd heard.

Lena smiled indulgently at Papa as he settled back in his chair at the head of the long cherry wood table. James Dennison, co-founder of Denwall Department Stores, claimed he relished the idea of a quiet house and fewer place settings, but Lena wasn't fooled. For all his talk, she knew Papa hated the idea of any of his children leaving the nest.

Lena sighed and gently replaced her cup on its saucer. It was sad, indeed, not to have Lou at the breakfast table. She was the quietest of the five Dennison offspring, yet her absence left an indelible mark on the room.

At least Max had joined them this morning, though he had his own house in town. He'd fallen asleep on the parlor settee after all the guests had departed. No one had the heart to wake him and insist he go home.

He hadn't slept well, if his wide yawn was any indication.

Alix, the youngest of the Dennisons, sighed dramatically, as if she were auditioning for the stage. "Lou looked so beautiful. Wasn't the wedding romantic?"

When Max groaned, Lena smoothed the napkin on her lap and turned to her sister to smooth what was sure to be ruffled feathers. On the cusp of nineteen, Alix could be offended quite easily. "It was *very* romantic. The church looked lovely, and the flowers were perfect."

Alix pressed a hand to her heart, still deep in her reverie. "The way Stuart looked at her during the vows. Like she was the only woman in the world."

"I *never* want to get married," Tris grumbled. "Too confining and restrictive. Who wants to be ruled by a man?" The thinker in the family, she had the distinction of being the first of the Dennison daughters to attend college.

Across the table, Max snorted into his coffee. "Yeah, well, I hope Lou knows what she's doing. That guy's a little too perfect, if you ask me."

"Max, you're so mean," Alix pouted. "Why don't you like Stuart?"

"He just rubs me the wrong way," Max said. "Too smooth-talking. And he wears too much pomade."

Alix huffed. "Lena, tell him to stop. He's being awful."

Lena patted her sister's hand and turned to Max with the warning look she'd perfected years ago as the oldest daughter and self-imposed mother-figure after Mama died. "Lou made her choice. And I think Stuart truly cares for her."

At least she hoped that was the case. Prayed it was—often and with great sincerity. She'd been the first to encourage Lou to accept Stuart Newbury's attentions. And it had all seemed so promising, from his manners and his compliments to the way he looked at her.

But now Lena couldn't help remembering all the little things Max had pointed out. How Stuart never really answered questions about his business ventures. How he always managed to flatter the right person at the right time.

Still, Lou had glowed like a lighthouse around him, and Lena believed theirs to be a strong love match.

At the far end of the table, their stepmother frowned. "Stuart is well connected," she said with a nod as if that statement said it all. "And his family is very respectable. That kind of marriage strengthens us socially."

Max rolled his eyes. "We own one of the largest chains of department stores in the country. How much stronger do we need to be?"

"Max," Papa warned gently.

"He's not wrong," Lena murmured.

Papa gave Myra's hand a pat, then reached for his coffee. "It never hurts to have allies in the right circles. Still, I think we're doing all right."

"Speaking of society." Alix tapped a finger on the society page of *The Philadelphia Inquirer*, which lay folded beside her plate. "Did you see this? Mary Langford is engaged to a duke. A real English one!"

"A duke?" Myra's eyes sparkled. "James, can you imagine? One of our girls marrying into the British aristocracy?"

Lena bit the inside of her cheek to avoid laughing. Myra could always be counted on to spin breakfast conversation into a full-blown social strategy. She'd been giddy over the rash of British American alliances the past few months.

"There are so many young men in England with titles and no money," Myra said in a dreamy tone. "They'd be grateful for a match with a good American family. It's practically our duty to offer them options."

Max muttered something under his breath, then said, "Next thing we know, you'll be planning Alix's debut in London."

"I'm not planning anything," Myra said. "But it doesn't hurt to be prepared."

Once upon a time, Lena might have shared her stepmother's fascination with fairy tale romances and grand European matches —when she was very young and had imagined her own Prince Charming riding up on his white steed and carrying her away.

She wasn't so young anymore, and those were girlish fancies. Dreams, she reminded herself, needed to be shelved. She had younger sisters to watch over and guide, as she promised Mama she would.

"You didn't sleep well." Her father's voice cut into her thoughts.

Lena raised her eyes to find Papa's narrowed gaze on her. "I did. Better than I have all week. I was a little anxious about the wedding, that's all."

"There was no reason to be. Everything went off beautifully."

Baxter, their longtime butler, returned to the room with a fresh pot of coffee, which he placed on the sideboard. "Is there anything else you need?" he asked the room in general.

Papa wiped his mouth with his napkin. "Would you bring in yesterday's mail? I don't believe I ever looked at it."

A few minutes later, Baxter returned with a silver tray stacked with envelopes. He placed it neatly beside Papa, then quietly left the room.

Papa flipped through the letters slowly. About halfway through, he stopped. His brow furrowed, and he pulled a silver letter opener from the tray. The room fell quiet as he slit the envelope and unfolded the single sheet of stationery.

He read silently and rubbed the back of his neck.

"James?" Myra prompted. "What is it?"

Papa didn't respond at first. Instead, he passed the envelope to Myra, his expression unreadable.

Myra scanned the return address. "Countess of Akethorpe? Who—" Her voice cracked. "Who is that?"

Max leaned forward. "We're getting mail from a countess?"

Lena blinked at her father.

Papa stood and went to the door to close it. Odd, that. They always left the dining room door open during breakfast. Instead of returning to his chair, he walked to the window and stared out at the street.

No one spoke. Only the faint ticking of the clock on the mantel broke the silence.

Finally, without turning, Papa said, "The Countess of Akethorpe was your mother's mother."

Myra gasped, and Max sat back as if struck.

Lena felt her breath catch. She set down her spoon, her appetite evaporating. "I thought Mama's family were distant cousins of some baron with an estate in Suffolk. And that her parents passed away before she ever came to America."

"We all did," Max said, glaring at Papa. "Was that a lie?"

Papa turned away from the window, sorrow in his eyes. "If you'll remember, your mother rarely spoke of her family. You were all so young. Too young to understand. She let you assume she had no family left in England."

"So, who was she, then?" Tris asked.

Alix grabbed Lena's hand and stared at Papa.

Papa returned to the table and laid a hand on Myra's shoulder. "Your mother was the daughter of the Earl of Akethorpe. Sarah was their only child from his second marriage. Her older half-brother—your uncle—is now the current earl."

Alix clapped both hands over her mouth. "We have a real live uncle who's a *peer*?"

"And a grandmother?" Lena's voice came out small. "She's alive?"

Papa nodded. "The dowager countess. This letter is from her."

Max folded his arms and glared at Papa. "Why now? Why reach out after all these years? Or have you been in touch with her all this time?"

"No, I've never had contact with the family. They disowned your mother for marrying an American—particularly one in trade. She wrote them now and again in the early years. I wrote when she passed, and never received a response. But now ..." He tapped the letter. "She writes that she regrets the estrangement. She says her husband—the earl—refused to acknowledge the marriage and forbade her from making contact. But now that he's gone ..."

"She wants to meet us," Lena whispered, and her soft heart warred with her pragmatic mind.

"She says life is short. That she wants to know her grandchildren before it's too late." Papa paused, then looked directly at Lena. "I don't know if this is a genuine change of heart or something else. But it's up to you children. I won't force a reunion."

"I want to go," Alix said, bouncing in her chair. "This is like something out of a novel. What would I even be called? Lady Alexandra?"

Myra's eyes gleamed. "It would depend on the titles held by the earl. You're likely 'the Honorable,' but we should consult Debrett's." She stood suddenly. "We'll need to pack! And we must stop in Paris first, of course. I know just the dressmaker—"

"This feels ... strange." Lena leaned her elbows on the table and folded her hands." I've spent my entire life thinking Mama had no family." She slowly shook her head. "Why would the countess wait so long?"

"She says she never stopped thinking of her daughter," Papa said gently. "But she honored her husband's wishes. It may be guilt that has her contacting us now. Or loneliness. Or both."

Max scratched his chin. "I don't like it. It smells fishy."

"You say that about everything," Alix huffed.

"I'm cautious."

Papa lifted his lips in a ghost of a smile. "There's nothing wrong with being cautious. Just make sure you don't miss the Lord's plan for you by being overly so."

Lena let the voices swirl around her. England. A countess for a grandmother. A dead earl who'd never acknowledged them. And a mother who had carried all of this in silence.

She pushed back her chair and stood. "I need air."

"Lena ..." Papa rose partway.

"I'm all right," she said quickly. "Truly. I just need to think."

Alix rose too. "I'll come—"

"No." Lena smiled, softening the word. "You stay. Enjoy your waffles. This might be the last quiet breakfast we have for a while."

Myra looked positively delighted at the prospect.

As Lena grabbed her coat and stepped out into the cool morning air, she drew in a long breath and let it out slowly.

Lou had just walked down the aisle.

Prince Charming, from what she could tell, didn't exist.

And now, the ghost of her mother's past was rewriting everything Lena thought she knew about her family.

She tucked a loose strand of hair behind her ear and looked up at the wide blue Philadelphia sky.

Apparently, this spring was going to be full of surprises.

Two

April 13, 1897
La Turbie, France

Bronley Jeffers adjusted his goggles and tightened his grip on the steering wheel as the motorcar crested another ridge along the Grand Corniche. The sea glittered to his left, blue and bold and entirely too far below. To his right, the rocky hillside clawed upward, flanked by vines and scrubby trees.

"Ridiculous," he muttered—not for the first time that morning.

Behind him, the sharp whine of a rival's engine echoed like a mosquito with a grudge. Bron pressed his foot to the accelerator. The motor growled, then roared, responding with all the enthusiasm of a thoroughbred being challenged.

Thirty kilometers remained in the final leg of an eight-hour race ending in La Turbie. Five other cars were still ahead. He'd passed more than a dozen competitors since dawn, overtaking them in clouds of dust and cheers. But now, with only this winding, cliffside stretch remaining, he wasn't sure whether he—or the car—had enough left.

The April sky sagged with pale clouds, the kind that threatened rain without ever delivering. Spectators had lined the road through Nice, and even more had swarmed the route near Monte Carlo, cheering like madmen for every passing vehicle. They raced past white houses with red geraniums pouring out of window boxes, and churches with steeples so high they seemed to touch the clouds.

One of his competitors said that he always started the first day of a race in church. Regardless of what town he was in.

Bron didn't have such a ritual. Didn't pray before races. He trusted gears and timing, not Providence. Faith, in his experience, had little to do with finish lines. It took skill, courage, and a good team of mechanics to reach the winner's circle. Luckily, he had all three.

He rounded the corner on a stretch of road with a hairpin turn and he slowed. Unfortunately, not all motorists were as cautious.

Just outside the Café de Paris, a driver lost control and plowed into one of the building's iron pillars. Before the dust settled, Bron slammed on his brakes and leaped from the car to offer aid. Fortunately, no one was hurt—just some broken chairs, a racer's dented pride, and a very loud Frenchwoman who shouted insults Bron didn't need translated, her voice rising above the acrid smell of dust and petrol.

Stopping had cost Bron valuable time.

It would likely cost him the race.

He eased the car into another sharp turn, the tires skimming the cobbled edge, and glimpsed La Turbie ahead—its ancient ruins rising like sentinels over the sea. The village perched on the mountain's spine, a crown of stone overlooking the Mediterranean.

Cheers erupted as he entered the heart of town. Pressed close to the finish line, people waved hats and flags, calling out the names of the most popular drivers. The wave of sound struck him like a wall when he passed under the checkered banner. No victory, perhaps—but not defeat either.

Bron pulled his 8HP—the Jeffers Motorworks' newest racing car prototype—beside a dusty De Dion-Bouton and peeled off his goggles. His hair was damp with sweat, his gloves streaked with grease. Despite the ache in his spine, he grinned.

A Frenchman leaned over and slapped his shoulder. "Better luck next time, Monsieur Jeffers!"

"Next time I won't stop for impromptu dining room demolition."

Another hand clapped his back. "Tough blow, my friend."

Bron turned—and grinned wider. "I thought for certain you'd be trapped at the roulette tables in Monte Carlo."

Harry Tisdale—Lord Henry Tisdale to the stuffy—impeccably dressed despite the dust in the air, gave a dramatic sigh and clutched his chest. "You wound me. I came all this way to see you triumph gloriously, and instead, you perform a public service by saving diners from destruction. Nobler than winning, perhaps. Less impressive to the betting crowd." Harry slung an arm over Bron's shoulders. "Come back to Monte Carlo. Let's get you cleaned up before someone mistakes you for a chimney sweep. I'll even buy you lunch. Consider it a consolation prize."

Bron winced as he stretched. "Only if you let me order something extravagant. With cream sauce. Training for this blasted race meant forgoing guilty pleasures for two months."

"Done."

They drove to the Hotel de Paris in companionable silence, this drive much slower than the one he'd just finished. The hotel gleamed like a sugar palace—cream-colored stone, balconies laced with iron, and windows catching every glint of late afternoon sun.

Inside, Bron shed his dusty coat and handed it to a bellhop. They followed the maître d' to a table by a window. Soon, a waiter brought them a basket of warm bread and filled their glasses with mineral water

"So," Harry said, lounging in a velvet chair opposite Bron, "how bad was it?"

Bron rubbed the back of his neck. "Accidents. Far too many. One man tried to lighten the car's weight by running ahead of it uphill. It knocked him flat and rolled right over both legs."

Harry coughed into his napkin. "Sorry. That's terrible. But also—why would anyone—never mind."

"Another collided with a motorcycle on the first day. And an elderly woman in Aubagne was struck."

Harry's smile faded. "That's no laughing matter."

"No," Bron agreed. "The public already thinks we're mad. That didn't help." He swirled his glass. "And yet they still show up. Hundreds of them."

"You're the future, Bron."

Bron gave a crooked smile. "Funny. My father imagines my future of robes and a barrister's bench in Lincoln's Inn, not grease and crankshafts."

Harry chuckled. "Ah, yes. The Honorable Auberon Jeffers —eternally disappointed that his only son became a lecturer and tinkerer."

"I prefer *mechanical innovator*, but yes. And I plan to return to university at the end of the summer. It's still law, just not in the courts."

"So, you've decided, then?" Harry looked Bron straight in the eye, not allowing him to deflect.

"Yes, I need to start behaving like a responsible adult and pick a lane to ride in."

"And yet here you are."

Bron sighed. "Driving gets in the blood." He'd raced gigs and trotting carts in his university days—light, two-wheeled contraptions that he'd worked on to make them fast enough to win almost every contest he entered. But those carriages were nothing compared to the horseless vehicles he first encountered at a French motor race the summer of '94. That experience lit something fierce in him. Then the Paris automotive exhibition later that year introduced him to a British engineer with the same wild glint in his eye, and together they'd cobbled Jeffers & Keating Motorworks into existence.

"Driving may get in your blood," Harry said, "but you also are moving around like you've just been through a boxing match and lost.

"The new crankshaft design was supposed to reduce vibration. And the steering kickback could dislocate a shoulder." Bron rolled his sore upper arm.

"I hope you're exaggerating."

"Only slightly."

Harry leaned back and surveyed him. "You always did like machines, maybe even more than people."

"I love people. I understand machines better. They're more predictable." Bron leaned forward, his heart picking up speed at the thought of his new car and the next race. "It wasn't just about winning. This race was a test. We're preparing for orders from Italy and Belgium. If this model doesn't perform under stress ..." He trailed off.

"Then you'll fix it. You always do." Harry fiddled with the stem of his glass. "Have you received any more offers to buy your company out? Although, frankly, they seem more like threats to me."

"One. That German group isn't likely to give up anytime soon. They know we have a superior vehicle and want to get their hands on it." Over his dead body would Bron let someone buy his business. And with Keating having left the partnership to work on something that gave him a steady income, it was now just Bron's company. It wasn't big enough to leave law behind—not yet—but now, with orders coming in, a new full-time engineer with viable designs, and two new models to test, the future no longer felt quite so theoretical.

Harry narrowed his eyes, causing Bron to squirm. "My concern is that if you don't give in willingly, they'll find other ways to force you into retirement."

Bron chuckled at his friend's concern. "You worry too much."

They lingered a while longer, discussing the race, old classmates, and the lack of good tea on the Continent. Bron had just begun to relax when a man in hotel livery approached.

"Monsieur Jeffers?"

"Yes?"

The man held out a telegram. "This arrived from London."

Bron took the folded paper, cracked the seal, and felt the world narrow to a single line of ink.

Harry sat up straighter. "What is it?"

"It's from the Countess of Akethorpe. My aunt—Lady Langston—she's very ill. Lady Akethorpe thinks I should return home." Eleanor Parr was the dearest, most important person in Bron's life. She'd taken the place of her sister—the mother Bron lost as a teenager—and given him the nurturing love every boy needed. He'd be lost without her.

Harry let out a breath. "Then we'll get you to London."

Bron looked back down at the telegram. The cheers, the dust, the coastline—they all felt very far away.

THREE

⁑

Calais, France
April 15, 1897

The wind off the narrow arm of the Atlantic Ocean that separated England and France whipped the ribbons of Lena's hat as she shifted her small travel case from one hand to the other. She wouldn't dare let it out of her sight while they stood on the crowded deck of the packet steamer bound for Dover. Every bump of a trunk or shout from a porter set her on edge.

The case, which held her Bible, camera, and journal, had been her constant companion for nearly two weeks. Across the ocean from Philadelphia to Le Havre, then by train through the green heart of France all because Myra insisted they go directly to Paris before arriving in London. The *best* modistes were Parisians, she'd said, and if the Dennisons wanted to put their best foot forward in London, they needed gowns from Paris.

Although Lena would never admit it out loud, it had been

fun indulging her stepmother's delight in the Parisian shops, though the entire affair had been dizzying.

"If neither of you comes home with a titled fiancé in tow, I shall never forgive myself," Myra had declared to Lena and Alix.

Lena had wished they could head straight to London and get this trip to meet their long-lost relative over with. A month was all they needed, if that, to meet this grandmother who'd not bothered to contact them before now. The quicker they were back in Philadelphia, the better. The distinct feeling that not all was right in Lou's very new marriage sat heavy on her heart.

Now, standing in the chill wind of Calais with her fingers cramped around the handle of that well-traveled case, she couldn't help thinking how strange it was to be between the world she knew and the one waiting across the water.

"Where's Max? The steamer leaves in less than an hour." Myra tapped her foot and turned to Lena as if she were Max's personal secretary.

The oldest Dennison offspring could look after himself. And besides, if Lena tried to manage him like she did her sisters, he'd get annoyed with her.

Just the same, she tried to assure Myra that all would be fine. "I'm sure he'll be arriving any minute. If he doesn't get here before we leave, he'll just have to catch the next ferry."

"I don't know why he insisted on traipsing off to Monte Carlo." Myra huffed.

"Because he didn't find any enjoyment in traipsing around Paris with us."

Myra's eyes widened as a porter threw a trunk onto a luggage cart. "Be careful with those trunks, young man. There are some expensive gowns in there." She placed a palm on her cheek. "I wish your father were here. Then he could take care of everything."

Lena slipped her arm through her stepmother's. "We're doing fine. Everything's handled. Why don't you go lie down?"

Truth be told, Papa had been reluctant to accompany the family to England to meet his first wife's family. He'd left it up to each to decide whether they would take up their grandmother's invitation but thought his presence would only hinder the bonds that might form between grandmother and grandchildren. Lena wished she could have stayed behind too, but she wanted to keep an eye on Alix who'd begged to go.

Tris had classes to finish, but they'd be back in time for her graduation in June. Myra, however, would not be left behind with Papa and Tris. There was no way she would miss the opportunity to be the guest of a bona fide countess.

Max said he'd join them for a laugh, yet Lena doubted he'd want to stay as long as Myra and Alix wanted to.

Two months. She could handle two months in England, but that was all.

"Maybe I'll go to our stateroom and write Deirdre about our visit with the most famous modiste in Paris. She'll be green with envy." Myra's eyes lit up, probably imagining her friend would spread the news far and wide. She turned and made her way toward the stairs, leaving Lena and Alix on the promenade deck to wait for Max.

Lena's lips twitched at Myra's enthusiasm. Once the family's connection to nobility had been discovered, she'd become one of the most popular society women in Philadelphia and promised to write her friends regularly about her experiences.

Lena leaned over the railing and searched for her brother. Max could be hard to nail down, but she didn't think he'd be so irresponsible that he'd miss the ship.

"There he is." Alix waved, and Lena shifted her gaze to see their brother making his way up the gangplank with a straggling group of passengers. The steamer's whistle blew, and many passengers went below deck, either to staterooms, the ladies' cabin, or the gentlemen's smoking room.

"Let's hope this crossing is smooth," Max said when he arrived at Lena's side. "The last time I made this trip, the steamer pitched and rolled the entire voyage."

Lena slipped an arm around Alix, who was prone to seasickness. "Do you think you should go below deck to our stateroom? You might be better off."

Alix slipped out of Lena's hold and gave her a pleading smile. "I don't really want to go to the room. I'll be fine."

"All right, then, if you're sure." Lena turned to ask Max if he'd like to go to the dining room for something to drink. But he was no longer next to her. "Where did Max go?" Frustrated that he'd managed to disappear already, Lena placed her hands on her hips.

"Oh, he stopped back there to join a game of deck quoits with a group of men." Alix slipped her arm through Lena's. "Never mind him, let's go wave to people as the boat leaves port. We can pretend we're royalty." Alix giggled.

Since many people had left the deck, they quickly found a good spot along the railing.

Alix waved to a little boy who then took off his hat and waved back. "How long do you think it will take us to get to Grandmother's house once we arrive in Dover?" Already, she'd taken to calling the woman "Grandmother" even though they'd never met her.

Lena wasn't so sure she'd ever be able to call her something so familiar and warm. The idea that someone had rejected her lovely mother weighed heavily on her heart.

"We'll take the train into London. According to the countess's last letter, her carriage will pick us up at Charing Cross Station. From there to Berkeley Square is about thirty minutes," Lena looked at the watch pinned to her bodice, "which means we'll be there by five."

"I wonder what she'll be like. Will she look like Mama, do you think?"

Mama had died giving birth to Alix. The only reference she had was the portraits Papa had commissioned of his beautiful wife.

"No one is as lovely as Mama was," Lena said. She was nine, Lou seven, and Max eleven when their mother passed away. And little Tris only two years old. She had no recollection of Mama either. Lena counted herself blessed that she'd been able to spend nine wonderful years with their mother.

"Oh, Lena, it's all so thrilling, and a little frightening! We'll have so much to do before we're launched into the London season."

Lena would rather be launched over the ship's railing, but she'd grin and bear the upcoming weeks in London. She hoped that Alix and Myra would hate it so much that they'd decide to return to Philadelphia as quickly as possible. She didn't want to stay in England any longer than was necessary.

They made their way along the ship's crowded deck. Up ahead, a throng of passengers gathered, blocking their way.

"I wonder what's going on," Alix said.

"I don't know. Let's go back the other way."

Alix tugged Lena's arm. "I think it must be someone important. I've heard you can encounter all kinds of famous people crossing the Channel."

Lena gave in to her sister's enthusiasm and allowed herself to be towed toward the crowd.

"Congratulations!" called a gregarious young fellow, giving a taller gentleman a hearty slap on the back. "I hear your motorcar nearly touched thirty miles an hour."

"Yes, we made good time on the wet roads, but another man won the race, and that's all that counts," the tall man replied.

"Well, had it not been for Michelin, you would have won."

Lena tried to edge past the growing knot of people, tugging Alix gently by the arm. The hum of laughter swelled around them as someone made a convoluted joke about racing that Lena didn't bother to unravel. Someone else blocked her way, and she gave him a gentle nudge so she and Alix could pass. Too late, she realized it was the man at the center of the attention.

His dark gaze caught hers—steady, curious, far too direct—and she felt her breath hitch before she could stop it.

"Pardon me," she murmured, attempting to step aside. But the man shifted instinctively in the same direction, as if heaven itself had conspired to keep them from passing cleanly by.

A doe-eyed young woman stuck a fountain pen and paper in front of the celebrity for his autograph, and he turned his gaze away from Lena.

Thank you, Lord, for small favors.

Several other people searched their pockets and reticules for scraps of paper to thrust at him.

Lena tried again to move through the crowd.

"Did you want my autograph, too?" The celebrity asked her with a smile, probably used often to make ladies' hearts flutter.

Lena's eyes widened. "*Your* autograph?" She laughed and then covered her mouth with a gloved hand. "No, I don't think so."

"You don't want his autograph? Are you serious?" exclaimed the doe-eyed woman, still in earshot.

"I don't even know who he is."

"Why, *he's* the Merry Barrister."

Lena laughed again, only this time she didn't bother to cover her wide grin. "Is he indeed?" She raised her eyebrows.

The tall man had the sense to look embarrassed and

shrugged his broad shoulders. When he grinned, his teeth looked very white in his tanned face.

"Lena, don't be so rude." Alix tugged at her arm. "I'm so sorry, Mr. Jeffers. My sister doesn't read the society columns." She turned her green eyes on Lena. "He's Bronley Jeffers. The motorcar driver. I read about his race in *The Times*."

"Well, then, may I give *you* my autograph?" The racer's gaze slid to Alix.

"Oh, yes, please!" Alix searched in vain for a scrap of paper.

Lena sighed and opened her travelling case. She tore a blank page from her journal and handed it to Alix, who then handed it to Mr. Jeffers.

He tilted his head, a quirk of a smile on his lips, and a fountain pen at the ready.

Dazzled, Alix could only stare back, wide-eyed.

Lena cleared her throat. "It's Alix Dennison. A-L-I-X."

He smiled a genuine smile—Lena was certain the others had been fake—and her traitorous stomach fluttered. "After the Princess of Wales?" he asked.

Alix blinked. "Why, yes! Most Americans don't know that."

"Well, Miss Dennison, I'm not American."

Was that a slight? For a man who raced around in a tin can, he was quite the snob.

Lena straightened her shoulders. "Good day to you, Mr. Jeffers."

"Good day, Mr. Jeffers," Alix called over her shoulder as Lena pulled her farther away.

"What an irritating showoff," Lena muttered as she and Alix strode the steamship's deck.

"He seemed perfectly nice to me." Alix squeezed Lena's arm and giggled. "Besides, he's so handsome. Did you get a look at those eyes?"

In school, Alix hadn't shown much interest in boys, unlike most of her friends. For a time, Lena even thought she might have a *tendre* for Ned Walraven, the youngest son of their father's partner and longtime friend. But Ned went off to college, and Alix no longer saw him as often as when they'd grown up in each other's pockets.

Then she'd had her coming out in Philadelphia this past winter, and her reluctance to form an attachment seemed to vanish. Now she grew starry-eyed over any handsome young man who gifted her a smile. Lena wanted to throw up her hands. There was already enough to worry about with the upcoming meeting with the Countess of Akethorpe.

Clouds were forming to the north, and the waters took on a sullen cast, their gentle chop turning to an uneasy roll. A sharp wind swept down the deck, whipping at Lena's skirt and sending a chill straight through her traveling coat.

"Let's go find some deck chairs and order some tea," she said to Alix.

"You're such a fuddy-duddy, Lena."

Someone tapped her shoulder from behind, and Lena turned. "There you are! We've been looking for you."

Max shot her a smile meant to disarm. Women had often told her that his dimples caused them to swoon. Lena couldn't see what the fuss was about.

"I was standing not three feet from you. Back there." Max tilted his head toward the crowd that still surrounded Bronley Jeffers. "So, you got yourselves some autographs from the Merry Barrister?"

"Alix got an autograph, not me," Lena said. She glanced sideways at her brother. "How do you know that Jeffers character?"

"I saw him race in Monte Carlo."

Lena groaned. "Of course you did." She shook her head and led them to a trio of unoccupied deck chairs. Once they'd all settled in, Lena pulled out her pen and journal. Not a diary, precisely, as she didn't write her dreams or emotions on the page like many other women did. She believed in pragmatism and thought of the notes as more of a logbook, keeping track of events.

After a short delay, the steamer was on its way, and she settled in for a pleasant journey.

The heavens, however, had other plans. A mere five minutes out from the harbor, the tossing began. The wind howled, and hats took flight. Empty chairs slid along the deck. Some travelers braved the battle above, but soon moans emanated from people in the throes of seasickness. One woman asked God to either calm the waters or let her die.

Her prayers went unanswered.

Lena glanced at Alix and Max in the chairs next to her. Both of her siblings appeared to be handling the rolling of the ship admirably. Good for them. As for her, she felt sick to her stomach.

The six-day journey from New York to Le Havre had been child's play compared to this Channel crossing. The steamer continued to pitch and roll the entire voyage. Although the trip lasted just over sixty minutes, the crossing felt like an eternity. When they finally docked, Lena wanted to shout for joy, but couldn't summon the energy.

A train bound for London sat at the Dover station, awaiting the steamer passengers from Calais. Porters stored the Dennison family's trunks, and Lena took a seat by a window and pushed aside the curtain. Men furiously worked to clear the tracks where storm water had breached the seafront, leaving piles of debris in its wake.

Lena prayed it wasn't a sign of things to come.

Four

"That was the worst crossing I've ever had the misfortune of experiencing," Harry grumbled as he and Bron planted their feet on terra firma.

Bron agreed. Though he had a cast-iron stomach, he felt a tad queasy.

Despite the rocky voyage, the young group of racing enthusiasts he'd met on board surrounded him as he marched to the train waiting to take many of the steamer's passengers on to London. "I clocked you at thirty-five miles an hour," one admirer claimed.

Bron's eyebrows rose at the number. A woman with a beguiling smile touched his arm. "You're amazing. I would be terrified to move at such speeds."

Despite the adoration, Bron didn't like losing.

"It amazes me how much attention you receive," Harry mused at his side. "Just for driving around in some contraption that doesn't have the sense to be pulled by a horse."

"Maybe it's my good looks, friend." Bron laughed.

"I guess that doesn't hurt."

"When's your next race?" a young man to his left asked.

"There aren't any races scheduled." Besides, Bron needed to get back to the university. The dean of the law school wouldn't appreciate his jurisprudence lecturer taking additional weeks off. "We'll see you in a few months, I imagine," Bron said to the group at large, effectively dismissing them.

Bron followed Harry toward the back end of the train bound for London. A headache drummed behind his eyes, and he was thankful they'd booked a private car. The farther they were away from the engine, the less noise there'd be. Maybe he'd be able to catch a few winks.

They passed a family who were also boarding the luxury cars. Americans, if the accent of the woman directing the group was any indication. A young woman with ginger hair stuffed under a wide-brimmed hat clutched the handle of a travel case. He chuckled under his breath. It was the same female who'd rebuffed him on the ferry.

"Now there are two pretty women I'd like to get to know better," Harry said at Bron's shoulder.

"The one on the left is a prude."

"You mean she didn't fall for your charms?" Harry laughed, obviously remembering her from the ship.

A conductor showed Bron and Harry to their private car, and they settled into their seats. Soon, the train was moving away from the platform.

"Have you decided whether you're staying the week in London?" Bron asked his friend after a few moments.

Harry shook his head. "No. I'm going down to Kempton to see my parents."

"Didn't you just visit them?"

"Yes, but with the Season approaching, my mother thought it wise to have a proper family conversation before London distracts us all." He leaned back, stretching his legs. "Nothing official—just the usual discussions about who will be where, and when."

Bron smiled faintly. "I don't envy you."

Harry laughed. "Oh, it's quite painless. One of the many advantages of being the spare to the heir—I'm expected to listen politely, offer the occasional sensible remark, and then return to my own life."

"Then I don't envy your brother. I'm fortunate my father is not a duke.'

Father may not be titled, and his property may be small, but the Honorable Aubron Jeffers's reputation in the fields of law and politics was quite large. His time in the courts was legendary. Since Mother's death, Father had spent less time at his law offices, urging Bron with great frequency and vigor to "cease his silly games" and return to the firm permanently. He thought it a waste that Bron chose to teach law rather than practice it. And don't get his father started on Bron's risk-taking hobbies. The words "foolish young man" were often heard from the elder Jeffers.

"When was the last time you visited the old man?" Harry asked after a few moments of silence.

Harry had the good fortune to have a close relationship with his father, who fully supported his son's obsession with medieval history and paleography.

"I admit, it's been a few months since I went home. Ever since Father ratcheted up his haranguing to include me settling down with a wife."

"Why *do* you have an aversion to marriage?" Harry's eyes crinkled with humor.

"Try not to point out the speck in my eye when there is a plank in yours. Why aren't *you* fat and married?"

"Point taken."

"Besides," Bron added, stretching his legs out, "marriage sounds like yet another responsibility. I've enough of those without adding a household full of expectations."

"So you remain a free man out of self-preservation?"

"Self-preservation," Bron agreed, "and common sense."

Harry rested his head against the seat cushion and closed his eyes. "Still, you should go see your father."

"It works both ways," Bron grumbled. He'd spent seven years in his father's practice under the man's thumb, drafting contracts for men who measured worth in acres and dividends. They called it work of importance, but to Bron it had begun to feel like justice priced by the hour and parceled out to those who could afford it.

Then a friend from the university brought him to the offices of the London Legal Aid and Advice Association, where clerks queued for advice on wages, and women came weeping about rent notices. That night, Bron had gone home with a sense of purpose he hadn't known in years.

The Association offered him a position, but the pay was meager. He'd promised to answer them by the end of the summer.

Harry mumbled a few incoherent words, and soon was snoring lightly.

Bron envied his friend's ability to easily fall asleep. He'd always been that way, even back in their schooldays when he'd come to Eton wide-eyed and impossibly shy. Bron, five years his senior, took Harry under his wing.

Ignoring Harry's last remark before he dozed off, Bron read the newspaper for a few minutes, but couldn't sit still.

He longed for a good cup of tea after several weeks of the swill in France. Quietly opening the door, he slipped into the narrow hall and headed to the rear of the train.

A porter nodded a greeting when Bron stepped into the first-class dining car, which sported upholstered chairs, wooden paneling, and tables laden with pristine white cloths and gleaming silverware. Thick curtains flanked the windows, and chandeliers hung from the elaborately painted ceiling.

As he walked down the aisle to find an open seat, Bron's

eyes snagged on the feisty American whose beautiful blue eyes widened before she shifted her gaze away. Seated next to her sister—who appeared fast asleep with her head propped against the window—she promptly picked up the newspaper, unfolded it, and hid her face from view.

Bron chuckled, stopped by her table, and tapped the newspaper. "You're amazing, you know that?"

The redhead lowered her paper slightly and peered over the pages with a frown. "What are you talking about?"

"I've never known anyone who could read the paper upside down." He chuckled again. "May I?" He tipped his head to the seat opposite her.

She looked around, probably trying to find him another vacant seat. But there were none. "Suit yourself." She went back to reading her paper.

"Avoiding me won't make me disappear."

"I was rather hoping it might."

Bron cleared his throat. He wasn't sure why, exactly, but he had the immense desire to get under this woman's skin. And, truth be told, he relished a challenge. Especially one wrapped up in an extremely attractive package. "I don't think we've been properly introduced. I'm Bronley Jeffers. My friends call me Bron."

She sighed and lowered her paper, taking the time to fold it neatly and place it next to her cup of tea on the dining table. "Miss Helena Dennison."

"You're from America, I take it?"

She cocked a brow. "My, my. Friendly *and* smart."

His lips quirked at her sarcasm. "Do you have a dislike of all men, Miss Dennison, or is it just me?"

"Oh, it's definitely just you."

Bron chuckled. "Well, at least you're honest. What have I done to offend you, pray tell?"

Miss Dennison hesitated and took a sip of her tea. After a

few seconds had ticked by, she sighed and placed the cup in its saucer. "I'm sorry, Mr. Jeffers. I'm not normally rude, but your type gets me a bit rankled."

"My type?"

"You know, the popular, attention-seeking type. The type that young impressionable females mistakenly fawn over."

"You aren't fawning over me."

"I'm not young and impressionable." When he started to protest, she raised a finger. "But I have an impressionable sister in my charge."

"Ah, I see." He shifted under the weight of her steady gaze, feeling a bit like a recalcitrant schoolboy. "And where are you and your charge from?"

"Philadelphia."

"The city of brotherly love."

Miss Dennison blinked. "That's right." She moved her fingers to the edge of the newspaper on the table, as if about to resume her reading of it. To dismiss him.

"Where are you and your sister headed?"

"To London. I'd assume that's quite obvious, as this train is bound for that city."

She had him there.

For all her prickliness, Helena Dennison interested him— if only to figure out what made a woman like her tick.

When the dining room porter approached the table, Bron glanced at the menu before him and ordered a steak and ale. Miss Dennison declined his offer to order something for her.

They sat in silence. She'd exchanged the newspaper for a book and stuck her nose in it until his food came. He caught her peering over her book a few times to peek at him.

"It's a good steak. Are you sure I can't order you one?"

"Uh, no. I don't know how you can eat after what we experienced on the steamer."

He swallowed a piece of potato and wiped his mouth with a snowy white napkin. "I have a strong stomach."

Twenty minutes later, the porter returned and took Bron's empty plate. "We'll be arriving in Charing Cross shortly, sir," he said.

Bron checked his watch. He'd need to return to his passenger car to wake up Harry. Otherwise, the man would sleep right through the stop. Of course, they'd part ways outside the train station, but they would no doubt see one another at university soon. For now, Bron had one objective —to go home and quickly change out of his rumpled clothes so he could get to Eleanor's townhouse within the hour.

Miss Dennison stood, book in hand. "If you'll excuse me, we should join our family for our arrival." She tapped her sister's shoulder. "Alix, it's time to wake up."

Bron rose as well. "It was nice chatting with you," he said with a cheeky grin. "Hopefully, we'll meet again."

Miss Dennison muttered something under her breath that sounded very much like, "Heaven, help us."

The train pulled into Charing Cross Station with a long sigh of steam, and Lena followed Myra onto the bustling platform, Max and Alix trailing behind. One of the countess's liveried footmen stepped forward with a slight bow, then hailed a porter to tend to the Dennison trunks.

Outside the station, an Akethorpe carriage gleamed like obsidian beneath the softened light of late afternoon. The family crest, featuring two silver lions, adorned the door. "Strength Through Honor," read the ribbon beneath—words that stirred curiosity in Lena. Surely there had been a knight in the Akethorpe line, some valiant ancestor who'd earned his title with sword and courage.

She stepped up into the coach and sank into the velvet-lined seat. The air held the faint scent of leather polish. A lace curtain at her elbow softened the light, offering modest privacy while allowing glimpses of the world beyond.

As they set off into the heart of London, the clip-clop of hooves kept rhythm with the city's pulse. Alix leaned toward the window, eyes wide.

London unfolded like a children's panorama book—Regent Street's wide curve of grand shops and row upon row of Georgian façades, stately and tight-shouldered. They passed several parks with tidy circles of hedges and benches and dotted with trees.

Before long, their carriage nosed its way to a stop before an imposing townhouse with dormered windows that appeared like watchful eyes.

Lena stepped down onto the cobblestones, her boots making a soft click. The butler met them at the door, tall and sepulchral in black, his voice like a distant thundercloud. "Lady Akethorpe awaits you in the drawing room."

Her name sat heavy in the air—Lady Akethorpe. Augusta Fenwicke, Papa had told them. The grandmother who hadn't contacted them in thirty years but who'd now summoned them to London like dutiful chess pieces.

Inside, the entryway gave way to a gracious staircase, its mahogany banister gleaming. Lena had seen many gorgeous homes in her life, and this one exuded not only luxury but also a sense of effortless grace, borne of its owner knowing their place in society.

"This way," the butler directed, and they followed him across the vast foyer and down a broad hall flanked by paintings of past Akethorpe family members. When there was time, Lena promised herself she'd return with her camera to photograph each portrait. If Tris were with them, she'd not be interested in her ancestors' likeness, but would research their pasts like a hound on the scent of a fox.

Off the great hall, Lena spotted a library and a music room. The butler turned and stood sentinel in the double doorway of the last room on the right.

Lena moved across the drawing room threshold first, quickly taking in her elegant surroundings from the silk draperies and Sheraton cabinets filled with porcelain figurines to the low conversation seats placed with military precision. She'd never before entered a room that seemed to look back at her and find her wanting.

And there—standing before an elaborate marble hearth as if she owned not just the house but the very air—was their grandmother.

The Dowager Countess of Akethorpe was draped in midnight-blue silk, the gown's bodice trimmed in Alençon lace and its train whispering across the floor. Her silver hair was arranged in a high twist, pinned with jet combs that sparkled under the chandelier. She turned, and Lena felt the full weight of her gaze—green eyes as cool as cut glass.

For one startled moment, Lena had the odd sensation of standing before her future. At the same age as the dowager. Dignified, but alone.

The dowager turned to Myra. "You must be the new Mrs. Dennison."

Myra dipped a practiced curtsy. "I am, Your Ladyship." She turned to the trio beside her. "And this is our eldest daughter, Helena, our son Max, and our youngest daughter, Alexandra."

Like a line of good little soldiers being inspected by a drill sergeant, they stood still while the dowager stepped in front of each of them, hand resting on an ivory-handled walking stick.

"Helena."

Lena dipped a curtsy that felt foreign to her American spine. "Your Ladyship."

"You have your mother's eyes."

"So my father says."

The dowager's eyebrows shot up, but she covered her surprise with a regal nod. Lena had no doubt the older woman was taking her measure—bodice to boots.

"I trust your journey was tolerable?"

"It was," Lena said.

The dowager nodded and stepped away to stand in front of Alix, who shook like a leaf.

"Alexandra," the dowager said as she gazed at her youngest granddaughter's face.

Lena had always wondered who Alix got her green eyes from. Now she knew.

Alix gave a wobbly curtsy while beaming. "It's wonderful to meet you!"

The dowager smiled. With teeth and all. Before now, Lena hadn't believed she could.

Last, their grandmother moved to stand before Max. "You're *just* Max? Not Maximillian? Maxwell?"

Max had joined them on this trip somewhat reluctantly. And it showed in his stiff posture and the lack of his swoon-worthy smile that disarmed females from nine to ninety. "It's just Max, Lady Akethorpe."

Something flickered in her eyes. A glimmer of recognition, perhaps. "I believe that was the name of your mother's dog."

When he said nothing, she gave him a slight smile. She turned with an elegant sweep of silk and gestured for them to follow. Once at the door, she stopped and turned, hand on the knob.

Her gaze landed on Max. "Heaven forbid that London society discovers an Akethorpe heir is named after a Labrador."

FIVE

Bron's carriage rattled to a stop before the tall white terraced house on Queen's Gate. He stepped down onto the pavement, glanced up at the symmetrical rows of sash windows, and felt the usual sense of relief at being back. Kensington suited him —near the parks and museums, close enough to Mayfair when duty called, yet far enough that he could breathe.

The black-painted door opened before he reached the steps.

"Welcome home, sir," his butler said with a dignified nod.

"Thank you. Send word to Lady Langston that I'll call on her after I've changed. I won't keep her waiting long, and I've asked the carriage to wait for me."

"Of course, sir."

Bron quickly bathed, dressed, and headed to his aunt's house in Cavendish Square, despite his aching head screaming that he needed sleep.

He let his head rest against the leather seat of the carriage and closed his eyes. Inevitably, the face of a spirited red-haired American intruded on his thoughts. Her wit had been sharper than a barrister's cross-examination. He told himself sternly not to let the memory dwell, yet found his lips curving into a grin despite it.

His aunt's townhouse stood solemn against the encroaching mist, a Georgian façade that had watched over generations of London society. Bron descended from the carriage and mounted the familiar steps, his chest tightening a little as he entered.

Inside, Pritchard, Langston House's longtime retainer, ushered him to the drawing room. The home was quieter now than in the days of his boyhood visits, but the fire burned brightly in the hearth, and the furniture gleamed with its usual polish. Lady Langston reclined in a high-backed chair near the blaze, her posture upright despite the frailty that illness had etched upon her.

"Eleanor." She'd requested Bron stop calling her "aunt" when he entered college. Said it made her feel old, and he'd never want that.

He bowed over her hand, startled by how slight it felt in his own.

For one unnerving heartbeat, he imagined a world without her in it, and the thought hollowed him in a way he'd never admit aloud.

"My dear boy." Her voice, though soft, carried the warmth of genuine affection. "You didn't need to come."

"I would have come sooner had I known," he said, settling into the chair beside hers. "You ought to have telegrammed me in France. I'm so glad Countess Akethorpe had the intelligence to do so."

A flicker of amusement touched her lips. "I'll throttle Augusta next time I see her."

Bron shook his head, half reproachful. "Shouldn't you be in bed? You should be conserving your strength."

"Strength is a fickle companion at my age," she murmured, adjusting the cushion at her side. "Besides, what strength am I using up by sitting in this blasted chair all day?"

"Point taken. Tell me what's happened in London since I've been away."

For a few minutes, they spoke of trivialities—the bleak April weather, the endless remedies her physician prescribed, the stubborn roses in her garden.

"We had to let go of a maid who was stealing," Eleanor said matter-of-factly, as if they were still discussing the weather.

"Stealing? You have an excellent staff that is very loyal to you! What happened?"

Eleanor waved her hand. "Some of my jewelry went missing from my dressing table. I didn't notice right away because they weren't pieces I wore very often. The house-keeper did a search of the staff's rooms and found them in one of the maids' trunks."

Bron's stomach clenched at the idea that someone would take advantage of his generous and sweet aunt. She paid her staff well and had a reputation for fairness. "I hope you noti-fied the magistrate."

"I let her go without a reference. I figured that was enough punishment," Eleanor said.

"You're much nicer than most." Too nice.

"Unfortunately, she was very well-liked, especially by the footmen, and there was some grumbling for a while. Many thought I should have given her another chance."

Bron disagreed. "Do you regret your decision?"

Eleanor shook her head. "There are some things I'll over-look. Stealing isn't one of them."

"You've been unwell," Bron said quietly. "That makes a house vulnerable. Are you certain the maid acted alone?"

"One can never be certain about anything, can one? But

no, the staff have all been with me for many years, or are the sons and daughters of retired retainers. I trust them."

"And I trust your judgment," Bron said, although he questioned how the thieving maid slipped through Eleanor's defenses.

Quiet for several minutes, she ran her finger round and round the rim of her teacup.

Bron sensed her circling another matter she was reluctant to broach.

"You have heard, I suppose, that Augusta has visitors?" she asked.

"No," he said. Honestly, what did he care if the countess had company?

"Her late daughter's children. They are grown now, of course. Americans."

Bron raised a brow. "I didn't know she had a daughter, let alone one who lived in America."

Eleanor's lips curved faintly. "The estrangement happened before you were born. Sarah ran off with an American merchant she met while he was in London on business. The old earl forbade anyone to speak of her and disowned her completely."

"The earl died several years ago. Why wait until now to forge a reconciliation?"

"The youngest grandchild is eighteen. Augusta wanted them to visit her of their own volition as adults. There are five of them. All girls but one."

Bron leaned back. "I imagine the young women are destined for strategic matches, if Augusta has her way."

"Undoubtedly. But it is the grandson who interests me." She paused for breath. "He is their eldest, perhaps two or three years your junior. He works for their family business in America."

"Good for him." Bron wasn't sure what else to say. Why

did he get the feeling, however, that there was more to this conversation than gossip about the countess and her family?

"Augusta and I were talking—"

"Uh oh. That doesn't sound good."

Eleanor raised a hand. "Hear me out. He could use a friend near his own age. And you, I daresay, could use a companion not wholly disreputable."

"So I am to be his bad influence?"

"Perhaps his good one." Her lips quirked. "You've managed a certain balance. You live as you please, yet you keep your head when others lose theirs. This young man could learn from you. And you, Bron, could do with someone who speaks plainly instead of flattering you. Americans tend to be plain speakers."

He studied her. He didn't relish the idea of shepherding Augusta's grandson around society. And yet—he could not ignore the plea in Eleanor's voice, nor the way her hand trembled slightly where it rested on the arm of her chair.

"I'll meet him," he said at last. "But only because you asked so sweetly." He wagged a finger at her. "Just so long as you and Augusta don't have matchmaking designs for one of the granddaughters and me. I've no desire to be anyone's eligible bachelor."

"I would never." The twinkle in her eyes belied the declaration. She patted his hand, and a smile warmed her pale features. "You're a dear."

"How long will these Americans be in London?" A fortnight would be more than plenty, he thought.

"Augusta is hoping they'll stay until the end of the summer."

"Four months?" Bron asked in a strangled voice.

"If she can convince them."

If the grandson had a business to run—and a backbone—Bron doubted he'd stay for the entire summer.

Silence fell, and Eleanor yawned.

"Don't fret over me, dear boy," she murmured, catching his troubled look. "My strength may fade, but the Lord's never does."

Bron stared at her, remembering the woman who had steadied him through grief and mischief alike. He hated seeing her so diminished. Although he'd never tell her for fear she'd think him a complete pushover, he'd never refuse her anything. Even if it meant escorting the entire group of the countess's American grandchildren around London for the season.

Hopefully, it wouldn't come to that.

⊹╌╌╌╌⊹

Lena closed her bedroom door behind the ladies' maid assigned to help her dress for dinner. She rolled her eyes and sighed. What a waste of staff.

Back home, Myra had insisted on a ladies' maid for her and all the Dennison daughters to share and a valet for Papa. Gowns and formal suits required multiple fastenings, corsetry, and meticulous presentation, so attendants were essential. Or so Myra said. But that was only for special occasions. Balls and fancy dinners, not for everyday affairs. Lena hadn't realized how heavily the British aristocracy leaned on staff.

About an hour earlier, Wilkins, the butler, had deposited Myra, Lena, Alix, and Max on the third floor of the townhouse. Each had their own room, and Lena found hers especially lovely with its tall sash windows overlooking the leafy square.

The maid had unpacked Lena's traveling trunk and carefully hung the clothes in an enormous armoire. A smaller case remained unopened on the floor by the dresser.

Lena picked up the case and carried it to the bed, where she carefully laid it on top of the plush counterpane. The leather traveling case, with its russet sides polished to a mellow sheen, had been a birthday gift from Papa, chosen not only for its sturdy brass corners and fitted interior but for the small indulgence of style he knew she prized. The narrow strap left her hands free, and she always carried it herself rather than leaving it to a footman.

When she lifted the buckle and eased back the lid, the familiar scent of oiled leather rose to meet her. Nestled inside lay her Kodak, snug in its velvet-lined compartment.

But the case held more than the camera. To one side, she had tucked her calfskin Bible and beside it a slim journal bound in blue Morocco leather, where she set down her daily activities in careful script. The arrangement left barely enough room for her camera plates, yet she preferred it that way. Her art, her reflections, and her faith. All in one place.

The familiar objects made her heart clench. Here in a house ruled by strangers, the case's contents were her anchor. Proof that she still belonged to herself.

Lena went to the writing desk that sat by the window. Someone had thoughtfully supplied a pen, an inkwell, and writing paper with the family crest emblazoned across the top.

She opened her Bible first, not sure where to find the strength she needed to get through the next several weeks. Almost without thought, she turned to Isaiah 41:10, a passage her mother had often quoted when storms gathered at home: *"Fear thou not; for I am with thee: be not dismayed; for I am thy God: I will strengthen thee; yea, I will help thee; yea, I will uphold thee with the right hand of my righteousness."*

Bowing her head, she whispered, "Lord, let this be true for me here. Help me not to falter in a place that feels so foreign. Keep me steady for myself and my family."

Her breath eased. Mama's voice echoed in memory, gentle

yet firm, as though she stood beside her even now. Lena traced the verse with her finger, willing the promise to steady her, then gently closed the Bible.

In her journal, Lena wrote the verse at the top of the page to remember what words she'd chosen that day to bolster her courage. She recounted the day's adventures in measured detail. The tumultuous Channel crossing. A train ride through the English countryside from Dover to London. The carriage ride from Charing Cross to Berkeley Square. Bunting and flags encountered on every street, on almost every building, proclaiming the sixtieth anniversary of Victoria's ascent to the throne. And a motorcar racer with an ego the size of a Denwall department store.

One thing Alix had correct—the man was handsome. Too much so. Most likely, a man lacking in character and not worth the time she spent contemplating him.

A tap sounded at the door, and Alix breezed in without waiting. She looked as pretty as a picture in a beribboned lilac muslin dress, her copper hair pinned up with a sprig of violets.

She stopped in the middle of the room, hands fisted on her hips. "Is that how you're wearing your hair?"

Lena touched the top of her head and remembered she still needed it seen to before dinner. "My maid will be back soon to finish it." She'd needed a break from the fussing and had sent the young woman away for half an hour.

Alix flopped across the bed, sighing contentedly. "Isn't this glorious?"

"The home is handsome enough," Lena admitted.

"I don't mean just the home. I mean, London! It's Queen Victoria's Diamond Jubilee—just think what we might see."

"Crowds, no doubt," Lena said dryly.

"And processions! Wouldn't it be lovely to catch a glimpse of the Queen herself?"

Lena gave a short laugh. "We've scarcely been here three

hours, and already you're planning an audience with Victoria. Don't get your hopes up."

Alix pouted. "You are such a spoilsport. We may not stay long, and I intend to enjoy every minute."

"We intend to behave as a guest in someone else's house," Lena countered.

"Oh, Lena, must you always be so cautious?"

"Better cautious than scandalous."

Alix rolled her eyes but smiled anyway. She sat up and scooched to the edge of the bed. "It's a shame that Grandmother's stepson is on the Continent. I would have liked to meet him."

"It's a good thing he isn't here. We have enough to contend with. From the looks of his portrait, he's not very friendly."

Alix sighed. "Perhaps you're right." She stood and moved toward the bedroom door. "Come get me when you're ready. We'll walk down together."

As she turned to leave, Alix paused on the threshold. "I do hope we'll see that Mr. Jeffers again. He was rather dashing, wasn't he?"

Lena's heart betrayed her with a quicker beat, though her tone was crisp enough. "Alix, he is hardly the sort of man you should encourage. A barrister with a reputation for reckless amusements behind the wheel of a motorcar? No."

Alix giggled. "You sound like Myra. He only spoke to us for a moment."

"All the better. A man like that will be surrounded by his own kind—fast friends, racing men, and women eager for excitement. We won't cross paths with him again."

"Wouldn't it be thrilling if we did?"

Lena forced a smile. "No, I can't say it would be. Besides, London is vast. Our circles will never overlap."

Six

From the moment she stepped inside, Lena thought St. George's Cathedral was different from how she expected it, despite what she'd read in her guidebook. It had a dignified simplicity that surprised her.

The galleries swept round on three sides, supported by slender columns, giving the sense of an open hall rather than a shadowed nave. Sunlight glimmered through the great stained-glass Tree of Jesse, casting jeweled color over the choir of men and boys as they began a hymn.

Lena glanced around at the congregation in their Easter Sunday finery. Ladies in gowns of satin and hats crowned with feathers, Easter lilies pinned to their bodices, rivaled anything she had seen in St. Crispin's back home.

At least in Philadelphia, the familiar faces of family and friends had steadied her. Here in Mayfair, amid strangers whose polish made even Myra blink with admiration, Lena felt every inch the outsider.

She took a deep breath and focused on the enormous painting above the altar. *The Last Supper* glowed in soft tones of amber and rose, its figures illuminated as if by candlelight.

The disciples leaned close around the table, their faces turned toward the calm radiance of Christ at the center.

On this Easter morning, with the choir's voices rising beneath that vision of devotion, the stillness reached her heart. The expression of Christ—the quiet strength of love triumphant—seemed to meet her gaze, and for a moment the restless ache of London and all that had yet to be resolved fell away.

The reverend's voice rose beneath the vaulted ceiling. *"Why seek ye the living among the dead? He is not here but is risen."* The words echoed down the nave, clear and unwavering. Despite the differences between here and home, the message was still the same—the most important of themes—no matter where they were.

Easter was not gowns or lilies or lofty ritual. It was this—hope stronger than death itself. Lena folded the truth quietly into her heart, a reminder she sorely needed in this foreign city.

Church bells rang out forty-five minutes later, and the congregants spilled out into the pale spring sunlight. Alix gripped Lena's arm, nearly bouncing with excitement.

"Wasn't it glorious? All the flowers and the music—oh, Lena, did you ever see so many lilies?"

"They were beautiful," Lena allowed.

Myra, of course, had been enchanted. She emerged from the church with a glowing smile and immediately began cataloging every gown she had admired in the pews. "The lady two rows ahead—her sleeves were Paris cut, I'd bet my diamond necklace on it. And the girl behind us wore last season's trim, poor thing. London is simply brimming with opportunity."

Max gave a crooked grin as he tugged his gloves snug. "St. George's may be impressive, but if every outing is this stiff, I'll need a map to the nearest boxing club before the week is out."

Alix gasped. "Max! You can't say things like that when

Grandmother might overhear." Yet her eyes sparkled, betraying amusement more than shock.

Myra fanned herself with her folded service program and cast him a reproving look. "London is *not* Philadelphia, Max. We are here to make a good impression, not haunt athletic clubs."

An Akethorpe footman stood waiting beside the carriage. Before any of them could climb inside, their grandmother turned on the step, her voice composed and carrying just far enough to silence Alix's chatter. "We shall not be returning directly home. A friend of mine, Lady Langston, has invited us to take tea with her this afternoon."

Lena blinked. The dowager had friends?

"An old friend," the countess stressed, as if she could read Lena's thoughts. "She resides in Cavendish Square. It is proper we call on her, and she has long wished to meet you."

Alix clapped her gloved hands together. "How delightful. A tea on Easter Sunday! I hope she has chocolate eggs."

The countess's lips curved—just barely. "I should expect nothing less from Eleanor."

"Does Lady Langston have some unmarried granddaughters, perhaps?" Max waggled his eyebrows.

"Hush," Lena said, but her lips twitched.

"Alas, she does not," the dowager said. "And before you ask, her nieces are all happily married."

"Such is my luck," Max grumbled good-naturedly.

The carriage rattled across town, wheels striking cobblestones in a steady rhythm. Alix peered out the window, pointing out every Jubilee banner and Easter bonnet.

Lena followed her sister's gaze. The city unfurled in quick vignettes—shopfronts draped in bunting, hansom cabs rattling along side streets, bootblacks already calling their wares.

Cavendish Square proved quieter than Berkeley, its garden

square bordered by dignified Georgian terraces. When the carriage stopped before a stuccoed townhouse, Lena noted the polish of the knocker, the fresh sweep of steps. Elegant, but not ostentatious. Unlike Myra, who clearly preferred grandeur, Lena found herself relieved by the understatement.

Inside, the drawing room exuded a sense of gracious comfort. Lady Langston—Eleanor, the dowager had called her—turned her head to greet them. Frail in build, yes, but her eyes sparkled with a warmth. "My dear Augusta, thank you for coming. And you must be the American grandchildren I've heard so much about."

Alix curtsied. "It's an honor, Lady Eleanor."

"Charming," the lady said, her smile softening. "So like your mother at that age."

Lena let her gaze wander as the others exchanged greetings. The tulips. The softly ticking mantel clock. The neat arrangement of silver and porcelain cups. The cake, fragrant with fruit and spice. A pair of chairs near the hearth.

And then—

"We meet again, Miss Dennison."

The voice, low and amused, cut through her thoughts.

Every muscle went taut. Wearing a mask of polite composure, she turned, her heart giving a betraying leap before steadying.

Bronley Jeffers. Again.

He stood at ease by the hearth, tall and insufferably self-possessed, those dark eyes gleaming with recognition. His sun-kissed dark blonde hair falling rakishly across his brow.

Her breath caught, then released. She straightened her spine and willed her features into cool civility. Heaven help her, London was far smaller than she'd imagined.

Bron had been listening to his aunt's lamenting of the sorry state of Parliament when the Dennison party had come through the door.

He'd expected Americans—Eleanor had warned him that Augusta's long-estranged grandchildren were at last in London. But London was crawling with visitors for the Jubilee. He hadn't expected the red-haired woman from the Channel crossing to step across Eleanor's stoop and turn those precise blue eyes on him like an indictment.

Miss Dennison. Helena.

He straightened, the reflex automatic. For the smallest beat, he only stared. On the train, she'd been spirited with a talent for deflating egos. Now, set cleanly into Lady Akethorpe's world, she looked different. A bit more subdued and less feisty. A shame, that.

The high windows threw pale light along the line of her cheek and touched copper into her hair. Her mouth, composed into politeness, nearly hid the wry curve he remembered. Nearly.

It made no sense. Eleanor had said there were four sisters and a brother. On the crossing, he'd only encountered two sisters—the fiery one and the younger, bright-eyed one to whom he'd given his autograph. And Eleanor had said nothing about a stepmother. Yet he knew the Dennisons had one because Helena had mentioned her on the train.

He glanced at Eleanor, who started to rise.

"Ellie, sit down," Augusta said with a wave of her hand. "You look as weak as a lamb."

Smart woman. He'd known Augusta for years, and although she came across as crusty and stiff to others, she possessed a heart of gold. Since Bron didn't need to worry about rescuing Eleanor from falling over, he turned his attention to the oldest of the sisters. "I never imagined seeing you again."

"Nor did I. I assumed London was too large." She turned her gaze to her grandmother, who raised her distinguished brow.

At least she didn't pretend she didn't remember him. Straight lines were easier to navigate than crooked ones. He turned to the brother, who was at least smiling, and held out his hand. "I had the good fortune to meet your sisters on the steamer."

"Yes, I heard. I'm Max Dennison," Max said with a nod. Tall by normal standards, Max looked Bron in the eye, and his handshake was firm. "I caught part of your race while I was in Monte Carlo last month."

Before Bron could answer, the youngest Dennison slid her arm through her brother's and gave Bron a wide smile. "Do you remember me, Mr. Jeffers?"

At least one sister could be friendly. "Of course. You're Alix, like the Princess."

Alix giggled, but then, in a sign of maturity and grace, she turned to the blonde woman beside her. "This is our step-mother, Mrs. Myra Dennison."

"It's good to meet you, Mr. Jeffers," Mrs. Dennison said with a polite smile. "A racecar driver. How ... exciting."

She looked about as excited as a law student before an exam.

"Come, sit everyone, I've had tea prepared." Eleanor made a slight motion with her hand.

Bron smiled at the assortment of treats. All his aunt's favorites, including a plate of small sandwiches, a bowl over-flowing with fresh berries, simnel cake—fruit and spice under a thick layer of marzipan—and hot cross buns still warm enough to steam the butter. At least she still had her appetite.

Her hands shook, however, as she tried to pour the tea.

"Would you like me to pour the tea, since I know how my family takes it?" Helena stood from her chair and moved to stand by Eleanor, bending slightly so that his aunt wouldn't have to look up at her.

"That would be lovely, dear," Eleanor answered, and Helena tucked in the corner of the shawl that drooped from Eleanor's shoulder.

So, the American had a soft spot, after all.

After Helena had filled cups for everyone but Bron, she turned to him, face unreadable. "Sugar?"

"Three teaspoons, please."

"Three?" Her brows lifted.

"And you, Miss Dennison, do you have a sweet tooth?"

"I take two," she said. "Three makes it sludge."

Polite conversation set its little sails. Church at St. George's. The crowds in the square. The season beginning like an orchestra tuning up. Eleanor's simnel cake was deservedly praised, and Augusta shared an anecdote about a duchess and a lapdog at a garden party. She didn't name the duchess.

He could have kept to the edge of it all, content to drink his tea and answer simple questions. But Helena's frosty gaze across the rim of her cup nipped at his ego. He tipped his own cup in her direction. "Are you enjoying London?"

"We only arrived three days ago." Helena sipped from her teacup with a grace that somehow felt like dismissal.

He almost laughed. "Plenty of time to partake in some fun."

That tiny crease between her eyes reappeared. He had the sudden, unwelcome sense that she was measuring him—and finding him wanting. Irritated, he looked away.

Max Dennison, meanwhile, proved better company than his bored expression suggested, and they briefly discussed the race to La Turbie.

Eleanor set her plate of cake on a side table. "Bron, you could make yourself useful and show Mr. Dennison the parts of town the guidebooks forget to include."

Helena was already bristling. Bron doubted she knew her grandmother had planned this with his aunt.

"Max isn't staying long," she said.

Max cleared his throat. "Long enough, Lena, to allow Mr. Jeffers to show me the sights."

When Bron asked if he had any particular place in mind, Max answered, "Whichever tells me most about London in the least amount of time."

"Then avoid the museums," Bron advised.

Max grinned.

Bron found himself liking the fellow, despite having decided beforehand that he would not.

Just to goad Helena, Bron said lightly, "I'm sure we can find something to keep us entertained."

At that, Helena's eyes traveled the length of him and back up again, but she said nothing. He couldn't decide whether she was judging his tailoring or his character, and neither possibility pleased him. So much for goading her.

"I'm free any time." Max said, without bothering to wait for anyone's permission.

"How about tomorrow at two o'clock?" Bron asked before Helena could erect a timetable like a fortress wall. "We'll begin with the courts. If you aren't bored to weeping, we'll walk to the Royal Exchange and eavesdrop on men who'd sell their hats if hats were listed."

Helena's cup paused, poised, then lowered with a slight clink. He would have paid a shilling to know the thought she swallowed.

Bron leaned back, cup and saucer balanced neatly in his hand. "So," he asked with studied casualness, "what do you ladies have planned for your stay in London? Surely Lady Akethorpe won't let you languish indoors while the Jubilee is in the air."

Augusta's lips curved in a smile. "Languish? Certainly not.

I've already secured places for Helena, Alexandra, and Mrs. Dennison to be presented at court next month."

The room seemed to tighten around the words.

Alix gasped, both hands flying to her cheeks. "Presented? To the Queen? Oh, Lena!" She turned, eyes wide as emerald saucers. "We'll be curtsying before Her Majesty herself!"

"Or maybe even the Princess of Wales," Bron interjected. "She's been the royal in the Drawing Room several times since Victoria's been ill. Or in mourning." Which she constantly was it seemed.

"My namesake! How wonderful!" Alix beamed, then leaned toward him. "I think I might prefer to meet her, truth be told," she said in a whisper.

Mrs. Dennison fluttered as if the air had turned suddenly thin, one hand pressing at her throat. "The gowns, the training—we must prepare at once! This is beyond anything I dared hope."

Not so much as a flicker of excitement crossed Helena's features. If anything, her eyes clouded, and Bron had the odd impression that the prospect of standing in glittering gowns before the Queen of England meant little more to her than another form of pageantry to be endured.

Max muttered something about "glad it's not me" and earned himself a glare from all the women in the room except Eleanor.

Bron hid his smile behind the rim of his cup. London, it seemed, had just grown considerably more interesting.

All the while, he kept an eye on Eleanor. Her color held. That was all he required of an afternoon—that it not drain her. When the conversation flagged, he picked it up with a harmless story about a motorcar mechanic in Aubagne who swore by garlic rubbed on bolts and a French matron who gave Bron a rosary at the starting line, as if it might keep him from harm.

Alix listened as if he were the most interesting person she'd ever met, while Helena looked as if she were filing away information to be used against him later. She'd probably make a good attorney.

Bron didn't mind. Better to be examined than dismissed.

Toward the end, Augusta rose with the finality of a gavel. Silk rustled. Gloves were retrieved. Alix thanked Eleanor with such sweetness that Bron saw his aunt soften visibly. And Helena—Helena held Eleanor's hand in farewell as though she genuinely liked her.

Bron met her at the threshold. Not blocking—just there, where departure narrowed everyone to a single file.

"Until next time, Miss Dennison." He kept his tone neutral—polite, nothing more—and stepped aside before she could decide whether he was blocking her path on purpose.

SEVEN

Lena sent up a prayer of thanks when, after a week of mostly dreary English drizzle and society hibernation, the weather finally granted them a clear afternoon—long enough, the dowager declared, to parade properly in Hyde Park.

Lena's first impression of London's famous park was similar to her first impression of Central Park. As in New York, carriages gleamed, horses pranced, and the ladies wore the same expressions of calculated indifference. Society on parade—whether in New York or London—seemed united in the purpose of being admired while pretending not to care.

The scene would make a beautiful photograph. But unfortunately, the dowager had forbidden her to bring her camera along on the excursion. "It's unseemly to take candid images of society without their permission," she'd declared.

Next to Lena, Alix practically vibrated with delight, craning her neck to take in every gown, bonnet, and passing phaeton. Myra, almost as giddy as Alix, smiled and waved at passersby as if she were the Queen herself.

Alix's excitement dimmed only for a heartbeat when a pair of English girls her age tittered behind gloved fingers. Alix held her chin a little higher, but Lena saw the flash of uncertainty in her eyes and slipped her arm through her sister's, giving it a quick squeeze.

Lady Langston—Eleanor, as she insisted they all call her—reclined among the cushions beside the dowager, pale but determined to take part in the fashionable ritual.

A few paces away, Mr. Jeffers and Max rode abreast. Even from here, Lena could see how easily Mr. Jeffers handled his mount—how the reins rested lightly in his hands, how the animal seemed to move by instinct under his command.

She caught herself watching for too long and snapped her gaze toward the passing phaetons.

Absolutely not. Just because he handled the horse like he'd invented the creature didn't mean she should stare.

The dowager's fan snapped open. "Dear heavens, here comes Viscount Eastmere," she murmured, her tone carrying concern that made both Lena and Alix glance up.

A rider approached—a tall, broad-shouldered man with a soldier's bearing and an expression carved from granite.

The dowager didn't deign him a smile like she had others who paid their respects. "Lord Eastmere," she said evenly, inclining her head.

"Lady Akethorpe." The man's voice was deep but cold. He tipped his head to Eleanor. "Lady Langston." His eyes then settled on Lena's side of the carriage. "And *these* must be the Americans."

The dowager gestured to them. "My granddaughters. Miss Helena Dennison, Miss Alexandra Dennison, and their step-mother, Mrs. Myra Dennison." She waved a hand toward Mr. Jeffers and Max, who'd stopped to talk to a rider several yards back. "Over there with Mr. Jeffers is my grandson, Max Dennison."

Lord Eastmere gave a curt nod. "I trust you are finding London instructive."

"We are indeed, my lord," Myra said, her tone respectful.

Lena was glad they weren't outside the carriage, or else she'd have to curtsy.

The viscount turned his cold gaze back to the dowager. "There are many who say the Queen is allowing too many foreigners into the Drawing Room."

The dowager lifted her nose and waved a gloved hand as if dismissing a servant. "And many who say that newcomers are a breath of fresh air in the otherwise stale room of our peers."

"It must be difficult, to be American—so exuberant—and learning how to be English proper," the viscount goaded them once more.

Lena felt her cheeks warm, but she met the viscount's gaze steadily. "We shall endeavor, my lord, to do credit to our family. Americans can muster a curtsy—though we're far better known for standing tall."

The whinny of a horse to her left drew Lena's attention. Mr. Jeffers and Max pulled up their mounts beside the carriage.

His smile didn't touch his eyes, but Mr. Jeffers inclined his head politely. "Lord Eastmere."

"Jeffers." Eastmere's mouth twisted slightly.

Tipping his hat to the viscount, Max said, "Lord Eastmere. A pleasure." Mr. Jeffers must have informed him of the viscount's identity before they reached the Akethorpe phaeton. Yet Max grinned and acted as though he were at a Philadelphia dinner party rather than speaking to nobility in Hyde Park.

Lord Eastmere's brows rose, though he offered no smile in return, and he shifted in his saddle. "I understand you've taken up time with Jeffers here. Motorcars, of all things."

"Indeed, Lord Eastmere, Mr. Dennison has a keen interest, and he's quick to learn." Mr. Jeffers spoke casually, but his eyes narrowed.

The viscount's mouth thinned. "Fascinations of youth. A man with responsibility should concern himself with matters that endure."

Mr. Jeffers clenched his jaw. A move so slight it was hardly visible. For all his bravado, he didn't take well to arrogance. Lena hadn't expected that.

"I'm certain motorcars will still be here long after you're buried in the family cemetery," he replied with a smooth smile.

The viscount huffed and turned to the dowager once more. "I wonder what Lord and Lady Akethorpe will say when they return to find their home overrun with strangers."

The dowager narrowed her emerald eyes. "As you know, the townhouse is mine, not my stepson's, and I'm sure he has more pressing matters as the Earl of Akethorpe than to worry about my guests."

"We'll see, won't we?" The viscount gave a curt nod and guided his horse back into the stream of carriages.

The air felt lighter the moment he was gone.

The dowager tucked her fan into her lap. "Impertinent man," she said.

"In Philadelphia," Myra said in a voice that carried, "we'd call him a sour pickle."

Lena choked on a laugh.

The dowager shot her the kind of look that could discipline a small army. "You managed yourself well, Helena," she conceded in an imperious tone. But her lips twitched, and she leaned forward. "Never was there a man who moved through life like he had a stick up his … shall we say, derriere?"

Alix burst into laughter, and Myra's shoulders shook with mirth.

Lena exhaled, the tension easing from her spine, while she wondered about her uncle, the Earl of Akethorpe. "Do you expect Lord and Lady Akethorpe to return to London anytime soon?" she asked the dowager.

"No. They'll remain on the Continent until the end of the summer. They always do."

Alix placed a hand on her brow. "It's all so confusing, what with you both being Lady Akethorpe." She glanced at Lena, then to the dowager, her smile tentative. "May we call you Grandmother?" she asked softly.

The dowager's eyes brightened. "How about *Grandmama*? I should like that very much," she said.

Lena felt her heart soften a tad at the exchange. She glanced up—only to find Mr. Jeffers observing her as if she were a puzzle piece that refused to fit where he thought it should.

She looked away first, determined to fix her gaze on anything but him. The sunlight gleamed across the Serpentine like liquid silver.

When the dowager caught her eye and gave her a nod of approval, Lena couldn't help the small smile that tugged at her mouth. She wasn't sure if she was ready to call this woman, who'd spurned her mother, "Grandmama" yet, but she would consider it.

⁘

Bron steadied his gelding as he watched Eastmere converse with a group in a carriage not too far away. The viscount nodded toward the Akethorpe carriage and then said something that made his conspirators laugh.

Max let out a low whistle. "Nice guy."

"London society is full of them, unfortunately." Bron's gaze shifted toward the Dennison carriage. Miss Dennison—the elder—sat very straight, chin lifted. The younger sister leaned close to her stepmother, cheeks pale with the strain, while Mrs. Dennison's smile held the brittleness of porcelain about to crack.

They were up against it, all of them. Four Americans dropped into a society that had measured and dismissed them before they even opened their mouths. And that was especially true of the women. Max could get away with more.

It was more than gowns and millinery that the Dennison women would need. They must summon steel in their spines. There had been a glimmer in Helena's poised remarks. That, at least, boded well.

Bron guided his gelding closer until he rode nearly level with the phaeton.

"You held your ground admirably," he said, low enough for only her to hear. "Few would have answered so evenly."

Her gaze flicked up, blue eyes bright as glass in the sunlight. "Americans are accustomed to frost, Mr. Jeffers. We call it January."

A startled laugh escaped him before he could stop it. He tipped his hat in mock salute. "Then may England beware the thaw."

For a breath, their gazes lingered. The murmur of voices, the clatter of hooves, even the creak of carriage wheels seemed to recede beneath the taut thread stretched between them. Then Helena turned back to her sister, her profile serene yet dismissive.

Bron straightened, unsettled by the odd tug low in his chest. She had more steel than he'd credited. Before he could say more, a familiar figure ahead caught his eye—a tall, lanky man on a bay hunter, brown hair sun-touched, bearing easy as ever.

Bron grinned. It had been ages since he'd seen his cousin. "Redgrave!" he called, spurring his gelding forward, weaving through a tide of riders until he drew alongside.

Cedric turned, his face breaking into a wide grin. "Jeffers, by thunder!"

Leaning over their horses' necks, they clasped hands hard, laughter bursting out like schoolboys reunited after too long a holiday.

"I thought you'd vanished into France for good," Cedric said. "Racing death on wheels, if the papers are to be believed."

"Exaggerated tales," Bron said, though the grin lingered. "And you? Still the best seat in Norfolk?"

"Everyone seems to prefer bicycles now," Cedric replied wryly. "Can you imagine?" He shifted, glancing past Bron. "Who's that with your aunt and Lady Akethorpe?"

"The dowager's American grandchildren and their step-mother." Bron waved Max over and made introductions. They all promised to meet at Bron's club for cards later in the week.

"Where's your lovely wife?" Bron asked.

"She's talking with Lady Blount." Cedric waved toward a tree, where a striking figure in emerald green guided her mount toward them.

Lady Haverleigh was breathtaking. Her riding habit clung in flattering lines, her blonde tresses tucked under a jaunty hat. When Cedric presented her, her smile was smooth, her voice velvet.

"Lady Haverleigh," Bron said, inclining his head.

"Mr. Jeffers." Her pale eyes met his, cool and unreadable, her smile so polished it gleamed.

Bron understood Cedric's attraction. Beautiful enough to still conversation, elegant enough to silence a room. Yet as she smiled again, he felt the distance—as though she were a portrait admired in a gallery. Flawless, but behind glass.

Oblivious, Cedric beamed at her before turning back to Bron. "You must come to Haverleigh. The hall misses your noise, and I—well, I've missed you, old man."

Bron's throat tightened. "And I you. It's been far too long."

They fell into talk of old hunts and schoolboy pranks, laughter ringing easily between them. For a few blessed moments, it was as if the years had never passed. Yet even as Bron reveled in the comfort of friendship renewed, his gaze strayed to Lady Haverleigh, now speaking with Eleanor at the Akethorpe carriage. If he had to guess, her clothes were from the most expensive of Parisian modistes, and she wore a diamond brooch that must have set Cedric back a pretty penny.

When Cedric and his wife turned to join another pair of riders on the Row, the youngest Miss Dennison sighed dramatically. "She's so beautiful."

Eleanor leaned forward in her seat next to Augusta. "There's a story behind the cool smiles of Lady Haverleigh," she murmured, her voice pitched low. "Cecilia once had hopes of marrying a third son of an earl—a handsome and charming young man, if not a wealthy one. But her father lost nearly everything at the gaming tables. Overnight, her prospects changed."

Mrs. Dennison gasped and waved her fan in front of her face. "How dreadful! Then what happened?"

Eleanor nodded. "It was a horrible situation. Her family pressed her into a match with Cedric. His father's estate at Haverleigh was secure—sheep, wool, solid rents. A sensible choice, given the circumstances." Her tone cooled. "But practicality is a poor substitute for affection."

Augusta's gaze turned thoughtful. "Sometimes the choices we make out of desperation become the burdens we carry longest."

Bron absorbed the story in silence, certain he'd never heard it before. He'd known about Cecelia's father's financial woes, but not that she'd promised herself to another before Cedric. He must have been her second choice, if she had a choice at all.

He felt sorry for the woman. Even though she was cold

toward him, she'd been very attentive to Eleanor while in town, from what his aunt said.

But more than anything, his heart ached for his cousin, who loved someone who didn't return that love. What a sad state of affairs. Why society thought marriages of convenience could be beneficial, he'd never understand.

Eight

Lena stared at the ornate ceiling above her four-poster bed. Since their arrival in London, a full night's sleep had proved elusive. You'd think the fast-paced schedule the dowager kept them on would exhaust her. But alas ...

She pounded the pillow into a ball and flipped onto her side.

Her nerves weren't helped by her stepmother's frenzied state. Ever since the dowager announced that Myra, Lena, and Alix would be presented before the Queen on May eighteenth, Myra had been in a tizzy of monumental proportions.

Though she'd bought more gowns in Paris than they could ever wear, Myra eagerly joined the dowager's parade to the modiste, the milliner, and the jeweler. All the while, Max —with whom Lena wasn't overly pleased at the moment— vanished into meetings with Denwall buyers.

Lena huffed and rolled onto her back, contemplating all that was required of them to be presented to the Queen.

In Philadelphia, debutantes were drilled from birth in the code of white gowns and long gloves. White, they were told, symbolized innocence and purity. Lena suspected the real reason was more practical—white stood out in a crowd. A goose among peacocks. Or was it peafowl? She'd have to look that up in the Akethorpe library.

Though not her debut season, she fell under the same rules as every debutante presented to royalty. Diamonds and pearls were acceptable. Sapphires and rubies were not. Colored flowers might be permitted, but only sparingly. Sleeves must be short, the bodice round and low, and the train long enough to trip over. If a young woman were ill on the day of presentation, she could modify her low neckline but only if she brought a doctor's certificate with her. Why anyone thought one should attend at all if sick, Lena couldn't imagine. Hadn't these people heard of contagions?

The headdress had a rule book of its own—three white ostrich plumes and a tulle veil. Even flowers failed as a chance for individuality. "Lilies of the valley," the florist said. "Everyone's choosing them this year." So much for originality. Two hundred white ducks in a row.

In addition to fittings, lessons on deportment were required. Miss Edith Derry-Ballister, who had launched "hundreds of young ladies, *even* Americans," took command of the drawing room.

"Not so low, Miss Dennison," she snapped, tapping her stick. "Bend don't bow. The curtsy is a ripple of the sea—graceful, contained. Eyes always on Her Majesty."

Alix giggled. "I feel as if I'm about to topple."

"You will if you lean so far forward," the countess observed. "A lady must appear effortless, not rehearsed."

By the end of each morning, Lena's legs trembled. They practiced curtsies, posture, the precise incline of the head, and how to glide without seeming to walk.

"Englishwomen do not stride like Americans," Miss Derry-Ballister lectured. "You drift. Shoulders back, chin lifted. Never bounce."

Alix twirled before the mirror. "It's like being a swan."

"It's like being in a straitjacket," Lena muttered.

"You must endure it," Myra said, though her smile was tight. "Your grandmother means to see us properly launched."

"Again, Miss Dennison," Miss Derry-Ballister commanded. "Your left foot strays half an inch."

Lena lowered into another curtsy, her knees quivering. The entire exercise felt absurd—hours spent mastering a gesture lasting mere seconds before a queen who would never remember her name.

"Better," Miss Derry-Ballister said, which was the closest thing to praise.

From the corner, the dowager watched like a hawk. "Not like that, Alix. Glide don't shuffle. Remember, your every step reflects upon our family."

After two weeks of instruction, Lena could curtsy in her sleep. Yet while the women rehearsed decorum, Max found diversion elsewhere, often vanishing with Mr. Jeffers on some motorcar escapade.

"He's remarkable," Max had said over dinner one night. "Knows law, politics—and he can handle a horse like nobody's business."

Let Max admire him. The man boxed, raced motorcars, and smiled as though he expected every woman to fall at his feet. Hardly the sort a sensible woman noticed twice. And reckless, worldly men were the last sort she admired—unless, apparently, she was losing all sense. She couldn't shake the memory of the spark in his dark eyes or the deep-throated laugh she'd heard at his aunt's.

Truth be told, Mr. Jeffers was the main reason she didn't sleep well. Unless it was the goose liver the dowager insisted upon nightly. "Good for the constitution," she said with unshakable authority.

One morning, during a particularly grueling lesson with

Miss Derry-Ballister, Mr. Jeffers arrived to collect Max. Alix had gone to fetch her new hat, and both the dowager and Myra had retired for a nap.

Lena had just executed an almost perfect curtsy when he appeared in the doorway—hat in hand, amusement tugging at his mouth. "I beg your pardon," he said smoothly. "I appear to have interrupted a ballet rehearsal."

"A Court presentation, sir, *not* a performance." Miss Derry-Ballister glared at Bron.

"Ah," he said, eyes sliding toward Lena, "could have fooled me."

Lena straightened, chin high. "You seem easily entertained."

"Only by the extraordinary," he replied, smile deepening. "I'm here for Mr. Dennison. Wilkins has gone to fetch him, I believe."

Max entered with a small traveling bag.

"What's in the bag?" Lena asked, though she suspected she already knew.

"We're headed to Bron's boxing club. I brought a change of clothes."

"Just don't get yourself banged up. Lady Akethorpe will have your hide if you appear at her ball with bruises."

"I'll make sure not to aim for his pretty face," Mr. Jeffers said, clapping Max's shoulder. He winked—confident, disarming, knowing exactly how unsettling he could be.

Lena lifted her nose and turned away.

He only laughed.

He was the sort of man who moved through the world as if it owed him nothing—and would still give him everything. She told herself she disapproved of that kind of ease, yet the thought of it tugged at her. What would it feel like to live with such effortless confidence?

"Are we going in one of your motorcars?" Max asked.

"Absolutely."

When they'd gone, Miss Derry-Ballister cleared her throat. "Now, Miss Dennison, shall we see if you can maintain composure under real distraction?"

As she bent once more under that eagle eye, Lena wondered—not for the first time—whether she'd rather be driving in that motorcar with the wind in her hair than curtsying before a monarch who would never know her name.

NINE

"I declare, English crowds are as solemn as funerals," Myra whispered as they shuffled through the third room of oil paintings at the Royal Academy's newly opened summer exhibition.

Lena nudged Myra in the ribcage. "You don't expect them to yell like fish mongers, do you?" A bubble of laughter rose in her throat.

She thumbed through the programme. According to her grandmother, the Royal Academy's annual exhibition was open to any artists who wanted to display their work. Many exhibitors were Royal Academy students, but the school didn't select the art at the exhibit.

A painting with subdued tones amid a riot of color surrounding it drew Lena in. Her heart stuttered at the scene of a woman bent over a child's bed, a candle cupped in her hand, its light trembling across the little one's sleeping face.

Something inside Lena gave a familiar twist. An ache for the mother she and her siblings lost. For the many times Lena did her best to comfort when one of the little ones was sick. It wasn't the same, however.

She moved away and joined Myra by the room's exit.

"Do you ever get the feeling we are being watched and judged?" Myra whispered, tugging at her gloves. "I can feel it from that gentleman with the walrus mustache. He doesn't care for Americans."

Lena followed her gaze toward a somber man who kept glancing their way.

"He doesn't care for sunlight either, from the pasty look on his face," Myra added in a louder voice.

Lena bit back a laugh and moved with the current into the sculpture gallery.

"Where's Alix?" Myra turned in a small circle, clutching her reticule as if it were an anchor in a storm. "I told her to keep to us."

"She's just there," Lena said, indicating where Alix hovered on the edge of a marble display, head tilted as if in an intense study of the figure.

They began to thread that way, pausing for a moment as a tide of viewers surged around a celebrated bronze. Someone behind them sighed the name of the artist with reverence. Ahead, Alix leaned in to touch the life-like form of a lion terrorizing a tortoise.

Beyond her, Mr. Jeffers and Max conversed beside a bust of a former Academy professor.

Lena noticed, too late, that Alix's arm was coming perilously close to a marble statuette behind her.

Alix stepped back, and elbow collided with marble.

The statuette rocked.

Lena's heart leaped to her throat. She caught a flash of motion at the periphery. Mr. Jeffers moved with a swiftness she would not have credited him. One long step, a hand outstretched—palm to marble. The unclothed female form never hit the ground, and Mr. Jeffers looked almost as surprised at his feat as Alix did.

A ripple of sound traveled through the gallery, that peculiar English scandalized hush that says everything without saying anything at all.

Alix froze, color draining fast. "I—oh—oh dear—"

"It's quite all right," Mr. Jeffers said, still with his hand cupped around the torso of the statuette. He cleared his throat, and Lena almost laughed at the look on his face.

"You've only given her a fright," he told Alix. "She's been standing still for hours. Anyone would wobble."

A laugh startled from behind them. "Well done, Mr. Jeffers," Max chortled.

Alix's eyes filled with tears.

"Good heavens," Myra breathed, one hand at her throat. "At the price they're selling that piece for, we would've had to sell the house in Rittenhouse Square."

Mr. Jeffers set the statuette back on its stand, checking that it was standing in the middle and not on the edge.

Lena looped her arm through Alix's and gave her a small squeeze. Enough to hopefully reassure her, but not enough to make Alix feel worse.

With the air of a conspirator, Mr. Jeffers leaned toward Alix.

"Between ourselves," he murmured, "the Duke of—well, never mind which—once toppled a Grecian urn in a gallery twice as crowded as this. Claimed it improved the composition. The curator did not agree. You've done no harm at all. And you've certainly done better than he did."

Alix hiccupped on a laugh. "Did he truly?"

"On my word," Mr. Jeffers said gravely.

Blessedly, onlookers had moved on. Alix wiped at her eyes, mortification pulling into a watery smile. Mr. Jeffers eased back half a pace and gave a small, gentlemanly bow.

Lena exhaled, and gratitude rose warm and quick as steam. *Thank You, Lord.*

"This is precisely why sculpture should be caged," Myra declared in a stage whisper. "At least with paintings, one only knocks a *frame* askew. With a statue, you could lose an entire head."

"Myra," Lena said, a thread of laughter weaving through her voice, "please don't suggest cages to the Royal Academy."

"Bars. Discreet bars." Myra dabbed at her brow, then brightened as if struck by inspiration. "Or a rope, implying one must not get any closer."

"A novel idea," Mr. Jeffers said with a smile.

Myra fanned her face. "How are you so adept at catching falling things, Mr. Jeffers? Do you practice?"

"Motorcars," Max said. "I imagine they teach quick reflexes."

Well, whatever the reason he possessed such a skill, Lena was glad he used it to prevent further disaster for Alix.

From the other side of the room, whispers reached Lena's ears. "They're Americans," a society matron uttered with disdain.

"Come," Myra said, plucking at Lena's sleeve. "Let's find your grandmother. It's getting rather stuffy in here."

⚜

Bron glared at the old biddies whispering behind their fans. People like that gave the English a bad name. He thanked his lucky stars that he'd managed to catch the statuette before it crashed to the ground in a thousand pieces. That would have been splendid fodder for the gossipmongers.

The truth was, he hadn't thought at all about what to do when the statuette began to topple. So when he looked down and found it cradled in his hands, he was as surprised as anyone.

Mrs. Dennison ushered them through to the watercolor gallery—the last room to visit. Max and Alexandra were close behind, leaving him and Helena to bring up the rear.

"Thank you," Helena said quietly.

He turned. She peered up at him, her expression composed, something softer moving beneath. Gratitude did not embarrass her, he noted. Nor did she try to make a hero of him, which most people attempted on the flimsiest of excuses. It was oddly restful.

"I got lucky. Nine times out of ten, I wouldn't have caught it before it hit the floor."

"I meant for your kindness to Alix afterward." A smile ghosted her mouth. "Although your catch was quite spectacular."

Around them, the air shifted with a thousand small social currents—the brush of silk, the creak of a floorboard, the cough of a gentleman. Helena's gaze flicked to Alexandra. "She would have been mortified if she'd broken it. She felt bad enough that she'd caused a spectacle—or at least, what she thought was one."

"Then I'm glad I was able to prevent a catastrophe."

"You'll be her hero now."

They had moved slowly enough through the crowd that they'd lost sight of Helena's family. She stopped and placed a hand on his arm.

The touch made him want to capture her delicate hand and brush a kiss across her knuckles.

"Mr. Jeffers," she said quietly, eyes on his lapel, "please be careful with Alexandra. She—likes you."

He went very still. "Ah."

"She's easily dazzled. And you are very bright at present."

"It's unintentional," he said.

"I know." She looked up then and met his eyes straight on. "Still."

He nodded. He would sooner have stepped into the path of a runaway motorcar than into a girl's unguarded longing. "You have my word."

"Thank you." She started away, then glanced back. "For everything."

Bron watched her cross to Alexandra—watched the way the younger sister's shoulders softened, as if a held breath had finally let go.

He wondered what it would be like to see Helena let go of the tight control she seemed to keep over her own life. He imagined it would be spectacular.

His gaze lingered a moment longer than was wise. He could still feel the ghost of her touch on his arm. That she would think him capable of hurting someone so young, capable of carelessness, troubled him. He'd spent half his life dismissing the notion that he *was* careless—too easily amused, too quick to charm the female population.

He drew a slow breath. The lady wasn't wrong. They didn't call him the Merry Barrister for nothing.

But did he want to continue being that person?

He glanced at Helena. No, he really didn't.

Max appeared at his elbow. "You all right, old man? You look a little pale."

Bron smiled faintly. "I think I could use some fresh air."

Or perhaps, some space between himself and Helena Dennison.

⊹

Augusta regarded the drawing room—her favorite space in the house—with quiet satisfaction. Evening light slanted through the tall windows, glinting off polished oak and the gilt edges of framed portraits. A faint scent of lemon polish lingered in the air, mingling with the sweetness of lilacs arranged on the mantel.

Across from her, Myra sat with a book in hand, her face touched by lamplight. Her posture remained faultless, though her expression held the lively self-consciousness Augusta had come to recognize. The poor woman had been intimidated from the first day—and perhaps with reason. Augusta had never made anything easy.

Yet now she felt oddly at ease in the American's company. The girls were upstairs, Max gone off with Bronley, and the house had fallen into an agreeable hush. Two women left behind, bound not by blood, country, or shared history—but by affection for the same young people.

Augusta reached for her teacup—though the tea had long since cooled. "London is all aflutter over the Jubilee. The processions, services, garden parties ... it will be a marvel. The girls would be much admired if they remained."

"We may not stay. Beatrice graduates next month, and I promised we'd return home for it. Whether we come back afterward ..." Myra exhaled. "That will be up to James, although I'd hoped he might join us on this trip."

James Dennison. The name curled through Augusta's chest with an uncomfortable weight. She turned the thought carefully, as though handling an unopened letter from decades past.

"I should like to meet him," she said at last. Her voice came out quieter than intended. "I owe him both an apology and a measure of gratitude. I judged him harshly—dismissed him because he was a young man in trade. But he did well by my daughter. Loved her, and that's more than I can say for her father." Her throat tightened.

Myra blinked rapidly. "You ... would apologize to him?"

"I would," Augusta replied simply. "If he will accept it." She pretended not to notice that Myra's eyes glistened.

The clock ticked gently, deepening the hush.

Augusta sipped her tea until her composure returned. "They are fine young people, my grandchildren," she said at last. "Particularly Helena. She has a steadiness not often found in wealthy young women."

A tender smile touched Myra's lips. "She earned that steadiness the hard way. When their mother died, Helena stepped in long before she should have. Nine years old and suddenly thrown into the role of nurturer to her younger sisters." Myra shook her head fondly. "Even after James and I married, she still tries to take care of all of us. I think she forgets she's allowed to enjoy life while she's still young."

"She carries herself with authority."

"She carries all of us," Myra said, a chuckle softening her words. "There are days I feel I ought to ask her permission before taking Alexandra to the dressmaker."

Augusta laughed—an unguarded sound that surprised even her. "That does seem exactly like her."

Myra's smile softened. "Underneath it, all she wants is to see her sisters settled and happy. She's always put them first."

Augusta tapped her cup lightly. "So that's why she withdraws from Bronley."

Myra's brows rose. "You've noticed it too."

"How could I not? He hardly knows whether he ought to admire her or avoid her, and she keeps him at arm's length because she fears what Alexandra might feel." Augusta shook her head. "And Alexandra, I suspect, has developed a touch of hero-worship."

Myra sighed. "Exactly. Alexandra is impulsive and beautiful but still impressionable. Yet, Helena would sooner break her own heart than let her sister be disappointed."

Augusta nodded slowly, thoughtful. "Bronley is not frivolous, despite appearances. Beneath the jokes and charm, there is a great deal of depth." Her voice gentled. "Much like

Helena, his childhood was not simple. He was just into his teens when his mother died. Loss left its mark on him."

"And his father?"

"Thinks his son should kowtow to his every wish. Aubron Jeffers is a sanctimonious prude."

"Bronley is nothing like him, then," Myra said with a nod.

"Not in the least. And he's learned to make light of things rather than to lean on anyone."

Myra absorbed this, her expression softening. "Helena would never risk her duty for a man who wasn't deserving."

"And Bronley, despite his flaws, is deserving."

A comfortable quiet settled between them, warm as a shawl laid across tired shoulders.

"So, you're saying you could see Bronley with Helena?" Myra asked after a moment.

Augusta allowed herself a small smile. "Possibly. They would balance one another. She would give him steadiness, and he would give her laughter. He needs someone who sees beyond his charm. And she ..." She exhaled. "She needs someone who reminds her she is allowed a life, not only a duty."

Myra's smile turned conspiratorial. "Perhaps we ought to help them along."

"Splendid idea," Augusta replied with a nod.

Their eyes met, and quiet laughter rose between them. It was an unlikely alliance of an American stepmother and an English dowager contemplating matchmaking. Absurd.

And yet, somehow ... delightful.

TEN

This day, Lena decided, marked the end of her education in absurdities. Three weeks of lessons in how to curtsy, glide, and hold a bouquet as if it were a frightened bird. Enough to make any sensible woman renounce London society altogether.

From what she could tell, a presentee's role at court came down to two rules: curtsy and escape without tripping.

Still, she had survived the training. Barely.

By the time the Akethorpe carriage reached the Mall outside Buckingham Palace, the crowd had already gathered— faces pressed to the railings, waving as though every passing carriage carried the Queen herself. One eager boy leaned in so close Lena half expected his nose to leave a smudge on the window.

Across from her, Alix sat pale but smiling, her bouquet of blue delphinium and periwinkle balanced across her lap like a declaration. Against a sea of white roses, it looked almost rebellious.

"The bouquet you picked is beautiful," Lena admitted, though she'd thought it a bit bold.

Alix's smile brightened. "I don't want to look like every other debutante."

"And there's nothing wrong with that," Myra said, adjusting her gloves. "Now remember—step forward, curtsy, rise, and back away. Smile, but not too broadly. And mind your train."

"Yes, Myra," Alix said dutifully.

Lena bit back a grin. "If I forget, I'll improvise. Americans are known for that."

Across the seat, the dowager lifted a brow. "If you forget, child, faint. It's more dignified than improvisation."

Lena's laugh caught in her throat. Lady Akethorpe's tone could freeze a spring bloom, yet beneath it lingered something like affection.

The carriage jolted to a halt, and footmen hurried to open the doors. Within moments, they were ushered through high arches and into the state rooms, where the air shimmered with anticipation—and too much perfume.

Sunlight spilled across polished floors and mirrored panels, dazzling enough to make Lena's eyes water. Jewels winked, trains rustled, and the low hum of conversation rolled through the room like a restless tide. Her fingers itched for her camera. The light alone was worth a photograph.

The dowager, lorgnette poised like a general surveying troops, scanned the crowd. "Ah, Lady Granard—violet plumes and three daughters dressed alike. Imagine, three debuts in one season. If that doesn't bankrupt the family, nothing will."

Alix leaned close. "They're lovely, though the middle one looks ready to faint."

"A few might," the dowager said drily. "I once saw a girl tumble headfirst into the dais in '67. Disappeared into a mountain of tulle."

Myra gave a nervous smile. "Surely that doesn't happen now."

"Fashion changes. Nerves do not."

A ripple of movement passed through the crowd as brighter light poured from the adjoining doorway. The Princess of Wales had entered—graceful, silver-spangled, her hair crowned with white plumes.

Alix drew in her breath. "She's smaller than I imagined."

"Small but perfectly proportioned," the dowager corrected. "A model of deportment."

"She looks kind," Lena murmured.

"She is," the dowager said softly. "And better than the Prince deserves." Her eyes narrowed. "Repeat that, and I'll deny it."

Lena's lips twitched. She loved these flashes of honesty—the little cracks in her grandmother's perfect composure.

The dowager's attention shifted again. "Ah—Lady Margaret Forbes in that butterfly gown. Overdone, but effective. And beside her, Miss Mary Goelet—one of your countrywomen. Quite the sensation this season."

"The New York heiress?" Myra asked.

"The very one. Her gown cost more than some estates. Money and ambition—an intoxicating combination."

Alix giggled. "Then she's making her mark."

"Oh, indeed," the dowager said. "Americans always do. You bring new fortunes and opinions no one knows how to manage."

Lena laughed quietly. "That sounds rather like us."

The dowager's fan flicked open. "You, my dear, are also a Fenwicke. That elevates you above your countrymen."

"I shall try to be worthy of the distinction," Lena replied, hiding her amusement behind her gloved hand.

"Do. And stand tall when your turn comes. I refuse to have our name associated with clumsiness."

Lena said nothing—too busy imagining her inevitable stumble across that shining floor.

The line crept forward, the air thick with heat and perfume. Ostrich plumes quivered. Jewels caught the light like stars.

"Notice the sleeves," the dowager said, tapping Lena's arm. "Smaller this year. Blessedly so. And the feathers—three plumes separated by osprey in the new Prince of Wales style. Every lady will copy them before week's end."

"And they'll all look equally ridiculous," Lena murmured.

Her grandmother's lips twitched. "You sound very much the Yank when you're nervous."

"It's my native tongue."

"More's the pity."

Before Lena could reply, the booming herald began the roll of names.

Myra went first, her curtsy deep and graceful enough to make the dowager nod. Alix followed, trembling but radiant as the Princess leaned down with a few quiet words.

Then Lena's name.

Her pulse drummed in her ears as she crossed the threshold. The Princess stood at the center of the room, serene beneath her diamond tiara and plumes. Rumor said she was nearly deaf, but her poise made it irrelevant.

A page tugged Lena's train into order. She took a breath. *So much ceremony for one impossible curtsy.*

She stepped forward. Down she went, skirts whispering, knees trembling, feathers swaying precariously. *Don't faint,* she prayed, imagining the headline: *American Girl Collapses Before Princess.*

When she rose, the Princess's eyes met hers—cool blue, shadowed with weariness yet kind. For one instant, Lena felt seen—not another white-gowned blur in an endless parade, but herself.

And then it was over.

She retreated as gracefully as she could manage, certain she looked like a backward-moving heron. Somehow, she reached the doorway intact, heart thudding, palms damp.

In the Withdrawing Room, the tension vanished like mist. Myra glowed, Alix looked ready to float away, and Lena was simply grateful to be upright.

"What did she say to you?" she asked Alix.

"That she was glad I was here, and that I wore her name well," Alix said, her voice tinged with awe.

Myra clasped her hands. "An omen. You'll be remembered, darling."

The dowager's eyes gleamed. "Indeed."

Lena exhaled, too afraid to ask how she'd done.

"You didn't trip or fall," the dowager said over her fan. "That will suffice."

Lena laughed, the last of her nerves spilling free. "Then I shall count it a triumph."

"Do," the dowager said. "And for heaven's sake, stop looking as though you wish you'd photographed the Princess. It's unseemly."

"I can't help it," Lena replied. "She's so ... symmetrical."

Alix dissolved into giggles, and even Myra's lips curved.

The dowager sighed, though her eyes twinkled. "An artist in the family. Heaven preserve us."

As they stepped into the bright afternoon, sunlight fell warm across the gravel. The crowd's cheer rippled faintly beyond the gates. Lena drew a long breath of freedom. She'd survived—no fainting, no scandal, no humiliation.

Perhaps she could endure London society after all. And if Mr. Jeffers dared tease her for curtsying to royalty—and he surely would—she would remind him that she'd done it in heels, feathers, and a gown that weighed more than his motorcar.

The faint strains of a violin drifted up to Lena's bedroom on the third floor of the Akethorpe townhouse. Below, the household swelled with the noise of final preparations. Footmen hurried through corridors. The scent of roses carried on the breeze through an open window. The dowager had spared no expense—the ball that followed their presentation at court would be talked of for weeks.

Lena fastened the clasp of her pearl necklace just as Alix swept in, her eyes glittering with excitement.

"Can you believe it?" She twirled, her skirts fanning in perfect circles. "We've been presented—and now, our first real ball in London! Can you imagine dancing in that ballroom?"

Lena smiled, though her stomach tightened. "You'll have no shortage of partners, as lovely as you look."

"But I want one in particular." Alix clasped her hands to her chest, eyes bright with a secret she had no intention of sharing.

Lena's breath caught. *Please, Lord, not Mr. Jeffers.*

Before she could ask, the hall clock chimed eight. "Come along. Grandmama expects us in the receiving line precisely on the hour."

They descended the stairs, the hum of the crowd rising to meet them. When Lena stepped into the great receiving room, light and sound seemed to expand all at once. The air shimmered with candle heat and perfume. The parquet floors gleamed dangerously underfoot, as though conspiring to test every woman's balance.

It was magnificent, yes—but also overwhelming. Lena couldn't shake the feeling that she was stepping onto a stage rather than into a celebration.

At the far end of the room, the dowager presided over the

introductions like a general before her troops—erect, serene, her cane planted firmly on the floor. Myra stood beside her, gracious and composed, her every gesture controlled. Lena felt a rush of affection. Myra might drive her half mad with match-making, but she did it out of love.

Max joined them within minutes, dapper and entirely too confident. Men had it easy. He would dance, charm, and leave England in a fortnight without worrying what anyone thought of him.

Guests streamed in, their voices blending with the orchestra's prelude. Fans fluttered and jewels flashed. Because of the dowager's rank, every introduction was respectful, though not all equally warm. Lena smiled until her cheeks ached.

At twenty past the hour, the dowager raised her cane like a conductor, and the orchestra began the first waltz.

The ballroom glowed. Candlelight fractured across mirrors, and silk skirts brushed in rhythm. Lena's photographer's eye stirred. Each moment begged to be captured—the blur of motion, the shimmer of color, the elegance. She imagined freezing it all in a single frame.

Beside her, Alix glowed in silver tulle over white satin, clutching her closed fan too tightly.

"Don't fidget," Lena whispered, steadying her. "Smile. Stand tall. You're the belle of the ball, and don't forget it."

Alix's nervous grin turned luminous.

Lena wished confidence could be shared like a fan between sisters. She inhaled, drawing strength from habit rather than actual courage.

Her dance card filled quickly—four sets promised before she even had her first sip of punch. Like in Philadelphia, she reminded herself, no more than two dances with the same gentleman.

After her fourth partner bowed away, she slipped to the edge of the room for a moment's peace, joining Myra and the dowager near the unlit hearth. The crowd moved like a current before her—colors, laughter, motion.

Alix was easy to spot, spinning across the floor with a young man whose grin bordered on smug. Lena smiled despite herself. Her sister had always gathered attention without trying.

She felt an unidentifiable awareness sift through her. And then—just past the open doors—she saw him.

Bronley Jeffers, in formal black, stood beside Max at the edge of the foyer, speaking to an older gentleman. He looked perfectly at ease, which was infuriating. The candlelight caught the sun in his hair, the curve of his mouth hinting at amusement. As if he'd expected her to look—and caught her doing it.

He inclined his head in greeting, subtle, almost teasing, before turning back to his conversation.

Lena's pulse gave a traitorous skip. She pressed a gloved hand to her middle. *So he came after all.*

He crossed the ballroom floor, pausing to greet Myra and the dowager, apologizing for his late arrival.

Then his eyes found hers.

"Miss Dennison," he said, bowing slightly, his voice a blend of charm and something beneath it.

"Mr. Jeffers," she returned, matching his composure, though her pulse had gone traitor again.

For a heartbeat, they stood amid the swirl of dancers, the orchestra swelling around them.

"You handled yourself well today, I understand," he said softly. "That was no small audience. I'm proud of you."

"Proud?" She tilted her head. "You sound like my tutor."

His smile curved, half amusement, half challenge. "Then allow me to prove myself a partner instead. The next set is ours."

Her protest withered before it reached her lips. The music

shifted, and his hand extended. She hesitated only a breath before setting hers atop it.

They stepped onto the floor as the next waltz began. His hand at her waist was firm, guiding. Her body remembered the pattern before her mind caught up.

"You're smiling," he murmured.

"I'm not."

"You are. Slightly."

"Don't presume to read me, Mr. Jeffers."

"Like your presumptions about me?"

She might have answered if her breath hadn't caught on the turn. The chandeliers blurred above them, light scattering like water. The rest of the room fell away. For one dizzy moment, there was only the music and the warmth of his hand.

When the waltz ended, he released her, but his gaze lingered, saying everything propriety forbade.

Lena stiffened her spine and summoned every ounce of sense she possessed. She would not be swayed by charm—or by the strange exhilaration that made her heart race.

ELEVEN

Bron enjoyed society balls, with the hum of conversation, and the music that set even the stiffest Englishman into motion. If ever there was a stage for the Merry Barrister to perform, this was it—an audience of eager young ladies, suspicious matrons, and half-bored husbands ready to be cajoled into laughter.

Tonight was no exception. The Akethorpe townhouse glowed with light and warmth, the ballroom a kaleidoscope of gowns and jewels. Bron had already danced twice, shared three witty remarks that earned ripples of laughter, and accepted a glass of champagne. He was in his element.

Until he remembered why his aunt wasn't here.

He'd left her earlier that evening, resting in her townhouse, the faintest pallor stealing across her face again. Her physician had diagnosed a chronic gastric inflammation, brought on, he said, by "rich food and too little fresh air." Bron tried to take comfort in the certainty of the man's tone. The treatment—a light broth, a tonic before bed, and absolute rest—sounded sensible enough. And yet, watching his aunt fade a little more each week, he couldn't quite silence the unease coiling in his chest.

"Jeffers," Harry called from behind.

Bron turned and shook Harry's outstretched hand.

"Lady Akethorpe informed me that your aunt is unwell?"

"Her doctor insists it's only a stomach complaint. Says she'll recover with the proper rest and diet." He paused, managing a faint smile. "I hope he's right. London feels less itself without her."

Harry nodded, sympathy flickering beneath his good humor. "A pity. Though if she were here, she'd see half the women in London angling to become the next Mrs. Jeffers. And eventual Baron Langston. It's a battlefield out there."

Bron groaned. "Don't start." He didn't want to be reminded that if the worst happened and his aunt passed away, he'd inherit the barony.

"I'm merely stating the obvious," Harry teased. "The eligible daughters of Britain are in fine form tonight, and yet —" he leaned closer "—you seem interested in only one."

Bron gave him a flat look. "One?"

Harry tipped his glass toward the far side of the ballroom where Helena Dennison stood, poised and composed in ice blue satin. "That one."

"You're imagining things."

"Am I? You've watched her since you walked in."

"I've watched everyone. It's part of the sport."

Harry laughed softly. "Sport, is it? I think you're a man already half caught."

"Caught implies a trap," Bron said dryly. "And I'm not foolish enough to walk into one."

Harry's eyes gleamed. "No? Then why are you still looking at her?"

"What do you know? You're barely out of your nappies."

"I'm five and twenty, as you well know," Harry sputtered.

Bron tossed back the rest of his champagne—not that it

helped—and set the glass aside. "It's my duty to dance with the dowager's granddaughter. That's all."

Harry grinned. "A noble sacrifice."

Bron ignored him, crossing the ballroom. Helena stood at the edge of the floor, her gloved hands clasped at her waist, her expression betraying neither boredom nor excitement. But when she turned toward him, her lips turned up in the faintest of smiles.

"Miss Dennison." He bowed. "May I have the honor of one more dance? I believe that's socially acceptable."

Her hesitation lasted a breath. "It would seem so." She placed her hand in his, her touch light but steady.

The orchestra struck up a waltz. Bron guided her onto the floor, his movements sure and easy. Her steps were measured, deliberate. Together, they found the rhythm.

"You don't care for waltzes?" he asked lightly. "Or is it just me?"

Her eyes flicked up to his. "I adore waltzes."

He caught the hint of a smile playing at her lips and smiled back.

Her chin lifted, and for a moment he thought she might laugh. It was absurd, the two of them gliding beneath glittering chandeliers while a string quartet played some Viennese confection. Yet it felt strangely easy.

"You've been in London nearly a month," he said. "Does it suit you?"

Her gaze drifted over the crowded room. "It's beautiful, certainly. Though one does get the sense it's all … performance."

He chuckled. "You've seen through it already. Most take a lifetime."

"And you?" she asked. "You seem to enjoy it."

"Of course. I've always liked a good performance."

Her brows arched. "Even when you're the one acting?"

He grinned. "Especially then."

For a heartbeat, their gazes held. The world narrowed to the rhythm of their steps, the rustle of her skirts brushing against his leg, the faint scent of roses clinging to her gloves.

He shouldn't have noticed any of it. He was here out of duty—to his aunt and to Augusta. But when she looked at him with that quiet defiance, he felt something he couldn't name stir beneath the layers of practiced charm.

"Do you always deflect questions with humor?" she asked suddenly.

"It keeps life interesting."

She tilted her head. "Or safe?"

The remark hit closer than she likely intended. Bron's grin faltered for the briefest second before he covered it. "Touché, Miss Dennison."

Before she could reply, a pair of dancers swept too close, forcing Helena to step nearer. Her hand tightened briefly on his shoulder, and he felt the warmth of her through the thin layers of evening fabric.

"Forgive me," she murmured, regaining her balance.

"Not at all." His voice came out lower than intended. "You're remarkably steady."

"Years of practice."

"I should have guessed. The English court system could use a few lessons in poise and composure."

That drew the faintest laugh from her—a soft, reluctant sound that settled somewhere deep in his chest, robbing him of his breath.

When the final notes of the waltz faded, he released her hand with deliberate slowness, bowing once more. "Thank you, Miss Dennison."

"And thank you, Mr. Jeffers."

She started to step back, but the movement caught her

train. He reached out instinctively, steadying her arm before she could stumble.

Their eyes met again—too close this time, too aware.

She drew in a breath, composed herself, and stepped away. "Good evening."

"Good evening," he echoed, watching her glide toward her sister.

Harry reappeared at his elbow, wearing that infuriatingly knowing expression. "A 'noble sacrifice,' you said?"

Bron didn't look away from Helena. "That's correct."

Harry chuckled softly. "Perhaps. But something tells me, old friend, you're not quite as detached as you think."

Bron exhaled, running a hand through his hair. "You're wrong."

"Rarely," Harry replied with a cocky grin.

Bron's gaze found Helena once more across the ballroom, radiant beneath the glow of a thousand candles. For the first time all night, the hum of conversation and the glitter of chandeliers faded to nothing.

He told himself it was curiosity. Nothing more.

But even as he thought it, he wasn't sure he believed it.

⚬

"I believe the next dance is mine, Miss Dennison." The pleasant voice came from behind Lena's left shoulder. She turned to find Lord Henry Tisdale standing with a smile and warm brown eyes.

Harry was everything Lena thought a gentleman should be—amiable, articulate, and possessed of a charm that made one feel welcome. He bowed as the orchestra struck up a gentle Strauss piece.

When she curtsied and called him Lord Henry—as was

acceptable for the second son of a duke—he instantly corrected her.

"Harry, please."

"And you must call me Lena."

"I'm told you survived Miss Derry-Ballister's training unscathed. Quite a feat," he said as he led her onto the floor.

"Barely unscathed," Lena replied, unable to suppress a laugh. "My knees may never forgive her."

"Ah, but you curtsy beautifully." His tone was complimentary without being forward. "The dowager must be proud."

"I think so. It's hard to tell with her. However, she's already planning which dignitary we should meet next."

"She's a formidable woman—but never dull." Harry guided her into a smooth turn.

"That seems to be the family motto."

He grinned. "And tell me—are you finding London tolerable so far?"

"Tolerable," she said carefully. "Though I'm not sure we're welcome by everyone. I feel like there are women here who would like to see us on the next ship back to the United States."

Harry's eyes twinkled. "Don't take it personally. Every unmarried lady in this room is watching Bron. And at this moment, he's watching you."

Lena glanced instinctively toward the opposite side of the floor, where Mr. Jeffers stood talking to a duchess she'd met earlier, but for the life of her couldn't remember her name. She was from Ireland, that Lena knew.

Mr. Jeffers's gaze, though polite, drifted toward Lena as if drawn by some invisible thread.

A tiny flutter stirred in her chest. "Surely you exaggerate," she murmured.

"I assure you, the jealousy is palpable. Half the mothers

here are recalculating their daughters' prospects because an American has captured the Merry Barrister's attention."

She rolled her eyes, though her cheeks warmed. "I would have thought they'd want their daughters to steer clear. Don't they want men with titles? And he has a reputation."

"His reputation is more myth than anything. And you must understand—Bron's something of a prize."

"Oh?"

"A respectable fortune, a future title, and the good manners to carry both without arrogance. It's a rare combination."

"A future title?" It was news to Lena.

"He'll inherit the Langston estate in East Anglia when his aunt passes away. The estate has more than five thousand unencumbered acres."

An estate not in debt up to its eyeballs was a rarity, from what she'd been told.

"I'm not sure I understand. How will he inherit the barony?"

"The original barony was unusual," Harry said. "It can pass to heirs, male or female. The late baron had no sons, only two daughters—Eleanor and Bron's mother. Since Eleanor never married and therefore has no children, the title passes to her younger sister. However, Bron's mother passed away when Bron was a boy. So, now, the title and estate will go to Bron eventually."

"And if he were to die—without children?"

"Then the title reverts to the next branch of the family descending from the fifth baron. That happens to be one Cedric Redgrave. His great-grandfather and Bron's great-grandfather were brothers."

Lena tilted her head. "Isn't he already titled through his father?"

"For the past year. He's the Duke of Haverleigh and has an

estate in Norfolk, but if rumors are true, Redgrave's estate is in financial straits."

The dance ended, and Harry escorted Lena to the refreshment table for a drink. "So, that brings us back to the original subject. The ladies who glare at you tonight have their eyes on the future prize of the very wealthy Langston estate."

Lena's lips twitched. "You have a rather cynical view of the women here."

"I see the battlefield clearly, and make sure I'm armed with knowledge and self-awareness." He grinned and took a sip of champagne. "Though I confess, it's entertaining. Every time Bron so much as looks at you, a debutante faints in spirit."

"Then perhaps I should keep my distance, for their health."

"Too late for that," he said lightly. "He's already decided you're interesting."

The words struck deeper than he perhaps intended. Lena looked away, her heart beating faster than the music.

"If I may say so, Lena, your sister is causing quite a sensation."

Lena glanced across the room. Cheeks flushed and eyes bright, Alix was surrounded by a small cluster of admirers.

"I'd better make sure she's behaving herself." Lena set her half-empty glass on a footman's tray.

Harry stuck out his elbow. "I'll walk you over there."

They arrived at Alix's side the moment Max and Mr. Jeffers did the same.

Max surreptitiously nudged Mr. Jeffers, who turned to Alix. "Miss Dennison, I believe the next dance is mine."

Alix glanced at her dance card. If Lena remembered correctly, the spot had been promised to someone else.

Alix, eyes lit, dropped the card and let Mr. Jeffers lead her to the floor. Her admirers drifted away in search of another female to lavish attention on.

"Did you plan that?" Lena asked Max.

"As a matter of fact, I did," he chuckled. "Those men were getting a little too friendly."

When the orchestra struck up another lively tune, and Mr. Jeffers led Alix into the swell of dancers, Lena couldn't look away. The two of them moved as though they'd known each other for years, his confident lead matching her youthful exuberance step for step.

When they returned, Mr. Jeffers made some remark that drew a bright laugh from Alix. Lena forced herself to smile. It would not do to seem disapproving in public.

All in all, the dowager's ball appeared a success. Lena even caught herself a time or two composing the scene in her mind as if for a photograph.

Through it all, Mr. Jeffers was nothing but attentive and polite, dancing again with Alix and once with Myra.

And yet, Lena found herself fascinated.

Get a hold of yourself. She was no schoolgirl to be carried away by devastatingly handsome looks and a roguish smile.

When the ball finally ended, she let out a sigh of relief.

At last, when all the guests' carriages had driven away, the family withdrew to their bedrooms. Lena felt the weight of the night settle upon her shoulders as she undressed. She extinguished the lamp, slid beneath the coverlet, and closed her eyes —only to hear the faint creak of her door.

"Lena?"

Alix slipped inside, a shawl drawn hastily over her nightgown, her cheeks still pink with excitement. She perched at the foot of the bed like a conspirator.

"You should be asleep," Lena whispered.

"I couldn't." Alix drew in a breath, her eyes shining in the dim light. "I had to tell someone. Lena—I think I've found someone I could truly fall in love with."

Lena's heart stuttered. "Who's that?"

"Bron," Alix breathed the name out, her smile dreamy. "He's everything a gentleman should be—kind, handsome, attentive. And when we danced—oh, Lena, it felt as though the whole room vanished."

Lena pushed herself upright, searching for words. The echo of his hand at her own waist, the memory of his easy grin, still lingered far too vividly. But she saw the eagerness in Alix's expression and knew she must not falter.

"Alix," she said quietly, "you barely know him. Do not mistake charm for constancy. Mr. Jeffers is ... practiced at this sort of thing. And he's at least ten years older than you."

Alix's face fell. "You don't like him?"

Lena hesitated. *Too much*, her heart whispered. "I only want you to be cautious."

Alix sighed, slipping down onto the coverlet beside her. "Perhaps. But I can't help it. He makes me feel—" She broke off, cheeks flushing deeper. "Different. Alive."

Lena drew her sister into a steadying embrace, even as her own pulse raced. "We've still so much more to do here before we leave. And leave we will. Don't be hasty in forming attachments."

But long after Alix returned to her own room, Lena lay awake, staring into the darkness. For all her warnings, she could not banish the memory of Mr. Jeffers guiding her across the floor, nor the unsettling truth that her sister's infatuation was not hers alone.

TWELVE

A pale morning haze hung above the rooftops, but by noon the sky had cleared to a bright, sharp blue—the kind of day that begged for speed. Bron stood in the mews behind his Kensington house, sleeves rolled, checking his newest motorcar's brass fittings.

Unlike the Fleetwing he'd raced in Monte Carlo, this vehicle was from their flagship Marquis line. A luxury model with eight horsepower for the wealthy who wanted speed and room for passengers. Their third model, the Vanguard, would be more affordable, stylish, and reliable.

Bron found immense satisfaction not only in racing his cars but also in working with his engineer on designs that customers would enjoy.

At the clatter of an approaching carriage, his gaze shifted from the car hood to the road. Max jumped from the vehicle and strolled to the coach house's open door.

"By Jove," he drawled, mimicking a stuffy British accent. "She looks like a black cougar that might take a man's arm off if he so much as touched her wrong."

Bron grinned and wiped his hands on a nearby cloth. "Then we'll see if she purrs for you. Step up—you've the honor of being her first passenger."

"My last hoorah before I head back to the States," Max said, climbing in. "How fast will she go?"

"She should get up to at least thirty miles per hour."

Max whistled. "So almost as fast as a first-class horse at Epsom."

"That's right."

"But you can't drive more than … What? … Fourteen unless you want to be arrested."

Bron nodded. The Locomotives on Highways Act, passed the year before, raised the speed limit from eight to fourteen. "Even so, the traffic in town makes it difficult to go over eight." Bron handed Max a pair of goggles and placed a pair over his own eyes. He turned and grinned at Max. "But I have other plans."

Bron cranked the engine. It sputtered, coughed, then roared to life, scattering a pair of terrified cats. They rattled out of the mews and onto the street, the motor growling beneath them.

"Where to?" Max shouted over the din.

"Out toward Richmond," Bron called back. "We'll find a stretch of open road there. The constables can't chase us that far."

They skirted around Hyde Park Corner, drawing curses from cabmen and cheers from boys waving their caps. When the last terraces of Hammersmith fell behind them, the roads widened, and the city loosened its grip. Bron eased the throttle forward, the motor answering with a deep, eager hum.

Max whooped, clinging to his hat. "Good heavens, Jeffers, you mean to kill us both!"

"Not at all," Bron laughed. "This is freedom!"

The words had barely left his mouth when something jolted beneath the chassis. A grinding shriek ripped through the air—the steering wheel jerked violently in his hands. Bron fought it, but the front wheels wrenched sideways as though caught by an invisible hand.

"Hang on!" he barked.

The car slewed off the road, struck the verge, and lurched into a shallow ditch. Metal screamed. Dust and gravel flew. The machine shuddered to a stop at a dangerous angle.

Bron's ears rang. For a moment, there was only the tick-tick-tick of the cooling engine. Then Max groaned.

"Blast," Bron muttered, scrambling out. "Are you hurt?"

"I'm fine," Max answered. But then he cradled his left arm against his chest, his face white.

Dust settled in Bron's throat, and he tasted blood from where he'd bitten his lip. He and his team had built this machine with precision and trusted every bolt. This shouldn't have happened, and he'd never forgive himself for putting his passenger in danger. His gut clenched at the odd angle of Max's arm. "We'll find a doctor."

They limped the motorcar to a nearby inn at Kew Bridge, where a local physician set Max's arm in a stiff starch-and-bandage cast—plaster of paris was still a rarity in the country, it seemed, but this improvised splint would hold until they returned to town.

While Max finished up with the doctor, Bron returned to examine his car. The steering appeared to have been tampered with. Loosened enough at the joint to come apart over time and distance. That wasn't wear—it looked deliberate.

Within the hour, Bron had hired a carriage to carry them back to Berkeley Square. He'd have one of his team fetch the motorcar later.

They reached the townhouse near dusk. Max's arm was

bound from wrist to elbow, and his face had gone gray from the jolts of the cab.

Across the road, just inside the park, Helena stood with her camera poised, Alix posing by the iron railings. Laughter filled the air until the sisters saw them.

Helena's smile vanished, and she dashed across the street. "Max?"

Bron didn't have the opportunity to explain before she was at her brother's side. "What happened?"

"Just a mishap on the road," Max said quickly. "Nothing serious."

"Nothing serious?" Her eyes flashed. "Have you broken your arm?"

Bron started to speak, but she rounded on him like a storm. "How dare you bring him back like this?" Color flushed her cheeks. Then, as though realizing how near she'd come to panic, she straightened, fury rushing in to fill the space fear had left. "I knew that machine was dangerous. You treat danger as amusement, and other people pay the price!"

Her voice cut deeper than she likely knew. Bron, used to deflecting criticism with charm, found none at hand. "It wasn't recklessness," he said quietly. "Something gave way in the steering, but I did my best to control the vehicle. As soon as possible, I'll have it examined."

"Examined?" she echoed, disbelief sharpening the word. "And if it had been worse? If you'd both been killed?"

Max tried to intercede with an awkward grin. "Lena, truly—"

"Be still, Max." Her voice softened as she turned to him. "Come inside. We'll get you settled."

She guided her brother toward the door, every line of her posture taut with fury and fear. Bron, stood on the sidewalk, hat in hand, and watched them disappear into the house.

Wilkins lingered a moment. "Shall I inform the family you're staying, sir?"

Bron hesitated. "No. Not today."

As he turned toward the street, he looked back at the windows of the townhouse. The crash replayed in his mind—the sudden give in the wheel, the unnatural way the metal had failed.

His prototype was a failure. A dangerous failure.

"Augusta said I'd find you out here," Max said as he descended the garden steps.

Lena set her camera beside her on the stone bench. "I needed the air."

"Or the space to fume?" Max winked. "Don't be upset with Bron. I'm fine."

"Your arm is broken, had to be set, and is now in a cast. You're *not* fine."

Sometimes Max's devil-may-care attitude grated on her nerves.

Like right now.

He gave a crooked smile and sat next to her, arm in a sling and legs crossed at the ankles. "I keep running it through in my head. It doesn't make sense."

"The accident?"

He nodded. "We weren't going that fast."

She turned her face toward him and narrowed her eyes. "Oh, really?"

"Well, not fast for Bron." His gaze drifted to the garden awash in spring blooms. "The road was clear. Then—just this clatter, like metal striking metal. Bron kept his hands steady, tried to correct, but the steering wouldn't take. Then suddenly we were in the ditch. I swear it wasn't him losing control."

Lena's stomach clenched at the thought of how much worse it could have been. *Thank You again, Lord, for watching over them.*

"Do you think something was wrong with the car?"

"I don't know. Maybe a loose part, maybe more." Max's gaze met hers, steady but troubled. "He said he checked it thoroughly after it was delivered from his company shop a few days ago—and that was after his team gave it a full examination. I have a suspicion—and it's just a gut feeling, mind you —that he'll find someone tampered with it."

Lena's pulse quickened. "Do you really believe that?"

"I'm saying it's odd." He leaned back, rubbing a hand over his jaw. "But that's Bron's problem now. Mine is getting back to Philadelphia before the month's out."

The abrupt shift caught her off guard. "You're leaving even though you've just broken your arm?"

"I need to get back. You knew I wouldn't stay the entire time, and it has been a month. My arm will be fine. Besides—" His expression softened. "Lou wrote me."

"Lou?"

He hesitated, then drew a letter from his coat pocket, looking as though he'd read it a dozen times. "It's not anything she says outright. But it's the way she says it. All cheer, all sunshine. She talks about the social whirl—dinners, shopping, how Stuart's been invited to this and that meeting in New York—but every line feels … thin."

Lena's throat tightened. "You think she's unhappy."

"I think Stuart's gone too often, and she's trying to convince herself she doesn't mind."

Lena picked a dying rose petal from the bush beside the bench. "Lou, as quiet and introspective as she is, hates being alone. She'll sit in a drawing room, quietly reading or embroidering, not really joining in the chatter—but as soon as everyone leaves, she feels the need to go too. Or at least that's what she told me once, a few years after Mama passed."

A sigh escaped Lena's lips, and she tossed the petal into the breeze. "So, I always made sure I never left her alone. Papa used to joke that I was like a mother duck. But maybe I just made it worse—made her think she couldn't stand on her own."

Max shook his head. "You gave her someone to depend on, and to look up to. But it was never your job to raise our sisters, Lena."

She smiled faintly. "I always believed it was."

"And you've done an admirable job." His grin eased the heaviness between them. "Honestly, I think Lou married Stuart so fast because he was the first man who made her feel grown. Special."

Lena folded her hands in her lap, tracing the edge of her cuff. "You never liked him."

"I still don't. But *she* chose *him*, and that means I bite my tongue."

"You? Bite your tongue?"

"Occasionally," he said with mock gravity. "I worry for her," he said, his tone softer. "But I'll see what's what when I get home."

A companionable silence settled, warm with affection. For all his teasing, Max had always been her anchor.

He studied her for a moment, then tipped his head. "What about you?"

"What about me?"

"You've been playing nursemaid to everyone since we landed in England—Myra, Alix, even Augusta. Now you'll do it to me since I'm banged up." He found her hand and gave it a squeeze. "When's the last time you did something for yourself?"

She blinked, caught off guard once again. "I have fun."

"Oh, yes," he said dryly. "Taking pictures of the family, with you rarely in the photographs—pure amusement."

"Someone has to be practical. I'm recording our trip for posterity."

He leaned forward, his good elbow on his knee. "You're allowed to be practical *and* alive, Lena. You have a romantic heart—"

"A romantic heart? Me?" She laughed outright.

He held up a finger. "I've seen the books you read when you think no one's looking. Don't worry, I won't tell anyone." He winked, but his voice held quiet sincerity. "Unfortunately, you keep your heart buried in everyone else's troubles. You'll end up missing your own story."

His words landed with quiet force.

She sighed. "Spoken like an older brother who's about to run away from all the chaos. And Alix could very well do something stupid on this trip."

"Like fall for a motorcar racer?"

"Exactly." She was glad she wasn't the only one who knew of Alix's growing attachment to Mr. Jeffers.

"I've spoken to Bron and asked him to take care. I don't think he realized what was happening. He has no designs on Alix, I'm certain. Thinks of her more like a little sister." Max stood and smiled down at Lena. "Don't worry so. It will all be fine. Let Alix make a few mistakes—it's part of growing up. And let yourself breathe. Dance, laugh, drive one of Bron's motorcars, because I know you secretly want to. Just—be Lena."

Something in her chest eased at his tone, that old mixture of mischief and tenderness she'd missed since he'd taken up residence in his own house. "I'll try," she whispered.

"Good. Because I want a full report, so write often."

Max held out his hand to help her stand. "For what it's worth, I like Bron. He's solid. You could do worse."

Heat crept up her neck. "I don't know what you're talking about. I'm not interested in him in the least. Besides, we're as different as chalk and cheese."

"Really? I'm not so sure." He tilted his head with a grin that was half challenge, half farewell. "Take care of yourself, little sister."

He turned toward the house and walked up the path, his footsteps clicking on the bricks.

The door closed behind him with a gentle thud, leaving Lena alone with her camera and her thoughts.

The breeze picked up, and the roses swayed in the sunlight, their petals trembling.

No, she had no interest in Bronley Jeffers. At least, not one she was ready to admit.

Besides, she was still annoyed at the man. Even if the accident hadn't been his fault, it was *his* motorcar, and he *was* driving fast—no matter what Max said.

⁂

A week had passed since the accident, yet the ashen look on Max's face and the state of his arm still flashed often in Lena's mind. She told herself she was grateful he'd sailed for home yesterday, arm bound tight and spirits intact. He'd joked that the voyage home would probably be smoother than Bron's driving. She didn't find it funny.

Since then, London had worked itself into a frenzy with the upcoming Jubilee festivities, while still maintaining its rhythm of carriages clattering over cobblestones, paperboys shouting headlines, and the ever-present hum of the city's life.

And peace, for Lena, remained elusive. Every time she

looked out a window that faced Berkeley Square, she caught herself glancing toward the street, half expecting one of Bron's motorcars to pull up to the curb.

She stared at the latest edition of *Lady's Pictorial* with its ten pages of articles, drawings, and photographs from the Drawing Room presentation they'd attended at Buckingham Palace. Apparently, it was also the last one of the season, so its significance was important. Alix was depicted in her gorgeous gown, and Lena thanked the Lord that she had been written about in the best possible light. Lena and Myra were barely mentioned, but that was just fine with Lena.

"Mr. Jeffers, miss."

Wilkins had the quiet walk of a house cat, and Lena's heart jolted at both his announcement and the thought of their visitor.

"He's here?" *As opposed to what, Lena, you fool.*

"Yes, miss. He requests a word."

She hesitated, willing her pulse to steady. A proper English lady alone in the room would send him away without hesitation. A proper *American* lady might send him packing, but not without first telling him precisely what she thought of his reckless pursuits.

But curiosity—a troublesome, persistent thing—made her nod. "Very well. Show him in."

Bron entered the room like a man uncertain of his welcome, hat in hand. His expression was composed, but there was a new tautness about him, a gravity she hadn't seen before.

"Miss Dennison," he said in measured tones. "I wanted to call sooner, but my aunt advised me to wait until you got Max settled on the ship and bound for America."

She set her magazine aside and stood to face him. "If you've come to apologize, it isn't necessary. You already did so in your letter."

"I did," he admitted. "But not properly."

Her lips tightened. "Very well—apologize properly, then. I'm listening."

He smiled faintly. "You make it sound like a court deposition."

"It feels like one."

He studied her a moment, as if weighing his words. "I am truly sorry for what happened. I would never have risked it if I hadn't believed the car sound."

"*Believed* it sound," she repeated. "That's hardly reassuring."

He ran a hand through his hair. Thick with a slight wave. Women would kill for those tresses.

Lena shook her head, hoping to clear her addled brain. "So what caused the accident?"

"Mechanical failure."

She opened her mouth to ask him what difference it made. Driver error or a vehicle that shouldn't have been on the road, let alone with a passenger. Either way, it was his fault that Max had a broken arm.

But he spoke before she could voice her thought. "I'm having it brought in from the village where I left it to have an expert in mechanics take a look at it. Someone outside my team. If it was a failure of one of *my* mechanics, I don't want them to know I'm looking into it."

She swallowed, her fingers twisting together before she could stop them. "And you think telling me this will ease my mind?"

"No." His voice softened. "But you deserve to know that your brother's injury wasn't the result of my carelessness with Max's life."

For a heartbeat, neither spoke. The faint tick of the mantel clock filled the silence.

Finally, she said, "Then I should thank the Almighty that

he gave you good reflexes. For your acting quickly and mitigating the damage, as Max told me you did."

Silence fell again, but this time it wasn't sharp-edged. The late-afternoon light slanted across the room, catching dust motes in a golden haze. She became aware of how close he stood, the scent of motor oil and clean linen mingling faintly in the air.

His expression hardened, though not with arrogance this time—with something like resolve. "I won't let it happen again."

She nodded slowly, uncertain what she felt—relief, perhaps, or admiration she didn't care to name. "Then I wish you success, Mr. Jeffers."

He held up a hand before she could see him to the door. "I wish you'd call me by my Christian name. It will be easier since we're going to see each other quite a bit in the coming weeks."

"What are you talking about?" Lena sputtered.

"Your brother asked that I make myself available to you and your family as an escort to the coming society events."

Why, of all the nerve! She'd give Max an earful when she returned home.

Bron held up his hand. "Before you protest, my aunt and your grandmother have insisted on the same. So here I am."

"It isn't necessary. My father and my sister Beatrice will be coming to London in three weeks, so we'll have a male escort."

"And what will you do until then?"

"Lie low. We don't have to attend any more events."

A noise at the doorway had both Bron and Lena turning toward the door.

Myra sailed into the room, followed closely by Alix and the dowager.

"What's this nonsense, Lena?" Myra waved a hand toward Bron. "Mr. Jeffers is being ever so kind. There are many events to attend between now and the time we leave."

Alix tugged at Lena's arm. "I already have my dress for the Oppenheim flower ball."

The dowager moved to her favorite chair. "And it wouldn't do for you to miss it. It's the talk of the season."

Bron chuckled and lifted his shoulder. "I guess you're outnumbered, Miss Dennison."

Lena sighed and sank onto the settee. "Oh, for heaven's sake, call me Lena."

Thirteen

Bron had attended his share of Mayfair entertainments, but Mrs. Oppenheim's flower ball outshone them all. Her Bruton Street townhouse rose like a shrine to horticultural excess. Light spilled from the tall windows, gilding the slick pavement where carriages inched forward, and footmen in splendid livery helped every female guest alight.

The scent reached him before the music. The interior of the stately home was a veritable bouquet of roses, lilies, and orchids. Garlands looped from the ceiling. Banks of flowers devoured the staircase. Every lady glittered, every gentleman bloomed. Society's theater was in full performance.

"By Jove." Harry shook his head as he murmured, "She's managed to cram Kew Gardens into her ballroom."

"Let's hope she's left room for the guests."

Harry leaned slightly closer. "Speaking of guests—I ran into Lady Haverleigh on my way up the stairs. Or rather, Lady Haverleigh's gown nearly ran into me."

Bron frowned. "The Redgraves are here?" He'd thought Cedric was to return to the country to see to some estate business.

"I didn't see Cedric, but his wife is wearing a Worth creation I understand," Harry said dryly. "Silk, lace, hand-embroidered roses—one-of-a-kind, mind you. She told Lady Wetherby it was made exclusively for her. Must have cost Cedric half a year's income." He took a sip of champagne. "Assuming he still has an income."

Bron's head snapped toward him. "What does that mean?"

"Rumor has it Haverleigh is bleeding money. Cedric inherited an estate already teetering after his father's misman-agement, and he's been trying new 'innovations' in sheep breeding and wool production. Unfortunately, he's throwing good money after bad." Harry shrugged. "London believes he's in trouble. Deep trouble."

Bron's stomach tightened. "He told me nothing."

"Perhaps he doesn't want you to worry."

Or perhaps Cedric knew that if he told Bron, Bron would *help*—and Cedric's pride couldn't bear it.

Bron swallowed the bitterness rising in his throat. "He should have come to me," he murmured.

Harry clapped his shoulder. "I know. You should make sure you corner him when he returns to London. Cedric's a good man. He'll listen to reason."

Before Bron could respond, Harry pointed toward the other side of the room. "I think I see Lady Akethorpe and her Americans over there."

Bron's eyes landed on the group.

Duty called. Although lately, escorting the Dennisons felt less like a chore and more like a delight.

"I'm going to grab a drink. I'm parched," Harry said as he moved toward a server with a tray of champagne in crystal glassware.

Before he could make his way toward Lady Akethorpe, Bron was surrounded by women offering flowers for his lapel.

Mrs. Oppenheim floated toward him, dressed, astonishingly, like a basket of poppies. Bron blinked, needing a moment to take it in. The bodice of her gown shimmered with intricate gold embroidery arranged in a lattice pattern while vivid poppies spilled over her shoulders and sleeves. It was theatrical and extravagant—exactly the sort of thing London society would declare the height of cleverness. "Mr. Jeffers, you are dangerously handsome tonight. And you're already drowning in flowers!"

Bron glanced down at his lapel with a rueful smile. Lilies, orchids, damask roses, and a sprig of sweet pea.

"I'll do my best to stay above water, madam."

Her eyes sparkled, and she turned to a group of women nearby. "Ladies, remember our little game for tonight! One blossom in a gentleman's lapel means 'I favor you.' There's no need to smother the poor man in blooms to make your point." Laughter rippled. She glided on, leaving the faint scent of poppies in her wake.

Harry reappeared with a glass of punch. "If your lapel gets any fuller, I'll prune it with shears."

A murmur rippled through the crowd near the dais. "Miss Goelet—there she is."

Bron followed the collective gaze. The famous American debutante was being presented to the hostess. A slim girl in white satin, her gown banded with violets and diamonds that winked like dew, she moved with the cautious grace of someone aware every eye in London watched her.

"Her father owns half of New York's Fifth Avenue," Harry murmured. "Every bankrupt estate owner will be vying for her attention."

Bron studied the popular, and quite pretty, young woman a moment longer, curious but unmoved. Then, across the ballroom, he caught sight of Lena Dennison, beautiful and poised yet not showy nor self-conscious, her expression thoughtful amid the whirl.

For a fleeting instant, he wondered which woman was more dangerous to a man's peace—the heiress who could buy him or the woman who asked nothing and therefore disarmed him completely.

She moved away, and he could no longer see her. Bron advanced through the crowd, extricating himself as quickly as was polite from several people who wanted to chat.

His gaze sought Lena again. Where others were exuberant bouquets, she was an elegant nosegay in emerald satin with a temperate fall of violets. Taste over display. But it wasn't her looks that drew him. It was how she noticed things. The way she eased her stepmother through a crush, shifted her body so Alix wouldn't be jostled, and measured each word before releasing it.

Finally, he managed to reach the group whose presence he sought.

"Oh, there you are, Bron." Myra extended her gloved hand, and he took it, executing a courtly bow. She tittered at his performance.

Beside her, Alix was fairly bouncing on her toes. "Hello, Mr. Jeffers. Isn't this just the best? Look at all the costumes swirling around the floor!"

"A garden of loveliness with you three women the prize flowers of the evening."

Alix stood on tiptoe and slipped a forget-me-not into his lapel. She either ignored or didn't see the frown her sister gave her, but instead pointed to her dance card. "It's almost full."

Bron nodded and smiled at the exuberant girl. "You are indeed very popular, Miss Dennison. Your sister will need to keep an eye on the young swains vying for your attention." He turned his grin on Lena, who stood next to her sister like a sentinel.

"Miss Dennison," he said as he took Lena's hand, "if this next dance isn't already taken, I'd be honored."

Lena's gloved hand settled lightly in his, but she hesitated. He thought she might refuse, but politeness was ingrained in her very being. "The dance is yours."

The orchestra unfurled a Strauss waltz, and they turned into the current of dancers.

She placed her hand in his, and her eyes strayed to his lapel. "My, my. You're a popular man."

He shrugged, never looking at the flowers he'd collected. "All these blossoms—and not one violet. Have you no mercy?"

Her mouth tilted, but she ignored his question. "Do you know the language of flowers?"

"I'm not certain I do. Do you?"

"Myra gave Alix a book for her debut. Violet for modesty, white lily for purity, red rose for—well, everyone knows roses." Her gaze flicked to his lapel. "Forget-me-nots mean true love and faithfulness, though if he's a man, I doubt the recipient recognizes the gesture." She hesitated and raised her eyes to his. "You should be careful, Mr. Jeffers."

"Am I being careless?"

"Not on purpose." No accusation, only concern. "But Alix *is* young and impressionable."

They turned past Mrs. Oppenheim, who beamed approval, and two matrons who whispered behind their fans. One murmured, "The Merry Barrister," and both tittered.

Once amusing, the moniker now grated.

"You dislike that name," Lena said.

"You're observant."

"It begs the question—what does it cost you to be merry?"

He huffed a laugh. "You ask targeted questions."

"And you answer with jokes," she countered, smiling now. "A formidable habit."

When the waltz ended, Bron guided her across the floor,

slipping her hand through his arm, reluctant to let her go. "Care for a walk outside? It's oppressive in here."

She nodded, although she hesitated at first.

"How is your aunt?" she asked after a few quiet moments of cool, night air.

Bron's thoughts veered to Cavendish Square. "Not well, I'm afraid," he murmured.

Lena's brow knit. "Worse?"

"She's been steady for weeks. Now she fades too easily. Sometimes in the middle of sentences." Realizing his lapse into melancholy, he looked down and gave her a small smile. "Forgive me. Not suitable ballroom talk."

"It's human talk," she said simply. She looked down at her dance card. "I've promised the next waltz to Viscount Southwell. I dare not snub him, or I'll receive a stern lecture from Lady Akethorpe."

He released her—reluctantly. "I'll return you to your family then, so you can wait for the fortunate viscount to whisk you away."

They found Myra and the dowager near a bank of palms, where Mrs. Oppenheim praised the "American freshness" of Alix's forget-me-not trims. Two of the season's most eligible bachelors, a university man, and a middle-aged baronet who fancied himself a poet, surrounded a pink-cheeked Alix.

"Gentlemen," Bron drawled, hoping that his stern face reflected the message that he was keeping an eye on their behavior with the Dennison women. Max had tasked him with watching after his sisters, and he didn't take his commitments lightly.

Alix placed a hand on his forearm. "Will you dance with me next, Mr. Jeffers?"

"Alix! That's not proper. Not here or at home," Lena whispered.

Not sure what to do, Bron turned to Alix. He didn't want

to anger Lena, but he couldn't embarrass her sister by turning her down either.

"Certainly, Miss Dennison. How could I forget you owe me a dance?"

He led her onto the dance floor and made sure not to move in as close as he had with Lena. Alix was an admirable dancer for someone so young. And she kept up a surprisingly interesting conversation, even if she did jump from one subject to the next.

The next few hours flew by in a whirl of dancing and engaging conversation with other guests. The hostess made certain that no one was bored. Even Bron, who considered himself worldly and perhaps a little jaded, enjoyed himself immensely.

The departure was pandemonium—cloaks retrieved and carriages called. In the crush, Alix slipped close and touched a tiny posy at his lapel. "You kept my flower," she whispered reverently.

"I did," he said, slightly shifting his body away from hers. "They are valiant flowers."

Her eyes shone. Lena, a pace behind, saw the exchange. Her mouth tightened. Bron caught her eye and gave a small nod. *I'll be careful.* At least that's what he hoped his face portrayed.

Outside, the May night was cool and fragrant with honeysuckle. He waited with the Dennisons and Augusta for the Akethorpe carriage. When it nosed its way over, he opened the door and handed Myra into the vehicle, then the dowager, then Alix, and Lena last. Her fingers rested in his, and his heart thudded. He, the Merry Barrister, had a heart fluttering over an American woman who showed little interest in him, other than to keep him away from her sister.

"Bronley," the dowager said before he closed the door and

stepped back. "Tell your aunt we pray for her strength. We'll pay a visit as soon as she's up to it."

He bowed. "I will. Good night."

"Good night," they said in unison. He tried to catch Lena's eye, but she was already looking away.

At the last moment, however, she turned her head toward Bron and the look on her face almost had him vaulting into the carriage.

Instead, he closed the door with a quiet click and stepped back.

In the distance, a clock chimed two. Before the carriage moved out into traffic, Bron caught his reflection in the window. Hair still in place, a polite smile on his face, and blossoms wilting in his lapel.

The Merry Barrister, all bloom and no root.

Yet, he strode to his own carriage with the distinct sense that he, who'd spent years walking in circles, had finally found the correct path.

FOURTEEN

The Akethorpe front door had scarcely whispered closed when the house began to still. A footman dimmed the hall lamps as Lena stood at the bottom of the grand staircase, trying to decide whether she would go up to her room or wander to the kitchen to warm some milk. She didn't want to bother the staff, yet they'd be offended if she performed such a task herself.

Instead, she found a suitable, boring book in the library. A dissertation on estate management would surely put her to sleep *tout suite*. She wandered into the drawing room and sat in her favorite chair in the room. After slipping off her shoes, she tucked her feet underneath her and opened the book.

Alix wandered into the room not long after. Still in her gown, she collapsed onto a settee with a happy gasp.

"I'll never be able to sleep," she declared. "I can't stop reliving the ball tonight. It was perfect. Truly perfect. Mrs. Oppenheim told me my forget-me-nots were *'exactly the thing for youth.'* And Mr. Jeffers said they were valiant."

"Valiant?" Lena asked, loosening her gloves. "How gallant of him."

Alix hugged herself. "He kept them. All evening. Did you see?"

Lena hadn't made note, since it was customary for a man receiving a bloom to keep it all evening, not dispose of it.

"And he asked me to dance twice," Alix went on.

Again, not significant, as many men marked their names twice on Alix's card.

"He's not at all like the solemn men Grandmama recommends. He's—" Alix flung out both hands, searching. "He's sunshine."

"Sunshine gives freckles," Lena replied, exhaling quietly.

Alix leaped from the settee, crouched in front of Lena, and clasped her hand. "You liked the ball too," she insisted. "You must have."

"I liked the orchestra," Lena said, smoothing a stray curl behind Alix's ear. "The beautiful decorations. And how Mrs. Oppenheim conducted a room like a maestro with a fan."

"And the dancing?" Alix pressed.

Lena hesitated. "I liked—some of it."

"Some?" Alix's eyes sparkled. "I saw the way Bron's friend Harry asked you twice. And he's to be a duke!"

Heat slid up Lena's neck—not because of Harry, but because all the while she danced with him, she had been thinking of Bron Jeffers. "Alix," she warned in a long breath.

"I'm only teasing." Alix softened, smiling dreamily. "You do like him, though. A little."

"Don't start imagining fairytales," Lena murmured.

Alix leaned her head briefly on Lena's knees, like she had as a child. "You always say that. But sometimes stories come true." With an impish grin, she rose. "Good night."

"Good night," Lena said, as Alix vanished in a rustle of taffeta out the drawing room door.

Silence settled. Lena caught the scent of the violets still pinned to her bodice. She rose and crossed to the window.

Almost all lamps in the houses around the square had been extinguished, the small park lit by a pale moon.

Moments later, Myra stood in the doorway, dressing gown wrapped tightly around her. "I thought I'd find you awake." She extended a warm glass of milk to Lena. "I warmed it myself. No doubt I'll catch the wrath of the housekeeper in the morning, but so be it."

Lena's heart clenched. *Thank You, Lord, for bringing this woman into Papa's life. Into my life.* She took the milk and leaned in to kiss Myra on the cheek.

Myra touched the spot, and tears welled up in her eyes.

"I don't tell you nearly enough, but I love you, and I'm so glad you're our stepmother."

"Even if I'm trying to marry you to a peer of the realm?" Myra sniffed.

"Even then."

Myra pulled a handkerchief from her dressing gown pocket and blew her nose. She turned her face toward the window and gazed out at the dark square.

They stood in comfortable quiet, the kind that had grown between them through four years of a shared household and unspoken understanding.

"You were splendid tonight," Myra said. "Both of you."

"Alix needed no help from me. She dazzled the entire ballroom."

"And you?" Myra's tone gentled. "You spent half the evening making sure everyone else was happy. Your sister, me, even your grandmother."

"Someone must," Lena said with an exaggerated sigh.

"Perhaps," Myra said, "but not always you."

Lena glanced from the window to take in Myra's profile and her words. There was an uneasy truth in them. "I don't see the harm in looking after my family. In being steady, reliable." At least that's what she'd told herself for more than ten years.

"It isn't harm," Myra said. "But it can be lonely. You're allowed to want something that isn't dutiful. To want a man and, eventually, a family of your own."

Lena looked down at the violets pinned to her gown. "I thought not placing a bloom in his lapel was the safest gesture." The words slipped unbidden from her lips. What made her think of Bron in that moment?

"It may have been," Myra murmured. "But sometimes you need to do things beyond what feels safe for the sake of joy. For the sake of love."

Is that what she was doing? Missing out on the joy of love? *Lord, I thought your plan for me was to take care of my sisters. To be the mother they lost. Was I wrong?*

Myra turned and moved to the settee. Once she sat, she patted the place next to her. Lena curled into Myra's side, lay her head on her shoulder, and yawned.

As though recalling something, Myra said slowly, "Mr. Jeffers spent a considerable amount of time watching you."

Lena's head came up. "He did?"

Myra nodded, a small, knowing smile at the corner of her mouth. "He was perfectly proper, of course. But when he spoke to me, his gaze kept drifting toward you."

The words sent a flutter through Lena's chest. She fixed her gaze on the unlit fireplace. "Really?" she managed.

"Really," Myra replied, her eyes widening dramatically. "I wouldn't be surprised if he calls on you personally soon."

Lena's laugh was small and helpless. "You're impossible."

"I'm observant."

"He's a roguish sort. Loose with women's hearts. A man with a degree in law but drives around in motorcars instead. He's hardly the type we should encourage."

Myra tilted her head. "It's not like you to be so judgmental, especially about someone who seems to be a good man."

Lena felt the creep of guilt up her spine. "I'm not saying he's a bad man, just not very grounded."

"Yet I see how you look at each other."

Lena busied herself with the fabric of her skirt.

Myra watched her a moment, then said softly, "It's a lovely color on you, that blush."

Lena leaned back and unfolded her legs, eyes narrowing, though her smile betrayed her. "It's time to turn in, Myra."

"Gladly," Myra said, rising. "But promise me this—when he does come to call, don't hide behind a wall of propriety. Let him see the woman who enjoys a handsome man's company."

Lena shook her head, but warmth lingered where Myra's words had settled.

Myra took the stairs and Lena followed behind. They said their goodnights at Lena's bedroom door.

Once inside, she closed the door with a soft click and looked around her room. Despite her yawn downstairs, she didn't think she could sleep just yet. She'd already told her maid not to wait up for her, insisting that she didn't need help to get out of the simple but elegant gown.

Moving toward the escritoire, she unpinned the drooping violets from her bodice and set them on the surface.

On a scrap of paper, she wrote the words that echoed in her mind.

For the sake of joy.

She tucked the blooms in the middle of the paper, folded the sheet in half, and pressed it in a book of romantic poetry she'd found in the library that her grandmother insisted she keep.

The act of creating the keepsake felt like a secret promise made to her own heart, witnessed only by the moon.

Fifteen

Lena set down her cup with a contented sigh. Nothing compared to a hot cup of freshly brewed coffee to start the day, especially after a late night.

It seemed that everyone must still be half asleep, because the dining room was awfully quiet. Sunlight slanted through the tall windows, and somewhere down the corridor, a clock chimed half past ten. The mouthwatering aroma of bacon filled the air.

At the head of the table, the dowager countess spooned a soft-boiled egg. Myra and Alix quietly ate their toast and marmalade, probably recounting the events of the flower ball in their minds.

"I was happy with the interest you received at the ball, Alexandra," the dowager said suddenly. Apparently, she'd been ruminating over the event as well. "Several eligible young men seemed quite taken with you, my dear."

Alix looked up from her plate, her expression serene—perhaps too serene. "Yes, they were all very gentlemanly," she said with studied politeness, then cast a sly glance across the table at Lena and winked.

Lena nearly choked on her coffee. *Oh no. Not Bron again.*

The dowager, oblivious to the mischief, dabbed at her lips with her napkin. "I should hope so. The Oppenheim balls attract only the best families. Still, I expect you to keep your wits about you. Charm is cheap in London, but character is not."

"Yes, Grandmama," Alix said sweetly.

"I was speaking to all of you," the dowager replied, her sharp green eyes sweeping toward Lena.

Lena fought the urge to smile. "Duly noted, Your Ladyship."

Satisfied, the dowager set aside her spoon. "Today I intend to call upon Lady Langston. It troubles me that she hasn't attended the last few society events. I've sent notes—she returned them with assurances she's only a little under the weather—but I know her better than that. She does not miss gatherings without good cause."

Myra nodded at once. "Of course, we'll come with you. We all like Eleanor very much. Shall we bring something for her? Perhaps flowers or something from the bakery?"

"Chocolate," Alix said promptly. "She told me that she adores chocolate. There's that confectioner on Bond Street—oh, Lena, the one with the gold paper boxes."

Lena smiled. "Yes, the shop with the scandalously expensive truffles. She'd love that."

"Then it's settled," said the dowager. "We shall leave at two o'clock. Wear something cheerful. She needs her spirits lifted." She dabbed at her mouth with her napkin. "Oh, and bring that camera of yours, Helena. When I told her about it, Eleanor mentioned she'd like to see how it worked."

Always happy to take photographs upon request, Lena nodded. "Of course." She'd bring her tripod as well in case Lady Langston wanted her to take some pictures. Even though

Lena often used her camera without a stand, keeping it perfectly still produced better results.

After breakfast, they all went their separate ways. Both the dowager and Myra had letters to write, and Alix wanted to flip through the latest edition of *The Ladies' Realm*, which covered the London season in great detail.

Lena decided to use the free time to capture pictures of Berkeley Square. The air outside smelled faintly of rain, and the London sky was its usual shade of pewter. By the time Lena finished a brisk walk around the square to get her blood flowing, the sun was peeking through the clouds. Thankfully, there was enough light to take a few candid photographs of the children and their nannies gathered at the park for playtime.

Not really wanting to go shopping, Lena reluctantly headed back to the townhouse and met the dowager, Myra, and Alix in the front hall at one o'clock sharp.

They piled into the carriage which then made its way to the confectioner on Bond Street.

"Be quick, girls," the dowager told them. "We've less than thirty minutes to get back to Cavendish Square, and you know how I despise tardiness."

Yes, their grandmother was the queen of punctuality.

Lena hopped down from the carriage, not waiting to be helped by a footman. She looped her arm through Alix's, and they darted into the shop.

A bell chimed above the door, and the sweet aroma of chocolate and berries hit their noses. Alix adored sweets of any kind, and Lena had to remind her they weren't there to browse but to quickly purchase a gift for Lady Langston.

Moments later, they emerged from the confectioner with a beribboned box of dark chocolates. "For medicinal purposes," Alix declared.

Within fifteen minutes, they reached Lady Langston's

townhouse. They alighted from the carriage with the help of a footman and the butler, who met them at the door and showed them to the drawing room.

Eleanor smiled warmly when they entered the room but didn't stand from her reclined position on the chaise. Probably knowing she'd get a scolding from the dowager if she did.

"My dears," she said in a breathy voice, "you've come to rescue me from boredom, haven't you?"

"Entirely our intention," said the dowager. "And we brought reinforcements." She gestured to Alix, who presented the chocolate box with a flourish.

Eleanor laughed softly. "My favorite. You spoil me."

As tea was served, conversation flowed easily—first about the ball, then about gowns, then about society gossip that made Eleanor's eyes sparkle.

Twenty minutes later, the butler announced not only Bron, but his cousin Cedric Redgrave—Lord Haverleigh—and his wife.

"Good heavens," Cedric said, bowing to the dowager. "I thought I heard your voice down the hall, ma'am. You do improve the tone of any house."

"Flatterer," the dowager replied dryly, though her mouth twitched.

Lady Haverleigh smiled faintly but said little, perching on a chair near the window. Her beauty was undeniable—sleek blonde hair, perfect posture. The type of woman every other female envied to at least a small degree.

Bron stood next to Cedric by the fireplace, his hair slightly windblown and his demeanor casual and warm.

Lena's heart tripped when he looked her way, and she found herself not listening at all to the conversation.

"Lena, my dear," Eleanor said suddenly, causing Lena to jump, "you've your camera with you, haven't you?"

Lena blinked. "Uh, yes, I do ..."

"Then I insist you take some photographs. To capture the moment."

"Certainly. Let's get a few with you and your family."

With a few quick instructions, Lena arranged Bron, Cedric, and Cecelia behind Eleanor.

Bron laughed at something Cedric whispered to him, and his chest shook with mirth.

"Hold still, please, Bron," Lena said.

He raised an eyebrow. "Do I look like a man who holds still?"

"Not remotely." She pressed the shutter.

"That photograph will be a blur," Cedric said with a laugh. "A true likeness."

When Lena finished, Bron gestured toward the camera. "Allow me?"

She hesitated. "You've handled one before?"

"Once or twice."

Lena, Myra, Alix, and the dowager exchanged places with the Redgraves, and they were soon smiling in Bron's direction.

"What a group of lovely ladies," he said as he peered through the viewfinder. "Broken any hearts lately?"

Cedric stood behind Bron, a grin on his lean face. "Speaking of breaking hearts, I heard you caused quite a stir at the Oppenheim ball last night. How many flowers did you receive, eh? I wouldn't be surprised if you were half buried under bouquets from adoring admirers."

Eleanor tutted. "Cedric!"

"Purely in the spirit of curiosity," he said, unrepentant.

Bron met Cedric's gaze evenly. "One bloom is quite enough, provided it's from the right lady."

The room erupted in easy laughter—Eleanor's soft, Myra's delighted—but Alix, who'd been nibbling a biscuit, shot Lena a quick look and mouthed, *See?*

Lena managed a polite smile, but her stomach had gone

oddly light, as though the air itself had thinned. *To whom did he refer?* Alix seemed to think it was her. And Lena—well, she hadn't given Bron a flower.

"You're a wise man," said Cedric approvingly, still chuckling. "Though I'll wager the ladies won't stop trying."

"Then I shall have to be steadfast," Bron replied, his tone dry.

Lena didn't dare glance his way, though she was aware of him—keenly aware—across the room, the faint amusement in his voice, the weight of something unspoken beneath it.

Bron shifted his weight and glared at Cedric who was still laughing, clearly delighted with the ripple his teasing had caused. "Don't mind me, Jeffers. I like to see a man squirm a bit—it keeps him honest."

"Then I must be the most honest man in London."

The others laughed, and conversation drifted easily back to the Oppenheim ball. Myra remarked that it had been *quite* the crush, while Alix eagerly supplied details about gowns, bouquets, and music.

Bron only half listened. His gaze slipped toward Lena, who stood near the window, adjusting her camera plates. Afternoon light fell across her elegant hands and glinted off the polished brass fittings. She looked entirely focused—yet every so often, her attention darted toward him before she returned to her work.

He exhaled quietly. *I shouldn't have said it like that. One lady's flowers.* It had sounded like he was interested in one of the ladies who'd given him a bloom, when in reality, he'd not received a bloom from the only woman he wanted one from.

Choosing the wrong words didn't happen very often to him. It was his job to speak effectively and with measure.

Cedric clapped him on the shoulder, not content to leave the matter alone. "A few more of these society affairs, and you'll have to hire a footman just to carry the posies."

Bron managed a smile. "If I do, you can have the job."

Cedric raised a brow. "I could use the income."

What was that supposed to mean?

Eleanor's hand flew to her chest. "Really, Cedric, must you make jests about money in mixed company?"

He inclined his head. "Forgive me, my dear—merely a bit of self-mockery."

Bron caught the faintest flicker of discomfort behind his friend's smile. Cedric's humor was effortless as ever, but something in it rang hollow. *Best not to pry in front of an audience, but Bron meant to get to the bottom of the remarks soon.*

"Lena," Eleanor called, brightening. "Do take one more photograph of us before you go. The light is beautiful just now."

"Of course," Lena said, picking up her camera once more.

Cedric struck an exaggerated pose. "Like this, perhaps?"

"Perhaps not quite so heroic," she replied, dry as dust. She looked through the viewfinder and said firmly, "Hold still."

The shutter clicked.

When they were all settled in their seats once more, the dowager turned to Alix and tipped her head. "Would you please favor us with some music? I'm sure Eleanor would enjoy it, and you are such a talented pianist."

Alix straightened her shoulders and smiled, fairly preening at the compliment. "I'd love to play."

Eleanor waved her hand at Lena. "Lena, dear, would you mind taking pictures of my garden? It's exceptionally lovely this year, even if you can't capture the colors."

"I'd be glad to."

Bron picked up her camera stand and hoisted it over his shoulder. "I'll take you out there."

Alix stuck out her bottom lip. "But you'll miss my song."

"We'll only be a minute," Lena promised.

The terrace doors opened on a rush of late-May air fragrant with lilac and damp grass. A thrush sang somewhere beyond the clipped yews. Lena's skirts brushed the flagstones as she followed Bron down the steps, the camera swaying lightly in his grasp.

"I'm perfectly capable of carrying that myself," she said.

"I know," he returned with a glance over his shoulder. "But then what excuse would I have to accompany you?"

Her lips quirked, as though caught between amusement and reproof.

He set the stand near a marble urn overflowing with geraniums and turned, waiting while she adjusted her camera just so. The afternoon sun slid between drifting clouds, gilding her hair with a red-gold sheen. He had the absurd urge to touch it —just to see if it felt as soft as it looked.

She glanced up at him. "Do you suppose Eleanor truly wanted photographs of her garden?"

"Maybe not," he murmured. "Though I'm not complaining."

She gave a little laugh and lifted the camera, composing her shot. "Hold still. I want to see how the arch frames the roses."

Bron leaned nearer, pretending to check the focus. "You're the only person I know who tells a baron where to stand."

"Future baron," she corrected. "And someone must."

He grinned, but when she glanced up, the humor faded from his face. Sunlight caught the curve of her cheek; her eyes, intent and luminous, met his for one suspended moment. Something in his chest lurched.

She moved slightly—whether toward him or away, he

wasn't sure—but she bumped her camera and her foot caught on one of the tripod legs. The camera wobbled.

"Oh—careful!" she exclaimed, reaching to steady it, but she was tangled in the stand. Their hands collided. Instinct made him catch both her and the camera at once.

"Forgive me," he said hoarsely, one arm tight around her waist, while he straightened the camera stand. He hadn't meant to pull her in quite so close.

But she wasn't moving away. Her eyes, wide and startled, lifted to his again. The garden seemed to hush around them— no birdsong, no distant notes from Alix's piano—only the faint crackle of a bee among the roses.

"Bron ..." she began, barely a whisper.

He should step back. He knew it—could feel the warning drum of his own pulse—but the scent of rose water and sunlight tangled with her breath, and all reason slipped.

His head dipped, almost involuntarily, and his mouth found hers.

The kiss was quick, almost clumsy, a breath of shock between them before she drew a trembling step away. Her hand brushed her lips, as if to confirm what had just happened.

He exhaled, contrite and exhilarated all at once. "That was —mad of me."

"Yes," she said faintly, eyes darting to anywhere but his face. Then softer, "But I suppose even the steadiest man in London may lose his head once in a while."

Her attempt at composure undid him utterly. He laughed under his breath, half in disbelief. He stepped away.

"Best take the picture quickly," he said. "Before I do something even madder."

Her cheeks flushed, but she bent to the camera lens. "The light is perfect," she murmured, the faintest trace of a smile on her lips as she captured her photograph.

She straightened and, for a moment, they both stood motionless, the faint click of the shutter still hanging in the air. Then, as if summoned, the music from the drawing room drifted through the open terrace doors—Alix's light, assured touch rippling across the piano keys.

"There. I think that will please your aunt." Lena stepped back from the camera.

Bron nodded, though his thoughts were nowhere near the photograph. The warmth of her against him still lingered, her scent—rosewater and clean linen—woven into the sunlight. He wanted to say something clever, or contrite, or anything that might make sense of what he'd done. But every word felt inadequate.

She began to fiddle with her camera, seemingly determined not to meet his gaze. "We should go in before it gets dark."

"It's only half past four."

"Then before someone comes looking for us."

That, at least, was practical. He took the tripod from her hands and fell into step beside her as they crossed the terrace. The waltz swelled, the rhythm quick and bright, and for one absurd instant, he imagined taking her hand, leading her into a dance right there among the roses.

Instead, he said, with a wry half smile, "For the record, I've never been particularly good at following society's rules."

Her lips curved, almost despite herself. "So I gathered."

They stepped through the doorway into the cool hush of the hall, the music wrapping round them as the door swung closed. And if anyone noticed the heightened color in Lena's cheeks—or Bron's uncharacteristic silence—no one remarked upon it.

SIXTEEN

In a quiet reading room on the first floor of Akethorpe House, Lena sat on the settee opposite her grandmother, who sipped her afternoon tea while reading *The Times*. Myra and Alix were off on a shopping excursion, which Lena and the dowager had declined.

An open letter from Tris lay in Lena's lap. She picked it up and scanned it once more.

It had been their plan to return to Philadelphia in time to see their sister receive her diploma, but Tris, having heard wonderful stories about London from Alix's letters home, begged them to stay longer so she could join them after gradu-ation. Apparently, Tris didn't give a fig whether they attended. Instead, she'd convinced their father to bring her to England as a graduation present.

In the beginning, Lena was determined to stay no longer than a month, but that month had stretched to ten weeks. Now, the idea of staying longer wasn't wholly unappealing. She enjoyed London, with its theatre, museums, and lovely parks.

She tried to dismiss the fact that many of these outings

were with Bron as their escort. But it wasn't easy to wave off a man who invaded her thoughts far too often. Especially since the day at Lady Langston's house.

And, specifically, that kiss.

She attempted composure, though her heart began a wild, traitorous flutter.

That kiss.

She could still feel the shock of it—the warmth, the faint scent of starch on his collar, the way time had folded itself into one breathtaking instant. It had been nothing like the clumsy declarations or polite kisses she had endured in her first two or three years after her debut in Philadelphia. This had been— well, honest. Disarming. The kind that rearranged one's sense of the possible.

The dowager set down her cup and leaned back. "I've spoken to Bron."

Lena startled. *Could the woman read her thoughts?*

"I'm worried about Eleanor," the dowager continued, as if she hadn't just upended Lena's pulse. "As is he. I should like us all to take a trip to the seaside. The doctor believes the air there might do her good. Besides, it will give you all a chance to see something of England beyond London."

"That sounds entirely sensible," Lena said quickly, grateful for the change of subject. "Alix will love the outing, and I can bring my camera. Perhaps the rest will help Lady Langston."

"That is the hope. Although Brighton might be the choice of most for seaside luxury, Eleanor loves Torquay in Devonshire. There are some outstanding hotels there, and we should be quite comfortable. It's a longer train ride, but the scenery and the quiet at the other end will be well worth the trip."

"It sounds lovely," Lena said, caught between ache and wonder. "Will Mr. Jeffers be content with his aunt so far away?"

"Oh, he'll be coming with us—for most of the fortnight, at least."

They would be in each other's pockets for nearly two weeks? Lena almost dropped Tris's letter.

The dowager's mouth curved faintly. "Now that's settled, tell me why you've been smiling at nothing since yesterday afternoon."

Lena blinked. "Smiling? I hadn't noticed."

"Mm. I take it the Langston garden was ... pleasant?"

Heat crept up Lena's neck before she could stop it. "Very. The light was ideal for photographs."

"Indeed. Though I daresay Bron had something to do with it."

Lena busied herself adjusting the tea tray, though everything on it was perfectly aligned. "He helped me carry the equipment. That was all."

"Was it?" The dowager's gaze was keen but not unkind.

Why was the room so hot?

"If I were young again, I imagine Bron would make me blush too. The man is ... intriguing, to say the least."

"That's one word for him," Lena murmured, half to herself.

"I shouldn't blame any woman for falling in love with him."

"I'm hardly in love—" Lena began, then stopped. There was no point in finishing. She didn't even believe herself. Truth be told, she'd rather call what she was feeling an infatuation. It didn't sound so permanent.

Her grandmother's smile deepened, knowing and amused. "I once had a tendre for an incorrigible sort, but my parents married me off to the earl. I wish I'd followed my heart and married the man I loved. Learn from that sad tale, child. The only good thing that came of my union with Akethorpe was your mother."

Heat pinched the back of Lena's throat. "I'm surprised to hear you say that. I've wondered why you didn't write," she said carefully. "When she was alive—or when she died."

Sadness filled the dowager's green eyes. "Because the last letter I sent her, before you were born, never reached Philadelphia. *He* intercepted it." She pulled a handkerchief from the lace cuff of her gown and dabbed her eyes. "My husband believed affection was a dwindling resource. He spent it like a miser and forbade the rest of us to spend any at all."

Lena's fingers tightened around the saucer. "The old earl."

The dowager's smile was brittle. "He made this house a tomb—orderly, silent, cold. He demanded obedience, and I —" She stopped, a breath snagging. "I obeyed too long. Waited too long. It will always be my greatest regret that I didn't make amends with your mother." She dabbed her eyes once more. "I only hope that you can forgive me."

Lena's heart clenched at the way she'd treated her grandmother since they'd arrived. Not rudely or disrespectfully, but without softness or love. Colossians 3:13 came to mind. A verse Papa often recited when her siblings were angry at one another for some slight or misdeed. *Bear with each other and forgive one another if any of you has a grievance against someone. Forgive as the Lord forgave you.*

"Of course I forgive you. And now I understand why you did what you did."

Silence filled the room; not awkward, but companionable.

The dowager sighed, a sound caught somewhere between fatigue and resolve. "Thank you for humoring an old woman's confessions. I've not spoken so plainly in decades."

"Thank you for telling me," Lena said. Her own voice surprised her with its steadiness. And in that moment, she did not think of this woman as the dowager or as Lady Akethorpe, but, for the first time, Grandmama, as she'd asked Alix to call her.

Her grandmother's eyes glistened, though she quickly disguised it by fussing with her handkerchief. "Well, assuming your stepmother and Alexandra agree, we'll be off to the seaside in three days. Make sure your maid doesn't skimp on the packing of your bags. There won't be as many shops to visit like there are in the city if we forget something."

A jolt of excitement rushed through Lena.

She had a feeling that her Kodak would be well used in Torquay.

<hr>

The sun hung low in the sky over Kensington as Bron stood alone beside his motorcar, slowly wiping a cloth across its hood. The mechanical expert's verdict echoed in his mind. The mishap and Max's injury a few weeks back hadn't been an accident. Someone had filed just enough through the steering rod to weaken it, then disguised the damage. A flaw so precise it waited for the right vibration, the right turn, to break.

Bron crouched beside the front axle, running a fingertip over the rough edge. His stomach tightened. That small, unseen stroke of a file could have ended both his and Max's lives.

"Sabotage," he muttered, the word foreign and absurd in the quiet. Who would bother with him? He had rivals, certainly, but enemies? None he could name.

He straightened, wiping his hands on a rag that left black streaks across his palms. He'd taken the mechanic's report with a kind of disbelief, but now, face-to-face with the evidence, there was no denying it. Someone had tampered with the machine. Someone had meant for it to fail.

The mews door creaked behind him.

Bron turned. "Harry, I wasn't expecting you until tomorrow."

His friend stepped into the coach house and laid his hat on a nearby worktable. "You send a note saying, 'It wasn't an accident,' and I'm supposed to wait until morning?"

"Fair point," Bron said, managing a thin smile. "Come have a look."

Harry crossed the room, his boots thudding on the sawdust-covered stone floor. He kneeled beside Bron.

"I suspected someone had tampered with the steering," Bron said, pointing to the condemning evidence, "and the mechanic's eagle eye confirmed my suspicion. Filed halfway through, then masked with grease. A clever hand."

Harry rose, brushing his knees. "You've made enemies on the racing circuit?"

"None who'd do this. It's not like I win every race."

"Rival inventors, perhaps? You've been vocal about your designs."

Bron gave a short, humorless laugh. "If I had anything worth stealing, I'd suspect it. But half of London still believes these contraptions are a passing novelty."

"Perhaps it wasn't about you." Harry scratched his chin.

"Meaning?"

"You weren't alone in the car. Max Dennison holds a high position in Denwall Department Stores, and those large emporiums aren't impervious to harsh criticism for ruining smaller stores."

Bron stilled. He hadn't considered that angle—had been too busy berating himself for endangering Lena's brother. "You think someone meant to harm *him*?"

"I think you should consider every possibility." Harry's gaze flicked to the door. "Who knew you were taking the car out for a test drive with Max?"

"Only a handful of men from my team. And you."

"A short list, then. All the better to start with."

Frustration simmered, and Bron raked a hand through his hair. "Still, *why?* What's to gain by nearly killing two men in an experimental motorcar?"

"Perhaps not to kill," Harry said. "Perhaps only to frighten you or Max—or to make the venture appear more dangerous than it is."

"No matter the reason, I mean to find who did this." Bron paced before the bench.

"You need to be careful, Bron. If this wasn't just a warning, someone might want to finish the job."

Bron stilled and met his friend's gaze. "Duly noted."

Harry left soon after, but not before insisting he be kept abreast of any developments. Bron doused the lantern, plunging the coach house into shadow save for a slice of moonlight through the high window.

He lingered a moment longer, the quiet pressing in until he could almost hear the echo of the crash again—the shriek of tires, Max's oath. Lena's fear and then anger.

She'd said that he treated danger as amusement. Was she right? There was a certain thrill in controlling such a roaring beast and taking it to its limit.

Yet tonight, staring at the dark curve of the steering rod, control felt like a fragile thing—an illusion, as thin as the weakened metal that could have ended him. He'd trusted the precision of his machines, the steadiness of his hands, the logic that kept all moving parts aligned. But all it took was one hidden flaw, one unseen hand, to undo it.

Perhaps Lena wasn't wrong to call it folly.

Perhaps he wasn't nearly as in control as he liked to believe.

Outside, a carriage rattled past on the cobblestones, the sound fading as it moved down the street.

For the first time, he wondered why the thought of surrender, of trusting something beyond himself, felt far more dangerous than the sharpest curve at full speed.

SEVENTEEN

As a little girl, Lena always thought the best family outings were the ones to the coast. She loved the sound of the waves, the smell of the salt in the air, and building sandcastles with her siblings. Life being what it was, it had been years since they last made such a trip.

The idea of seeing the sea once more, but from an unfamiliar beach, made her heart feel lighter than it had in weeks. And when the Akethorpe carriage rolled into Paddington Station for the six-hour train ride to Devonshire, the afternoon bloomed with promise.

The station itself was a marvel—a cathedral of glass and iron designed by Brunel. Beneath its soaring arches, sunlight filtered through the mottled panes, striking the brass fittings and curling steam with a hazy glow. A Great Western Railway express, painted in deep Brunswick green, waited for passengers.

"Torquay Express! All aboard!" shouted a porter, his voice echoing beneath the iron ribs of the roof. Trunks were loaded quickly, and another porter directed their party to their private first-class compartment.

"There you are!" Eleanor said when the door opened. "I was worried you wouldn't make it."

Eleanor was already settled in a seat of crimson velvet, next to the window, a blanket draped across her lap. Bron stood and laid his newspaper on the seat.

"I never doubted them," he said and shot a wink and a crooked smile at Lena.

Her heart flipped at the gesture.

Grandmama took the seat beside her friend while Myra slipped into the seat opposite, with Alix and Lena close behind. Bron sat next to Grandmama in the spot closest to the door.

When the guard's whistle sounded, and the locomotive gave a great sigh, the train glided forward, wheels clattering into rhythm. Paddington Station slipped away, replaced by rows of brick terraces and distant gasworks.

No one said much in the first minutes of the trip. Alix yawned several times, and Lena yearned for a cup of coffee. Unable to sleep, she'd risen much too early that morning, and with everything that needed to be done before they left, she'd skipped breakfast, other than a quick bite of toast.

Before long, the express gathered speed—thundering past Reading and Newbury. Presently, stewards in GWR livery moved down the corridor, announcing lunch service in the dining saloon.

Bron folded his newspaper and laid it aside, while Lena closed her book. Myra and Alix were already in the aisle.

"I'll fetch something for you, if you'd like," Bron said to his aunt.

"Oh, I don't feel like eating, dear." Eleanor lifted a faintly trembling hand.

"Nonsense," Grandmama interjected. "You must eat *something*, Eleanor. You're as thin as a rail."

"Very well," she relented with a faint smile. "A ham sandwich, if you please—and a cup of tea."

"I'd be glad to help with that," Lena offered, rising. "Grandmama, may I bring you something as well?"

Grandmama looked momentarily startled, then softened. "That would be lovely, dear. I'll have the same—and perhaps a pastry, if they look good."

Bron and Lena followed Myra and Alix toward the dining car. Myra secured a table, and while they settled, Bron placed the orders to take back to Grandmama and Eleanor.

"That was thoughtful of you to offer to bring something for Augusta," he said to Lena as the steward departed. "She's very accustomed to servants tending to her needs—but not relations."

Lena nodded. "I get the feeling that her stepson isn't particularly attentive."

"An awful thing—to not have a close family. Even if they aren't blood." His voice was sincere.

She glanced up at Bron's handsome face. His warm brown eyes reminded her of the best Dutch cocoa. How could she ever have thought him self-absorbed? "I'm beginning to understand more of what my grandmother endured after being estranged from my mother."

"It's always good to see the other side," he said.

They took a tray back to Eleanor and Augusta and returned to the dining car. Their meals arrived soon after, and the steward set before them cold roast beef, poached salmon with dill sauce, new potatoes, and a bottle of chilled Moselle.

Alix finished her luncheon and fairly pressed her nose to the window as the countryside rushed by. "Isn't it lovely?" she enthused.

It *was* lovely—the hedgerows, the thatched cottages, the church spires flashing in and out of sight. Lena caught Bron chuckling.

"What's so funny?"

"The novelty with which Americans regard England's rustic charms," he said, his eyes glinting with amusement.

With their hunger satisfied, they soon returned to their compartment, and everyone but Lena and Bron nodded off to sleep.

Not able to nap, Lena sat at the window, watching the changing landscape.

Every once in a while, she glanced across the way. Bron read *The Times*, from cover to cover, it would seem.

The countryside unfolded in ever-changing scenes as the train sped west—Berkshire's gentle hedgerows soon giving way to the pale sweep of the Wiltshire downs.

Bron folded his newspaper and set it aside, shifting from his seat to crouch by the window. He touched Lena's knee, and a lovely warmth skirted through her. "Keep looking," he whispered, apparently oblivious to her reaction.

She did as he directed, and soon a white figure carved into the hillside came into view.

"Is that a horse?" Lena leaned forward, careful not to wake the others dozing around them.

"Yes. It was carved into the chalk, probably a hundred years ago," he murmured. "No one quite knows who made it, only that it's watched travelers pass this way for generations."

"It looks enormous. That was quite an undertaking."

Bron nodded. "It's probably about two hundred feet tall and almost just as wide."

He stayed there for a while longer, his spicy aftershave tickling her senses. Not overpowering. Just right. It made her want to bend close and bury her nose in his neck.

She straightened and cleared her throat.

He glanced from the window to her face, his smile knowing. But he said nothing, thank the Lord, and returned to his seat.

As they moved farther southwest, they left miles of green farmland for red cliffs that dotted the landscape. With a sudden brilliance, the English Channel appeared—blue and endless beside the track. Lena gasped at her first sighting of beach and water.

"That's Lyme Bay. We crossed into Devonshire a few miles back." Bron said.

Lena opened the window and breathed in the scent of the sea.

The express finally drew into Torquay Station, the platform lined with palms and white-painted lampposts, the air warmer, almost Mediterranean. Porters in pillbox caps hurried forward to unload trunks, their voices mingling with the hiss of steam.

Before long, their group was bundled into a waiting carriage. Beyond the station gates, the road curved steeply downward toward the crescent of the bay, dotted with yachts and the pale façades of hotels and villas gleaming in the late sun.

"My, it's quite the *Riviera of England*, just like the guidebooks say!" Myra exclaimed. "It almost reminds me of Newport!"

Lena had never cared for Newport or for its popularity among New York's Four Hundred. She'd even heard that Brighton, which Grandmama had first considered, would be far too bustling for their needs. Here, Torquay seemed much more to her liking. Elegant yet tranquil, with its fragrant sea breeze and endless beauty, instead of society's relentless scrutiny.

After a good night's sleep and their first full day in Torquay ahead, Bron's heart felt light with the anticipation.

He set one foot atop a knee-high stone wall and shaded his eyes with his hand. He stared out at the panoramic view across Torquay and the South Devon coastline as he waited for the Dennisons to arrive at their appointed spot in front of the hotel.

When Eleanor said the views from the Imperial were the best in the south of England, she wasn't exaggerating. From this balcony, and every room in the hotel, the view was nothing short of magnificent.

They hadn't had time to explore yet, but had spent their first evening in Torquay settling in—unpacking trunks, arranging rooms, and ensuring Eleanor had every comfort.

However, this morning, over a light continental breakfast in Augusta's large suite, she insisted that Myra, Lena, Alix, and Bron set off to explore the town while she and Eleanor relaxed at the hotel.

Sunshine lay brilliant upon the bay, the air so still that neither leaf nor wave seemed to stir. From this vantage point, the town spread in graceful terraces over the hillside, its villas half veiled in foliage and bloom.

"This must be one of the most striking scenes I've ever seen," Lena said from behind him.

He glanced down to see her profile as she looked out at the same view he'd just been admiring. She wore a navy skirt, a matching jacket over a crisp white blouse, and a straw hat trimmed with ribbon. A camera case, with a long strap, hung from her neck.

Myra and Alix appeared a few moments later, both looking refreshed and ready for adventure.

"I understand the Princess Gardens are a wonderful place for afternoon tea," Myra remarked from under a hat the size of a small country.

Bron chuckled. Trust an American to believe that tea could only be enjoyed with a meal, rather than at any time one needed a restorative. "I'll leave that pleasure to you ladies, but yes—by all means, indulge while we're here."

Together they crossed the gardens toward Park Hill Road, where a hotel attendant had told them they might hail a hansom cab.

The sun was strong, and the women drew their parasols while they waited. The wait was not long—this was not yet the high season—and soon Bron helped them step into a hired carriage and directed the driver to take them to Anstey's Cove, a must-see according to every guidebook.

Their driver, a genial man with a fondness for local history, entertained them with tales of famous visitors. "The Princess of Wales herself stayed here once—up at Sutherland Towers, with the late Duchess of Sutherland," he said, pointing out the estate.

Alix leaned forward eagerly. "Oh, I adore the princess. I met her once. Did you see her?"

"Oh, indeed, miss," the man replied with a grin. "Couldn't mistake the carriage—or the entourage of high-falutin' neither."

Bron smiled at Alix's delight and caught Lena's amused glance. The cab turned inland, passing the entrance to Kent's Cavern before winding sharply downhill toward Anstey's Cove, one of Torquay's loveliest inlets.

At the beach, Bron arranged for the driver to wait, promising a generous tip, and they followed a narrow footpath down to the water. Lena paused often to frame her photographs, adjusting the exposure with that quiet focus that made the rest of the world vanish for her. Bron found himself watching her more than once—how completely she lost herself in capturing the beauty around her.

The water shimmered a deep, impossible blue beneath the

red cliffs, and the air was rich with salt and honeysuckle. A small teahouse perched at the base of the cliff, its striped awning fluttering in the breeze. From the shore, the coastline stretched north toward Teignmouth and Exmouth, the view so clear that even distant sails glimmered white against the horizon.

"Mind the incline," Myra called as they began the climb back up. "It's steeper than it looks!"

Lena waved in acknowledgment of her stepmother's word of caution. "It's lovely, even if it feels endless."

At the top, they paused to rest, and Bron stole a moment to catch his breath—not that he'd admit it. Alix ran to the rock wall and peered over the edge, while Lena untied the ribbons at her neck and pulled off her hat. Sunlight caught her hair. It looked like liquid fire, and Bron's fingers itched to pull out her hairpins to watch it fall. *Did it extend to her waist?*

He shook his head to clear the wayward thought that had his heart pounding.

Then they returned to the carriage, driving past Bishop-stowe, once home to the formidable Bishop Philpotts, the renowned mathematician and Prince Albert's chaplain, before descending again toward the bustle of the Babbacombe Road.

By the time they reached the post office, they dismissed the cab and continued on foot along the Strand, peering into shop windows. Uriel's Library drew them in—a fashionable establishment exhibiting Caton Woodville's battle sketches, including those from the Crimean War, which Bron examined with genuine admiration.

At Myra's insistence, they had afternoon tea at the Princess Gardens, and Lena and Alix joked about how uncomfortable Bron looked in such a feminine setting.

When they finally emerged, the afternoon light had mellowed, casting a honeyed glow across the promenade.

"Torquay has the soul of a painting," Lena said softly.

Bron smiled. "And you intend to capture it, I suppose?"

"Perhaps—if I can catch the light before it fades."

They left Myra and Alix enjoying a little more shopping before everything closed for the day, while Bron escorted Lena to the end of the pier.

"Turn around and face toward me with the bay at your back," Lena directed as she pulled out her camera. "A few more steps back."

"Are you hoping I'll step one too many and end up in the water?"

She poked her head around her Kodak. "Why, Mr. Jeffers, I had no idea you were the suspicious type." She laughed, and the sound caught him off guard. He wasn't sure he'd ever heard her laugh so freely.

He liked it.

Too much.

A young man passing by stopped to observe Lena taking pictures. "I have a camera myself," he said. "Would you like me to take one of both of you together?"

Bron gave him a quick grin. "I think that's a brilliant idea."

Lena hesitated, as if weighing her options and considering letting a stranger hold her camera. Considering whether she wanted a photograph taken with Bron.

Finally, she nodded, handed her Kodak to the man, and walked to the end of the pier to stand by Bron.

He shifted so that their sides were touching, and he felt her intake of breath.

The camera clicked, and she jumped forward. "Thank you so much," she said to the photographer.

"I hope it turns out as nicely as it looked through the viewfinder." He tipped his hat and continued on his stroll down the boardwalk.

The walk back to the Imperial Hotel was pleasant, the evening air tinged with salt and honeysuckle. Only Alix had not grown quiet, chattering away about the caverns they'd heard of earlier.

"May we go to Kent's Cavern tomorrow?" she asked brightly.

"Perhaps not tomorrow," Myra replied, patient as ever. "We should spend a quiet day with your grandmother and Lady Langston first. We've two whole weeks here, Alexandra."

Alix sighed but smiled in resignation.

By the time they reached the hotel, the last rays from the setting sun glowed along the promenade, casting golden reflections across the bay. Inside, the tiled floor gleamed beneath chandeliers, and faint piano notes drifted from the public lounge.

Bron escorted the ladies upstairs, waiting until they were safely in their chambers before retreating to his own. Through the open window, laughter carried faintly down the corridor, and a smile tugged at his lips.

He changed for dinner, though his thoughts strayed to the day—the sunlight on Lena's hair, the soft concentration in her expression, the quiet grace she carried as naturally as breathing. There was steadiness in her that drew him, a sense that she would meet both beauty and trial with the same quiet courage. He'd known women who demanded admiration. Lena earned it without trying.

When he joined the party in the private dining room reserved for Lady Akethorpe, dusk deepened over the bay, the first lamps flickering to life along the waterfront.

Dinner was as it should be by the sea—fresh sole in butter, cold lobster salad, and new potatoes with sprigs of parsley. The scent of lemon and wine mingled pleasantly with the low murmur of conversation.

"Did you enjoy yourself, my dear?" Eleanor asked Lena once they'd begun their meal.

"I did," Lena replied, smiling. "I hope you'll feel well enough to take a tour yourself before long."

Bron watched her as his aunt responded, noting the graceful turn of Lena's wrist as she lifted her glass, the light in her eyes when she spoke. He wasn't sure when attraction to her beauty had turned into something more dangerous. There had been that moment in Eleanor's garden when they'd clumsily kissed.

He'd kissed women before.

None, however, had taken his breath away as it had with Lena. And now, being in close proximity and getting to know her better, the attraction had shifted to admiration. But he suspected he'd fallen for her when she took his picture on the pier and laughed at his joke.

Augusta's laughter drew him back. "This is so much nicer than Brighton," she declared.

"Just a little farther to reach," Bron offered good-naturedly, earning a ripple of amusement.

"Oh, but well worth the six-hour train ride," she countered.

Bron inclined his head with a smile. "Yes. Quite worth it."

Conversation flowed easily, yet now and then his gaze drifted toward Lena—who, at that instant, caught his eye and looked quickly away, color rising faintly in her cheeks.

He hoped she'd show him the photographs from today's outing when she developed them. Especially the one the young man took of the two of them at the end of the pier.

Bron's gut told him they looked good together.

Eighteen

<hr>

Lena hadn't ridden a bicycle in over two years, and, for the life of her, couldn't say why, when it was all the rage back home. Just never had the time or the inclination, she supposed. But now, as she wheeled along Torquay's quaint streets, she was glad Bron had suggested they rent cycles that morning for Alix's requested visit to Kent's Cavern.

To everyone's surprise and delight, even Myra came along, declaring she'd learned to ride not long before she married Papa.

The ride northeast from the seafront took them past luxurious villas and palm-lined terraces. The roads grew narrower and more uneven as they climbed from the bustling harbor toward Lincombe Hill, giving way to shaded lanes bordered by hedgerows and stone walls. It was a gentle ascent at first, then a brisk downhill run toward the wooded hollow where the ancient caves awaited—a route both scenic and, at times, thrillingly steep.

They parked their bicycles and met a guide at the small wooden door that opened to the cavern. Lena was grateful for her sensible attire: a riding skirt, stout boots, and a light jacket against the chill.

The guide led them into the vast chamber he called the Lecture Hall. By lantern light, he told them of the human and animal remains once unearthed in the cavern's depths.

The air was cool—no more than fifty degrees—and carried the scent of earth and minerals. Water dripped from unseen heights, each drop landing with a soft *plink* that multiplied in the silence. The walls glistened like wet marble, candlelight creating wavering shadows that danced over the stalactites and stalagmites rising in frozen motion from floor and ceiling.

Bron, looking dapper in a straw boater and linen coat, asked educated questions, surprising Lena once again at the many layers that made up the man.

They continued deeper into the caves, and the path twisted and narrowed unexpectedly. The ground was slick underfoot, and more than once Bron offered his arm to Myra, for which Lena was grateful.

When the guide raised his lantern to reveal a towering column of stone, the shadows eerily leaped in all directions. Alix gave a nervous laugh at the tale of a visitor who had lost his way in the dark and had to be rescued hours later.

"Oh dear," she whispered dramatically while she latched unnecessarily onto Bron's arm, "I believe I shall stay close to you, Mr. Jeffers."

Bron laughed, gently disengaging his arm and stepping back so he could gesture toward the formations. "You'll be quite safe, Miss Dennison. The cavern hasn't swallowed a guest in decades."

Alix pouted but obeyed, falling in beside Myra instead.

Lena noted the exchange with a complicated swirl of admiration and worry. Bron managed Alix's theatrics with unfailing good humor, but her sister's infatuation—however harmless—was becoming harder to ignore.

"It's very eerie," Myra murmured, slipping her arm through Alix's.

Bron's tone was light. "That makes it all the more entertaining, does it not?"

He turned slightly toward Lena and gave her a wink. She smiled despite herself, then looked away, pretending to study the mineral formations glistening before them.

"Well, that's the end of my tour, I'm afraid," their guide said as they moved toward the entrance.

"Oh, no!" Alix gasped, patting frantically at her bodice. "My watch brooch!"

The guide, already closing the gate behind them, looked apologetic. "We'll be locking up for the midday break, miss, but if you think it's not far in—"

"It must have fallen off when I slipped on that rock ledge," Alix said. "Near the first chamber, I'm sure of it."

Bron caught the guide's eye. "We can find it quickly enough. No need to trouble you."

The guide hesitated, then handed over his lantern. "Mind you stay on the main path, sir. It twists more than you'd think."

"I'll come with you," Lena said. "Alix, stay here with Myra." All she needed was to lose Alix as well.

Inside, the lantern's light wavered across the rock. Lena's boots scuffed the damp path as they retraced their steps.

"If Alix is correct, it was near here," she said, crouching to examine the ground. "The whole idea of buying her that brooch was so she wouldn't lose her watch."

Bron's chuckle reverberated softly in the hollow chamber. "Careful. You're perilously close to sounding like an elder sister."

"I've been accused of worse," she said, smiling faintly.

They moved deeper, the lantern's circle of light shrinking

as shadows pressed closer. Then, without warning, the flame sputtered—and died.

For a heartbeat, there was nothing. Only the absolute, consuming dark.

"Bron?"

"I'm here." His voice came from somewhere very near, though the darkness made it impossible to tell how close. A hand brushed her sleeve—then his fingers closed over hers. "I need to relight the lantern. Give me a moment."

He turned slightly, bumping her shoulder. The clatter of metal echoed as the lantern slipped from his grasp and struck the floor with a hollow ring.

"Sorry, I'm quite the butterfingers today," he murmured.

She laughed softly at the self-deprecating humor in his tone.

He bent to pick up the lantern. The hinge on the glass door squeaked as he opened it, and she heard the faint click of the knob as he raised the wick.

"Can you hold this while I find a match? I have one in my pocket somewhere."

"Of course." She groped until her hand closed over his, and he passed her the lantern.

A match struck in the darkness, flaring sulfur yellow. For an instant, its tiny flame lit his face and the rough walls behind him. Soon the wick caught, glowing steady once more—and Lena realized how close they stood.

Her heart beat so loudly she was sure he could hear it.

He took the lantern from her hand and, slowly, as though uncertain of her permission, tilted forward and kissed her.

It was soft at first, hesitant—the kind of kiss born more of instinct than intent. The faint metallic taste of the air mixed with the warmth of his breath.

She had meant to resist, to be sensible, to remember every

rule drilled into her. But one look at him—so near, so intent—and sense scattered like petals in a storm.

The last time he'd kissed her, it had been an accident. Clumsy. Quick. And she'd blamed the circumstances—surprise at him catching her camera before it fell to Eleanor's garden floor, and the rush of a moment best forgotten.

But there was nothing accidental about this one.

Of all the men alive, why did Bron Jeffers have to be the one who made her forget every rule, every warning, every sensible thought she possessed?

And whatever this was, it felt dangerously close to joy.

When he drew back, she could still feel the imprint of the touch—real, shocking, and utterly unforgettable.

The lantern flared brighter a moment later, flooding them with light that felt almost indecent.

Bron blinked down at her, expression unreadable. "We should ... find that brooch."

"Yes," she said faintly. "Of course."

They found it a minute later, on the ground near a rock ledge. When they stepped back into the daylight, both squinted at the brightness—and neither mentioned the kiss.

But as they rejoined the others, Lena was acutely aware they'd soon have to decipher whatever lay between them.

***

Bron stood outside the Imperial and looked up at the sky. The morning broke in shades of gold and pink. Even the sea seemed to be in an obliging mood.

He'd never seen England look so un-English—sunny and cheerful.

Next to him gleamed a black and red motorcar he'd had

delivered by a friend in Portsmouth. A prideful-looking machine, it was sure to resent a full load of women.

"Good heavens, it's a monster," Myra exclaimed as she approached, her parasol snapping open. "Do you mean to drive that all the way up the hill?"

"Only as far as it will go," Bron said. "After that, we push."

Alix's eyes brightened. "How thrilling! May I drive?"

"No," came Augusta's crisp reply before Bron could speak. "You'll sit behind Bron and pray fervently that you make it back in one piece." Since the car could only fit four people, Augusta and Eleanor had been more than willing to stay behind for a few hours. Bron promised them their own ride later, if they so desired.

"Oh, Grandmama, I'm sure we'll be fine." Alix grinned and climbed in with commendable grace.

Myra settled into the rear seat beside Alix, and Lena took the front beside Bron, her hat tied down with a ribbon that matched the pale blue of the morning sky.

"Ready?" he asked.

"Ready," she said, her smile uncertain but genuine.

The motorcar coughed, protested, then caught. A teenager standing on the walkway applauded. They set off through Torquay's narrow streets, the sea glittering on their right. Shops spilled color in the sunlight—striped awnings, bright ribbons, and racks of postcards commemorating the Jubilee.

Lena turned slightly toward him, and the wind lifted a wisp of hair from her temple. "Do you often drive in such public areas?"

"Only when I want to frighten pedestrians," he said. "It keeps them alert."

She laughed, a sound that caught him squarely in the chest. It wasn't polite laughter, the kind he was accustomed to at society events. It was unguarded. And that, more than anything, undid him.

They climbed past the villas of Wellswood, where magnolia trees spilled over stone walls and morning light slanted through palm fronds. The air grew keener as they rose along the cliff road toward Daddyhole Plain. The bay curved below them like polished glass, and gulls wheeled in the blue distance.

Myra declared that the view was positively breathtaking.

Alix insisted the wind would ruin her hat.

Bron grinned into the breeze. He'd never taken any woman for a drive in one of his motorcars. At this moment, with Lena beside him, wide-eyed with wonder, he was immensely glad he hadn't and that she was the first.

He'd promised Harry he would take a week's holiday, but this felt less like rest and more like revelation. The ordinary world had receded. Here, there were only sky and laughter, and Lena beside him, one gloved hand braced on the edge of the seat, a huge grin on her face.

At the overlook on Daddyhole Plain, he stopped the motorcar in a wide pull-off, and everyone spilled out to marvel. Below, the headland dropped sheer to the glittering water, where whitecaps dashed themselves against the cliffs of Meadfoot. Farther out, Thatcher Rock rose from the sea like a sleeping giant's shoulder, sunlit and wild.

"It's like standing on the edge of creation," Myra said.

"It's like standing in a hurricane," Alix countered, clutching her hat.

Lena lifted her camera. "Hold still. All of you."

"Not possible in the wind, I'm afraid," Myra said, though she smiled.

Bron helped Lena find her footing on a rocky ledge so she could steady the shot. The hem of her gown brushed against his boot, and his hands poised near her waist, instinctively ready to catch her should she stumble.

"You needn't hover," she said without turning. "I'm quite steady."

"Forgive me. It's an occupational hazard—I'm used to preventing catastrophes."

"Are you?" She focused on the viewfinder, the corner of her mouth twitching. "From what I've heard, you rather invite them."

He laughed, then fell silent as the shutter clicked. She lowered the camera and looked out over the headland. The wind lifted her ribbons again, and this time he reached to hold them down before they whipped across her face.

His fingers brushed hers—an accidental contact, yet it lit something steady and dangerous beneath his ribs.

"Thank you," she said, her voice softer than the wind.

"My pleasure."

For a moment, they stood like that, side by side, the world spread open beneath them. He wanted to say something—anything—but language seemed an inadequate vessel for what filled him.

"Bron!" Alix's voice broke the spell. "You promised to teach me how to start the engine!"

Bron stepped back as if waking. "Did I? Then I was a fool."

Lena's smile held both amusement and mercy. "You'd better dissuade her of that notion before she drives your motorcar into a stone wall."

"Or the Channel," he muttered, and went to show Alix enough of the car that she'd be satisfied without risking life and limb.

When he returned, Lena sat on a low stone wall, sketching in her notebook while the camera sat next to her.

He joined her quietly. "You draw as well?"

"Only outlines. The camera never quite captures everything I see."

"What does it miss?"

She hesitated, then looked up. "Color, certain light, laughter, love. The world's better moments."

He followed her gaze to her family—Myra taking in the beauty of their surroundings, and Alix sitting farther down on the wall, face to the sun. "You may be right," he said. "Some moments are meant only to be captured in the heart."

Their eyes met again, the understanding between them so effortless it frightened him a little. He wanted to reach for her hand, to claim something of this improbable peace.

Twice now he had kissed her—once in reckless surprise, once with full awareness of what he was doing. And being here with her so close, he felt the quiet ache of wanting something he dare not.

What would it be like to kiss her here, in the open—like a married couple might—without worry or guilt? To let the world see what his heart already knew.

The thought unsettled him—dangerous, impossible, and yet terribly, beautifully tempting.

But he did nothing. He only sat beside her until a carriage full of people pulled up next to their car and broke the quiet.

Back in the car, they descended the hill. The wind carried the faint scent of coming weather and the distant sound of the sea.

Bron kept his eyes on the road, but his thoughts were miles ahead—on a future he wasn't sure he had the right to hope for, and a woman who, without meaning to, had already become his compass.

When they returned to the hotel, they changed and had a light dinner together in Augusta's suite.

Tomorrow, they'd return to London.

A fine mist drifted in from the Channel, softening the lamps along the hotel's promenade until they glowed like halos. Bron went in search of Lena and found her standing at the terrace rail, the cool damp curling the tendril of hair at her cheek.

Inside, laughter drifted through the open windows. Myra was winning another round of double dummy whist from Augusta, who feigned irritation but was clearly enjoying herself. Eleanor, pale yet visibly stronger, reclined on the chaise with her embroidery, while Alix read a book about the history of the area to her.

"I thought you might have escaped out here," Bron said as he approached.

Lena didn't turn but continued to look out at the water.

Bron came to stand beside her, resting his forearms lightly on the rail.

"The sea's showing off again."

It was—a wide sweep of argent light, the mist breaking into long veils that drifted past the moon. Somewhere below, a man and woman spoke in low tones. Probably on a romantic stroll.

"You've been quiet since our outing," he said after a moment. "Did my driving terrify you into silence?"

"Not at all. I was impressed."

"Truly?"

"Impressed that we returned with everyone still alive."

He grinned. "High praise indeed."

The banter faded into a companionable hush.

Lena's hands gripped the railing. "I've enjoyed my stay here."

"As have I." And he meant it.

"It's not too quiet for you? There aren't any motorcar races or young women chasing after you for your autograph," she said with a small smile.

He bumped her shoulder with his upper arm. "Don't tell anyone, but I used to think life was about outpacing everyone else. Now I'm beginning to wonder if it's about learning when to stop."

"Did the sea teach you that?"

"Perhaps the sea," he said, "or perhaps a certain photographer who sees beauty in every scene. Stillness isn't my strength."

"It might be one day."

Their eyes met, and for a moment the distance between them narrowed to breath and heartbeat. The mist thickened, the sounds of the hotel suite dimming behind the glass.

Augusta's voice called through the open window, breaking the spell. "Lena! Do come in and settle this argument about who has the best modistes, London or Paris."

He sighed and straightened. "Rescued by your grandmother."

"She has impeccable timing," Lena murmured.

He lingered half a step longer. "We leave tomorrow for London. Are you ready to exchange sea air for soot?"

"I suppose I must be." She glanced back toward the water. "I'll miss this."

"So will I." And he meant it.

She went inside, the door closing softly behind her. The faint murmur of conversation resumed, blending with the hush of the tide.

Bron remained a while longer, watching the fog unravel itself across the shallows.

He thought of everything that had happened in a mere fortnight—Eleanor's color returning, Augusta's frequent laughter, Lena's loosening of the tight control she held on her life.

And as for himself, well, he'd found that elusive joy that before had felt out of reach.

A gull's cry echoed from the pier.

Bron whispered a brief, uncertain prayer that once they returned to London, he wouldn't lose his way again.

NINETEEN

The air in London had changed since Lena viewed its streets on the way out of the city a fortnight ago. There was a pulse of expectation—the quickened step of cab horses, the flutter of flags along Piccadilly. Jubilee bunting hung from every available balcony and shop window.

The Akethorpe carriage waited, as requested by a telegram the day before, just outside the station. Augusta directed her driver to take them to her townhouse first and then return Eleanor and Bron to their respective houses.

The Akethorpe townhouse gleamed in readiness—windows open, servants bustling with the cheerful fatigue of preparation. It felt odd to think of this place as home, yet Lena felt a pinch of fondness at the sight of the familiar black door and Grandmama's impeccable row of geraniums standing at attention.

Bron jumped out of the carriage and turned to help Lena and her family alight.

"Welcome back," he said as he offered his hand to her. "I'm sure London missed you terribly."

"I doubt London noticed," she said, though her smile betrayed her.

Augusta was issuing instructions to the footmen before her boots touched the cobblestones.

And then a familiar voice rang out from the doorway, "At last, you're back!"

"Tris!" Alix all but flew up the steps. Tris laughed and caught her in an exuberant hug. She moved past Alix and joined Lena and Myra in a group embrace.

Lena's heart soared at seeing her sister after two and a half months of being apart.

Arms wide, Papa emerged from the house into the sunlight, his hair a touch more silver than it had been when she'd left home. "My girls! You've managed to make England even prettier than it was."

Lena found herself laughing as he drew her into a hug that smelled achingly of starch and cigar smoke. "We were afraid your ship would be delayed," she said.

"And miss the Jubilee? Not likely." He released her, his eyes crinkling.

Alix threw her arms around Papa's neck, tears streaming down her face. "Papa, I've missed you so!"

Papa wrapped his arms around his youngest child, cleared his throat, and set her down. "Now, now," he said thickly. "I doubt you even thought of me."

Myra moved to his side. "Well, *I* certainly did. Every moment."

Lena's throat tightened at the sight of her father and stepmother in a loving embrace. She never once doubted their love for one another. Oh, she'd been resistant at first to the change of going from a motherless household to one with a stepmother, but now she realized Myra was the best thing that could have happened to Papa.

Grandmama waited patiently to the side, not saying a word, but her green eyes were misty with unshed tears.

Lena looped her hand through her grandmother's arm. "Papa, Tris, I'd like you to meet our grandmother, Lady Akethorpe."

"Your Ladyship," Papa gave her a short bow of respect, and Tris executed an awkward and reluctant-looking curtsy.

Grandmama stiffened. "Please, we don't stand on formalities, do we, Helena?"

"Of course not, Grandmama." Lena gave her grandmother's arm a reassuring squeeze. "Why don't we go inside, freshen up, and you can get better acquainted?"

Movement at the corner of her vision had Lena turning. "Oh, Bron! Eleanor! Let me introduce my family. My father, James Dennison, and my second youngest sister, Beatrice. Call her Tris, or she might not answer." Lena smiled and tipped her head to the carriage. "This is Lady Langston, and her nephew, Mr. Bronley Jeffers."

Eleanor smiled from the carriage window. A healthy bloom now resided on her cheeks. "Please, call me Eleanor. It's so good to meet you both at last."

Papa stepped forward and bowed to Eleanor. "Lady Langston, it's a pleasure." He held out his hand to Bron. "Mr. Jeffers, we've heard so much about you. And I've followed your racing career."

Bron shook Papa's hand. "Please, it's Bron, and don't believe everything you read."

"Even if the words are Alix's?" Papa winked at his youngest, who huffed in mock offense.

A faint blush tinged the tips of Bron's ears.

What had Alix written in her many letters home?

"Bron's motorcar exploits are the stuff of legend," Lena said, trying to smooth things over without giving air to Papa's words. "But why don't we allow Eleanor and Bron to get on their way? I'm sure they're both tired."

They said their goodbyes and followed Grandmama up the front steps.

Lena lingered by the carriage a moment longer.

"Goodbye," she said to Eleanor. "Thank you so much for showing us Torquay. I can see why you love it so."

"Goodbye, dear. We'll see you soon, I'm sure." Eleanor ducked her head back inside the carriage and settled against the seat.

Bron, hand on the carriage door, cleared his throat.

Funny, the Merry Barrister seemed at a loss for words.

"Thank you, Bron, for everything you did for us in Torquay. I'm sure it was the last place you wanted to be." A shyness crept over Lena that she'd never felt.

"It was my pleasure." He took her hand and placed a kiss on her knuckles. Despite the glove she wore, she felt the gesture to her toes.

She turned and moved up the steps, stopping at the door to wave. Bron was still standing on the cobblestones, his dark eyes on her face.

She moved inside, the hall buzzing with greetings, luggage, and overlapping voices. Grandmama stood by like a small, imperious general while servants whisked away hats and parcels.

Tris looped her arm through Lena's as they climbed the stairs. "You've a lovely color in your cheeks. Did the sea agree with you—or has someone made you blush?"

"The sunshine, probably," Lena said, but she could feel the heat flooding her cheeks.

"You must tell me everything," Tris insisted. "I've been living among academics and would give anything for a story that doesn't involve Latin declensions."

"Later," Lena promised. "Once we've settled."

In her room, she found someone—Tris most likely—had deposited a small parcel atop her writing desk—a packet of letters tied neatly with blue ribbon. The top envelope bore Louise's familiar hand.

Lena untied it and unfolded the letter. The handwriting was as elegant as ever, with perfect loops and a light touch.

Dearest Lena,

You will laugh, of course, when I tell you that marriage is proving far more complicated than novels led me to believe. Stuart is kind, but kindness does not always equal understanding. I sometimes think he married an idea rather than a person. Do you suppose that's common? Please don't mention this to Papa—he'd worry for nothing. I'm quite all right, truly, but there are moments when I miss our long talks more than I expected.

With love,

Lou.

Lena read the words twice, then folded the paper carefully and slid it back into its envelope. A chill of unease pricked her despite the warm afternoon. Lou rarely confessed anything, preferring to keep her own quiet counsel.

She glanced at the clock on her desk, startled by the late hour. Moving away from the window, she stepped into the washroom for a quick bath. The maid had already filled the tub. Afterward, Lena slipped into a simple evening gown and pinned up her hair in a simpler fashion. Before she could leave her room, a tap sounded at the door.

Tris entered first, followed by Alix. They perched on the edge of Lena's bed, chatting all at once—Alex bubbling over with tales of Bron and Torquay, while Tris listened, smiling. Lena, for her part, said little.

When the clock chimed seven, Alix gasped. "Oh dear! I'm not even ready, and Grandmama will have my head on a platter next to the roast duck if I'm late for dinner." She flew from the room, leaving Lena and Tris alone.

Tris tilted her head. "Isn't he a little old for her?"

"Who do you mean?" Lena asked, though she knew perfectly well.

"That Mr. Jeffers. The motorcar driver. Alix has written volumes about him in her letters to me."

Lena's stomach clenched. She knew Alix had a schoolgirl type affection for Bron, but she didn't realize it was worthy of mentioning to Tris. Multiple times, it would seem. "Yes, he's rather too old for her."

"Is he leading her on?"

"Oh, no, not in the least. Bron's wonderful. He's simply been kind, and I fear Alix has misunderstood his attention."

Tris's eyes lingered on Lena's face. "And you? What do you think of this Mr. Jeffers?"

That was the question that kept her up at nights. Were his kisses purely impulsive, or was there something deeper, more meaningful behind them?

Lena hesitated. "He's kind—very attentive to his aunt, who is ailing. He made an excellent escort while Max was away."

"Ah." Tris said. "I see."

Lena frowned. "What does that mean?"

"Only that I'm wondering if there's more here than what you're saying."

When Lena refused to answer, Tris grabbed her hand and tugged her out of her chair and toward the door. "Come, or the countess will have our heads on the platter with Alix's. We can talk about this more later."

No, they wouldn't. Not if Lena could help it.

TWENTY

The Jubilee dinner at Akethorpe House was a dazzling affair with enough glittering diamond jewelry that Lena's eyes ached. The extensive guest list included nobility, dignitaries, and well-known poets. Papa and Myra were in animated conversation with the Prime Minister of Canada, while other discussions ebbed and flowed across the long table like a tide, from political talk to finding and keeping the best household staff. The clink of silver punctuated it all.

Grandmama sat at the head of the table, of course, with Eleanor on her right and the Prime Minister on her left. Lena, Alix, and Tris were spread out, and Grandmama had made sure they were seated next to eligible bachelors. Lena stopped short of thinking the men were unsuspecting. She was sure they understood exactly what the countess was up to.

Bron was seated across the table from Lena, but a tall candelabra hid him from full view. If she tried to speak with him, she had to lean her head to the right or left, thereby getting too close to her dinner partner.

Once, she caught Bron's lips twitching at her predicament. When the final course was cleared, and music drifted from the drawing room, she slipped through the French doors onto the terrace. The night air was cool against her cheeks, carrying the scent of roses from the lower garden. Beyond the lanterns, the lawn of Akethorpe House stretched pale under the moon.

She had come out only for a bit of quiet away from the hum of family and guests. At the far edge of the terrace, she rested her arms on the balustrade, taking a deep breath to think about her predicament. Wanting to be steadfast for her family yet indulging in some of the pleasures of still being a relatively young woman.

Sometimes she wondered who she might have been if she hadn't spent almost two decades—*had it really been that long?*—being half sister, half mother. Not that anyone had asked or expected her to do so. Mama had only asked her to look out for her younger siblings, not give up her life for them.

For the first few years, she'd seen to their needs because it kept her from falling apart altogether. Then it became a habit for both her and her sisters. Now, they probably wished she'd just leave them be.

"Escaping the company?" Bron's voice held its familiar warmth and irony.

"Only for a moment," she said, turning toward him. He'd shed his coat, and his snow-white shirt created a contrast to his tanned face. His oh so achingly handsome face.

"It's stifling in there," she said as he approached.

"The room or the company?"

"Both."

He smiled a little, then glanced toward the garden steps. "Walk with me?"

She hesitated but followed him down the stone path bordered with lavender. The lamps behind them threw long shadows ahead. For a few minutes, they said nothing. Somewhere nearby, a nightingale began to sing.

"You're leaving soon," he said at last.

"In a fortnight," she replied. "Papa means to book our passage this week."

He nodded slowly. "All of you?"

"Tris wants to stay longer—to get to know our grandmother better. Papa has promised to think about it."

He was silent for a moment. "And you?"

"I'll go back with the others."

"I wish you wouldn't."

She stopped, startled. "You wish—?"

"That you'd stay," he said simply. "For a while longer, at least."

Her pulse caught. "Bron, that would be impossible. We—"

"Why impossible?" He turned to face her. "Because of distance? Or because you've already decided there isn't a future for us?"

She folded her hands tightly before her. "I need to be with my family. I think my sister Louise's marriage is in trouble. Alix is still young ..." Gazing across the dark garden, her heart clenched. Tears threatened to fall like rain if she lost her composure. She hated to cry. "Our worlds are so different."

He took a step closer. "I'm not talking about the world. I'm talking about us. Let me court you, Lena. Let's see where it leads."

The earnestness in his eyes unsettled her more than any charm ever had. "Bron, I don't know where such a relationship could go. You belong to England, to your work here, to—"

"I think I belong to you," he said quietly. "I want the chance to figure that out."

She shook her head, struggling for steadiness. "You don't mean that. You're caught up in the moment, the stars—"

"I mean it." His tone deepened. "You've changed how I

see my life, my future. Don't send me away with polite excuses."

The words broke something inside her restraint. She looked up—and in the half-light saw only sincerity and longing in his eyes. When he bent toward her, she didn't move. His kiss was gentle at first, then fierce with all the feelings they had tried to ignore.

A sharp cry shattered the stillness.

"Lena!"

They sprang apart. Alix stood on the path, her face white with shock. "I—Grandmama was looking for you," she stammered, then turned and fled toward the house.

"Alix—wait!" Lena called, but her sister had already vanished behind the yew hedge.

Lena pressed a trembling hand to her lips. "Oh, what have I done?"

Bron caught her wrist before she could follow. "Let her go."

"She saw us, Bron. She'll think—"

"She'll think what she chooses," he said evenly. "You can't undo it."

Tears stung her eyes. "This was a mistake. I should never have—"

He stepped back, pain tightening his jaw. "A mistake? Because your sister is upset?"

"You don't understand."

"Don't I?" His voice hardened. "You live your life only for others. When are you going to let your sisters live their own lives? When are you going to live for yourself?"

The words struck deep. She could only stare at him, unable to answer.

He turned away first, the moonlight catching the edge of his profile. "I can see this subject causes you distress. I won't speak of it again," he said quietly. "Good night."

He walked back toward the terrace, leaving her alone among the roses, her heart pounding with longing and something perilously close to shame. The nightingale sang on, unheeding, and somewhere inside the house the small orchestra began a waltz.

Lena drew a trembling breath. *Lord, forgive me. I wanted so much to be the best sister I could, to be the mother-figure my sisters needed—and instead I've made a mess of everything.*

She turned toward the lights of the house, knowing that nothing between her and Alix—her and Bron—could ever be the same again.

Bron didn't return to the house right away, but instead moved behind a hedgerow and waited for Lena to return to the gathering.

So much for bravery, you fool. It would shock the racing world to see him hiding behind a bush rather than crashing through it.

For a long moment, he remained where he was, staring at the place she'd been, the words *When are you going to live for yourself?* echoing back at him.

The words sounded harsh now—proud, even selfish. Yet he couldn't shake the conviction behind them. She lived for duty, for family, for the safe course of things. He only wished she could see what life might look like beyond all that.

No, he hadn't meant to speak so sharply. Hadn't meant to kiss her either—not there, not then. But every careful restraint he'd built since Torquay had given way beneath the look in her eyes—that fragile mixture of longing and fear.

He drew a slow breath and forced himself toward the house. Through the open terrace doors, the spill of music and laughter struck him like a discordant tune. Nothing had changed, except him.

A footman offered champagne, but Bron waved it away.

Across the room, Lena paused by her father, said something too quiet to hear, and left a moment later with Tris at her side. Her face was pale, expression unreadable.

Alix was nowhere to be seen.

Bron tried to rejoin the conversation near the fireplace, but every topic—politics, the Jubilee festivities, some endless discussion of garden schemes—felt miles away. The room seemed overly bright, every laugh grating, every note of the orchestra sharp enough to pierce.

When Eleanor found him at last, she studied him with the clear-sightedness he'd never been able to evade.

"Are you the reason all of Augusta's granddaughters have disappeared?" she asked.

"I'm afraid so," he replied.

Her eyes narrowed. "You look like you've been hit by an omnibus."

He managed a low chuckle. "You're very astute, Aunt, because that's exactly how I feel."

"Whatever has happened, you'll get past it. Don't let the Jeffers pride make it worse."

"Pride? I don't think I have any of that left. I practically groveled at Lena's feet."

Eleanor took his hand in hers and squeezed. "I'm not referring to *that* kind of pride. I mean the kind that keeps you from bringing your worries to the Lord." When he looked away, she raised her hand and placed it against his cheek, her voice softening. "You are the child I could never have. I know you as well as any mother could know a son. Ever since you went away to Oxford, you've lived as though you had to steer your own course. Always in control, never asking for help."

She hesitated, her eyes glistening with quiet wisdom. "The

Scripture says we're to trust the Lord with all our hearts and not lean on our own understanding. You know what that means? Stop trying to carry the whole of life by yourself. Let Him do the steering for a change."

He didn't know what to say, yet the words struck a chord within. For a man used to mastering machines, roads, and timing, surrender didn't come easily.

"Why don't you have a footman summon the carriage? I'm tired, and you look like you could use some quiet," Eleanor said after a moment.

They said their goodbyes to Augusta and some of the other guests, and soon they were in their carriage.

The ride home was hushed but not uncomfortable. His aunt's presence had always steadied him, even when her words pricked his pride. He watched the lamps flicker past the windows, the fog curling low across the road.

He replayed the garden encounter again and again—Lena's scent of rose water, the tremor of her lips, the shock in her sister's voice.

He knew he should regret it. And he did—the timing, the setting, the hurt it caused. But not the kiss itself. Nor the request to court her. Never that.

When Bron slipped into his quiet house twenty minutes later, he shrugged out of his jacket, cummerbund, and shirt. The housekeeper had left a single lamp burning in the hall, its faint glow spilling into the study beyond.

Instead of readying for bed, he wandered toward the window overlooking the park. He pressed a hand against the glass, the cool surface chilling his palm. He'd wanted to ask Lena to stay—and instead, he'd driven her further away.

Drawing the curtain closed, he stood for a long moment in the half-light. Weary to the bone, yet far from slumber, he sank into the leather armchair near his unlit fireplace.

He stared at the cold grate. The ache in his chest wasn't

only for Lena—it was for everything he'd kept bottled up these past few years. The constant striving, the loss of direction, the fear that he'd somehow misread the road altogether.

He tipped his head back against the chair and exhaled. "You've always been here for me, Lord. Even when I didn't want to acknowledge You." His voice was barely above a whisper. "I'm listening now. If there's a way forward—through this, through to her—show me how to take it. Because I can't seem to find it on my own anymore."

The words lingered in the dim room, quiet but honest.

Outside, the bells from a nearby church chimed the hour, the sound soft and steady. He closed his eyes, the rhythm tugging him toward stillness. And for the first time since the garden, he let himself breathe.

Twenty-One

Breakfast at the Akethorpe townhouse had never been so quiet. Lena startled when the footman dropped a serving spoon on the polished marble of the dining room floor.

Alix's chair stood empty.

Not surprising, really. When Lena had followed Alix to her room the night before, Alix had slammed the door in her face and locked her out. In a panic, she'd knocked until her knuckles ached, pleading for her sister to let her in. "Go away" was Alix's only reply.

"She's still unwell, poor thing," Myra said, pouring coffee for Papa. "Said she doesn't have an appetite."

A pang of guilt tightened Lena's chest for allowing matters to spiral so badly.

She kept her gaze fixed on her untouched breakfast, willing the others not to notice the tears burning at the corners of her eyes.

Papa looked up from his newspaper. "She'll be right in a day or two. London's pace wears on the constitution. A dose of fresh air and rest will mend her. Maybe we should take a ride out to the country."

"Or home," Myra said softly. "That would mend her."

Grandmama's cane rested against the table beside her, her hand folded over its carved handle. "So, you mean to return so soon?"

Papa nodded. "I only intended to stay through the Jubilee."

Myra placed her hand on Papa's. "And I need to return with him. I've spent long enough away from Philadelphia that I actually miss it." She smiled across the table at Grandmama. "Although I've enjoyed our time in England tremendously."

Tris set down her teacup, her brow furrowed. "But must we all go? I'd like to stay longer, if Grandmama doesn't mind."

Grandmama blinked rapidly. "Mind? Of course not, my dear. I should be delighted for the company." Her voice cracked with sentiment.

Papa cleared his throat. "Let me think about it some more. I don't like you traveling back alone, so if Max has business in London any time soon and is willing to bring you back, I might be amenable."

Tris beamed. "I'll telegram him today."

"You've spoiled us here, Augusta, truly," Myra said with a gentle smile. "We'll all come back again soon. I promise."

"I shall hold you to that," Grandmama said, dabbing discreetly at her eyes.

Folding his paper and placing it next to his plate, Papa's gaze landed on Lena. "How about you, my girl? Ready to leave London behind?"

Lena hesitated. "Yes—though I admit, a big part of me will miss it."

That was an understatement. Yes, she'd miss the excitement of London, the pageantry of the Jubilee, but that would wane. Her heart, she feared, would break when she left behind Grandmama, and Eleanor, whom she thought of almost as another grandmother. And, of course, Bron. The hole in her heart already gaped, and she was still on English soil. Once she was back in America, she doubted she'd ever be able to heal the wound.

The conversation drifted to a discussion of the voyage home—when to book passage, and all the extra gowns that would return with them, much to Papa's chagrin. Tension knotted in Lena's stomach with every word.

She excused herself soon after, blaming a headache that didn't exist.

The air in the conservatory was cool and still, scented with damp earth and lilies. It had become her refuge these past weeks—a place where no one expected conversation, where her thoughts could stretch without being observed.

Grandmama had generously allowed the use of the conservatory storeroom for Lena to develop her photographs. Now, she rolled up her sleeves and set about preparing her darkroom corner, the familiar rhythm steadying her. She adjusted the crimson lamp, uncapped the developer, and arranged the glass plates taken in Lady Langston's house into neat rows.

Prayer came to her best this way, with her hands busy, her mind anchored to quiet tasks.

Lord, forgive me for last night, she thought, though the words felt insufficient. *Forgive me for wanting what I shouldn't —for confusing my heart until I hardly know what's right.*

She breathed deeply, willing the ache in her chest to ease.

One by one, she slid the plates into the developer. The images bloomed slowly in the red light. Eleanor's house. The faces, the room full of flowers, the marble terrace. She smiled faintly at the familiar figures.

And then, in the corner of one plate, something odd caught her eye.

Cecilia Redgrave stood slightly apart from the others in the photograph Eleanor had requested Lena take. Her eyes were wide with something that resembled fear. The picture had also caught Cedric in a frown. *Funny, that.* Bron's cousin had always seemed so jovial. Yet this photograph told another story.

Lena shook her head of the silly notion, rinsed the plate, then hung it carefully to dry. As the acrid smell of chemicals filled the air, her thoughts wandered back to the breakfast table, to Tris's eager expression, Grandmama's tearful smile, and the unspoken absence of Alix.

She'll forgive me. In time, she will.

The image of Bron rose unbidden—the warmth of his hand, the steadiness of his voice, the look in his eyes when he'd said he wished she would stay.

She closed her eyes and pressed the heel of her hand against her heart. *No, don't think of him now.*

The sound of a carriage on the cobblestones outside startled her. She peeked through the window. It was a delivery cart, nothing more. Still, the sight of it reminded her of all that awaited—departure and distance. Leaving Grandmama and even Eleanor caused her heart to ache.

Leaving Bron ... well, that left a gaping hole she didn't think she'd ever be able to fill.

She turned back to the tray of photographs, her movements slow and careful. Each image felt like a small world she could control. Outside, the bells of a nearby church began to chime the quarter hour, their sound soft and resolute.

Lena whispered another prayer, not for forgiveness this time, but for clarity.

"Show me what I'm meant to see, Lord. Even if I was blind to it before."

The clock in the upstairs corridor had just struck twelve when Augusta tapped lightly at Alexandra's door. No answer came, though she could hear faint movement inside—the rustle of skirts, the scrape of a chair.

"Alexandra, my dear? It's Grandmama."

A pause, then a quiet, "Come in."

Augusta pushed the door open. The curtains were half drawn, letting only a ribbon of gray light into the room. Alexandra sat at her writing desk, a shawl pulled about her shoulders, her face pale and blotched from crying. A tray of untouched breakfast sat on the table beside her.

"You've been hiding away all morning," Augusta said gently as she closed the door behind her. "That won't do. You'll have the servants thinking you're ill."

"I told them I had a headache."

"Ah, yes. So I'd heard." Augusta crossed the room and rested a hand on the back of Alexandra's chair. "But headaches don't leave eyes quite so red."

Alexandra's chin trembled. "Please, Grandmama, I'd rather not talk about it."

Augusta studied her a moment. Part of her wanted to respect the girl's wishes and leave her alone. But the other meddling part of her—her right as a grandmother—had her seating herself in the chair by the window, next to the writing table. "Very well," she said. "Then perhaps I'll talk instead."

Silence stretched between them, soft and strained. Outside, a sparrow trilled somewhere in the ivy.

"I was young once too, you know," Augusta said at last. "Long before I became the terrifying dowager everyone speaks of."

That earned her a reluctant smile. "You're not terrifying."

"I can be," Augusta said dryly. "But not to you, my dear. You may tell me what's truly troubling you."

Alexandra twisted the fringe of her shawl between her

fingers. "I saw something I shouldn't have. And now I can't stop thinking about it."

"I imagine you mean Lena and Mr. Jeffers."

"How did you—?" Alexandra stared with wide eyes.

"I wasn't born yesterday." Augusta folded her hands in her lap. "You forget, I've spent the better part of my life watching people make fools of themselves over love. The signs are not difficult to read."

Alexandra stared at the floor, her voice trembling. "It wasn't ... improper, exactly, but it felt wrong. She's my sister, and he—he's so kind to me. I thought—" She broke off, tears glinting at the corners of her eyes. "I thought he liked *me*."

"Oh, my dear child." Augusta's voice softened. "Of course he likes you. You're bright, charming, and quite impossible not to like. But affection and attachment are two different creatures."

"Then why did he spend so much time with me in Torquay? He was always so attentive." Alexandra sniffed, wiping her cheek with the back of her hand.

"Because he's a gentleman," Augusta said simply. "And because you're the youngest sister of someone he cares for very deeply."

"And she cares for him."

"Yes."

"But I confessed to her my feelings for Bron. Did she just ignore them? Or care how I'd feel if she pursued him?"

"I think she'd only begun to realize that your feelings may be more than just a passing fancy. By that time, she already had feelings of her own, although I think she felt guilty about them. Tried to ignore those feelings for your sake."

"Do you think she loves him?" Alexandra tilted her head.

"I think she could, if she let herself."

Alexandra bit her lip. "Then why hasn't she said anything?"

"Because she won't."

Augusta leaned forward, hand resting on her cane. "Helena has carried responsibility since the day your mother died. She stepped into a role far too heavy for a girl her age—comforting your sisters, taking care of a motherless baby, making sure you grew up into the lovely young ladies you are today. It became her habit to think of everyone else first. Her heart is generous, but it's cautious. She will not reach for happiness if she thinks it will cost someone she loves their own happiness."

"You mean me."

Augusta nodded. "Precisely. She won't pursue a relationship with Bron now. She'll convince herself it's best forgotten."

For a long moment, neither spoke. The light shifted, falling across Alexandra's desk where a small vase of wilted forget-me-nots stood. Augusta reached out and gently turned the stems, straightening them. "You mustn't be angry with her, darling. She didn't mean to hurt you. Nor did he. These things have a way of happening despite our best intentions."

Alexandra drew a shaky breath. "It's just—I've never seen her like that before. So ... unguarded."

"That's because she finally allowed herself to feel." Augusta smiled faintly. "It frightens her, I think. Love often does when it comes to those who've spent years keeping the world at arm's length."

"Do you think Bron loves her?" Alexandra's words came out in a soft whisper.

"I do. And if I'm any judge of character, he's just stubborn enough not to let her retreat forever." Augusta reached down and brushed a lock of hair from Alexandra's temple. "Now dry your eyes, my dear. Pride is a poor substitute for a sister's love."

Alexandra caught her hand and squeezed it. "Thank you, Grandmama."

"Think nothing of it. I'm far too old to let my opinions go unspoken."

As she moved toward the door, Alexandra's voice followed her, hesitant but sure. "I'll try not to be angry with her."

"That's a good start," Augusta said without turning.

Closing the door quietly behind her, she paused in the corridor to steady herself against the banister. The conversation had left her oddly moved. She had seen too many young hearts ruined by pride and misunderstanding—her own among them, once.

"Lord," she murmured under her breath, "teach these girls what I never learned soon enough—that love is worth a little courage."

The light through the window glowed soft and golden, falling across the portraits of long-dead Fenwickes. Augusta squared her shoulders and started down the hall, her cane tapping a steady rhythm. There was life yet in her old house, and she meant to see it bloom while she still could.

TWENTY-TWO

"Five thousand guests," Grandmama announced with satisfaction. "Her Majesty does nothing by halves."

Lena poked her head out of their carriage to find they were in a long line streaming through the main gates of Buckingham Palace, where the Queen's Guards stood at rigid attention.

The invitation for the Queen's garden party had stated five o'clock, yet the gates had opened at four, and already guests poured steadily into the palace gardens. It seemed half of London society had decided that arriving early was a mark of superior cleverness. Or perhaps simply eagerness.

Tris leaned forward in wonder. "I can hardly imagine so many in one place."

Beside her, Alix made a faint sound of agreement but kept her gaze fixed on the passing scene. She hadn't met Lena's eyes since they'd left the house.

Lena adjusted her gloves, an ache behind her ribs. She'd rehearsed apologies, explanations—but Alix had made it plain she wished for none. Not when it concerned *him*.

The carriage rolled to a soft halt, its wheels crunching over the gravel near the Constitution Hill gate.

Myra followed Grandmama from the carriage. She fussed with her parasol, her gown of pale celadon silk catching the light. "Remember to walk naturally," she said, fluttering her hand. "Do not stare. We don't want to appear like country yokels."

Lena almost smiled. More than likely, people would stare at *them.*

The gardens appeared before them—broad, sweeping lawns, the air threaded with roses and clipped yew, the palace façade hidden partly by great old trees that created an air of pleasant seclusion. A large number of white marquees had been erected, their scalloped edges stirring softly in the breeze. Under one, musicians tuned instruments, and under another, long tables held silver tea urns along with plates of small sandwiches and teacakes.

Across the pretty lake, bargemen in scarlet rowed boats slowly back and forth like gondoliers, their bright uniforms mirrored on the water's surface.

Lena had to admit—it was enchanting.

"It's like a dream," Tris breathed.

"A very crowded dream," Papa murmured.

Her gaze sweeping over the throng of ladies and gentlemen moving toward the royal pavilion, Lena silently agreed.

Augusta tapped her cane with satisfaction. "We're to meet Eleanor and Bron on the steps of the West Terrace."

Lena offered her arm. "Let me help you, Grandmama."

"Stubborn girl," Augusta said fondly, but took Lena's arm anyway.

They moved slowly through the crowd, the grass springy beneath their steps. Somewhere overhead, peacocks shrieked from the balustrade, their jeweled tails cascading over the stone. A group of bagpipers marched by playing a lilting Scottish ballad, and Lena hummed softly, enchanted by the melody and the skill of the pipers.

She found herself committing everything to memory—the glitter of gold braid on a uniform, the light glancing off the lake, the way laughter carried across the water. It was easier than noticing Alix walking two paces ahead, speaking only to Tris.

The wisest course was to forget what had happened that night in the Akethorpe gardens, to treat Bron as no more than an acquaintance. And yet the memory of his voice, his nearness, would not leave her.

The first of the royal party soon appeared beyond the marquees, and murmurs rippled through the crowd. Hats dipped and parasols lowered.

Her Majesty moved slowly through the procession, seated in an open carriage next to the Princess of Wales. The crowd parted as they passed, faces softening with affection and awe.

Tris clasped her hands. "She looks so small—and yet so grand."

Lena smiled. "That's the power of endurance. She's carried the Empire on her shoulders for sixty years."

Augusta sniffed approvingly. "And with better posture than half the women here."

When the anthem began, everyone turned toward the dais. The voices swelled—*God save our gracious Queen, long live our noble Queen.* Lena sang softly, her throat tightening. The harmony of thousands joined in a single song.

When they reached the terrace, Lena glanced out at the faces in the crowd. No sign of Bron or his aunt yet. Part of her was relieved—she wasn't ready to face him—but another part ached at the thought of his absence. She told herself she only worried for his aunt, that she merely wanted Eleanor to be well enough to attend. Which, of course, was true. Just not the full truth.

A cluster of foreign dignitaries in elaborate dress passed by, and laughter rang from a group of officers at the bottom of the steps. For all the color and movement, she felt curiously detached, as though the world were happening at a distance.

And then, through the blur of hats and parasols, she saw him.

Bron, with Eleanor on his arm, was making his way up the path toward them—a tall silhouette against the late-afternoon sun, his expression unreadable. Her heart gave a treacherous leap before she could stop it.

So this is love.

Not the comfortable affection she felt for family or the fondness of friendship, but something deeper—an all-consuming ache that both steadied and shattered her at once.

⁂

"Are you quite sure you're up to this?" Bron asked for the third time that day as he guided his aunt carefully through the throng of people.

"My dear," she answered sharply, clearly frustrated with his attention, "if the Queen can preside over her Jubilee at seventy-eight, I can manage an afternoon of tea." Her voice was firm, though her cheeks were pale.

She *had* been better—so much better that she'd insisted they attend not only the garden party but the earlier events at St. James's Park. He had yielded, half relieved to see the old sparkle in her eyes, half fearful it would cost her dearly.

Lena and her family stood with Augusta beneath a striped marquee. James and Myra smiled at something Alix said, and Lena's face turned toward Tris. Even amid the finery, the

Dennison daughters drew notice—three shades of summer—Alix in pale rose silk, Tris in mint green, and Lena in cornflower blue. Bron caught the flicker of recognition in Lena's eyes as they approached, but then she turned her gaze away.

"Good afternoon," Eleanor greeted them. "You girls look charming. Like a veritable garden."

Bron shook James's hand and tipped his hat to the ladies.

Eleanor tugged at Bron's jacket sleeve. "Keep an eye out for Cedric and Cecilia. I told them to meet us here." She turned and began speaking animatedly with Augusta, her lace parasol tilting at a precarious angle. The older ladies compared recollections of earlier state garden parties, both insisting this was the most splendid by far.

The atmosphere in the palace gardens was beyond anything Bron had ever experienced. Even better than the end of his last motorcar race in Monte Carlo. Bands played on the lawns. Attendees wore their finest garden party attire. And color blazed everywhere, from the scarlet tunics of the Life Guards to the white plumes of Grenadiers. Above their heads, the royal standard with its brilliant red, gold, and blue emblems floated above the palace roof, signaling the monarch's presence.

The sight of Viscount Eastmere, however, dimmed the atmosphere, and Bron's stomach clenched. *Would the man be as rude here as he was in Hyde Park a few weeks ago?*

Eastmere approached through the throng, his smile like the polished edge of a blade. "Jeffers! So the colonials brought reinforcements," he drawled. "How charitable of you to guide them through the maze of etiquette. America can hardly prepare one for such company."

Next to him, Lena stiffened.

Bron gave the viscount a feral smile. "True, my lord. They lack instruction in condescension. But I'm sure you could teach them a thing or two."

A ripple of laughter passed among nearby guests. East-mere's lips thinned. "You'd do well to respect your betters, Jeffers."

Bron's tone turned to ice. "When I come across them, I'll be sure to remember your advice."

Eastmere reddened. "Someone needs to put you in your place," he whispered harshly and retreated.

Tris clapped her gloved hands softly. "You've routed him entirely."

"Don't encourage me," Bron murmured, though he thought he caught Lena's lips twitching.

Eleanor clasped his arm again and pointed to the great tent where the royal standard hung. There, in full view of her subjects, the Queen took tea, a large lace serviette spread care-fully across her lap. She looked, Bron thought, not merely a monarch but an emblem—England itself, venerable and unyielding.

Around him, parasols dipped, and murmurs swelled again, admiration and loyalty twining in a single sound. Eleanor lifted her chin, eyes shining. "How lovely she is," she whis-pered. "To have seen her again—what a gift."

Bron noted the tremor in his aunt's hand as she raised her fan.

"Fragile, yet unstoppable," Bron replied. He meant it about the Queen *and* his aunt.

For nearly an hour, the crowd ebbed and flowed between tents and terraces. Bron fetched lemonade for his aunt and returned to find her seated beside Cedric's wife, who bent solicitously to adjust her shawl.

"You shouldn't tire yourself," Cecilia murmured. "You must conserve your strength."

"I'm not made of glass, my dear," Eleanor replied, smiling, though her hand trembled slightly.

Cecilia rose as Bron approached. "Your aunt insists she's

recovered, but I fear the day's excitement is too much. Perhaps you'll persuade her to rest?"

He dipped his chin. "I was about to suggest the same."

Eleanor waved him off. "Nonsense. One doesn't come to Buckingham Palace to rest." She dabbed at her forehead with her lace handkerchief. "Besides, your father's note said he would meet us here."

It was a veritable family reunion, for heaven's sake!

Since when did Eleanor—his mother's sister—exchange correspondence with Father? He'd thought they despised each other.

Bron's stomach tightened when the esteemed Aubron Jeffers appeared almost on cue, immaculate in morning coat and grey waistcoat, every inch the barrister. His bow to his sister-in-law was correct, his glance toward his son glacial.

"You seem determined to make a spectacle of yourself," Father said once they'd moved aside. "Racing machines, teaching in colleges, escorting Americans around England— when you've obligations at the practice."

Bron kept his voice low. "I never agreed to work in your law office permanently."

"It's why I sent you to Oxford. Not to waste your talent or education on teaching night classes and running a silly motorcar company."

A surge of irritation rose, then receded. "I'm not going to waste my education. I'm thinking of working for the London Legal Aid and Advice Association."

Father's eyes flashed. "I won't see your defiance paraded before half of London."

Bron stiffened. "Then avert your eyes." He turned away before the argument could draw notice. His pulse hammered. Regret and anger tangled in his chest.

Eleanor had risen again, greeting acquaintances with practiced grace. Yet as he rejoined her, he saw the pallor in her cheeks, the faint sheen of sweat along her temples.

"I think it's time I took you home," he said when he reached her side.

"Just a few minutes more," she murmured, but then she swayed on her feet. The parasol slipped from her grasp, and Bron caught her around the middle just as her knees gave way.

TWENTY-THREE

All chaos broke loose when Eleanor collapsed. One moment she stood laughing with Grandmama beneath a lace-trimmed parasol, and the next, her face drained of color, her knees buckled, and the parasol sagged like a wilted bloom.

Bron caught her before she struck the ground, his voice sharp over the startled gasps. "Eleanor!"

The crowd drew back at once, murmurs rising as fans fluttered. Lena dropped beside him, slipped off her gloves, and pressed two fingers to Eleanor's wrist. The pulse fluttered weakly under her touch. She glanced at Bron, whose face had gone almost as white as his aunt's.

"I knew she was overdoing it," he murmured.

Someone pressed a glass into Lena's hand. She dipped her handkerchief in the water and gently applied it to Eleanor's face and neck.

Eleanor's eyes fluttered open. "What happened?"

"You fainted," Bron said. "I'm taking you home and fetching your doctor."

Papa, who'd been standing nearby, touched Lena's shoulder. "Help Bron—I'll see that the doctor is sent for at once." He turned to Bron. "What's his name?"

Bron gave him the name and address, all the while carefully gathering his aunt into his arms. His expression looked calm enough to reassure those around them, but Lena could see the tension in his jaw.

Grandmama was already ordering a Guardsman to see that a carriage—any available carriage—was brought around to the south gate immediately. "Lena, you and I will go with Bron and Eleanor to the Langston townhouse."

"Straight to Cavendish Square," Bron told the driver as soon as they were all settled in the hansom cab.

The door closed on the hum of voices and music, sealing them off from the bright swirl of parasols and brass bands. The sounds of London took over instead—wheels rattling, hoofbeats echoing against stone, the distant cheers of the crowd still celebrating the Queen's day.

Bron cradled Eleanor close, one hand beneath her chin to keep her airway open as she drifted in and out of consciousness. "She was well enough this morning," he said, his voice tight beneath the control. "Since Torquay, really, she's been doing so much better. Better than she's been in months."

On the seat across from Bron, Lena kept an eye on Eleanor's breathing. "She was," she said softly.

"She's overexerted herself," Grandmama nodded as if to convince herself. "Rest will put her right. Women faint at such functions every summer." Her lips quivered, and she worried the gold pendant that hung from a chain at her neck.

Truthfully, Lena wasn't convinced it was that simple. Eleanor's pallor wasn't the passing sort caused by heat or excitement—it was waxen, lifeless, as though every ounce of strength had drained from her veins.

Lena glanced out the window. The Union Jack hung from

balconies. Thousands of people who couldn't attend the Queen's garden party stood outside the palace gates, cheering every carriage that came and went. The celebratory atmosphere felt cruelly out of step with the quiet panic inside the carriage.

Eleanor stirred once, whispering something that no one could make out, then fell silent again. Bron tightened his hold. "It will be all right," he murmured, though his voice betrayed the effort it cost him to sound certain.

The two-mile drive seemed endless.

At last, they reached the Langston townhouse, where Bron carried his aunt upstairs to her bedchamber and laid her gently upon the counterpane. Her head rolled to one side, her skin slick with perspiration. Bron hovered at the foot of the bed, coat rumpled, breathing as though he'd run the whole way.

Grandmama stood near the door, issuing orders to the housemaid. "Keep watch for the physician—he's to be shown up the instant he arrives." She turned to Lena. "If we don't see him in the next ten minutes, we'll send for a physician close by. Any physician at this point."

The doctor appeared within ten minutes—a stout, self-satisfied man with a gold chain across his waistcoat. "Ah," he said, after briefly examining Eleanor. "A fainting fit. The heat, no doubt." He took her pulse with perfunctory fingers, gave a cursory listen to her chest, and nodded. "Yes, yes, the system is taxed." He stood and faced Bron. "Her heart is failing, I'm afraid. You must make her comfortable. I'll leave a draught to ease her rest."

"What are you saying?" Bron's voice came out in a harsh whisper.

The man spread his hands. "At her age and in her condition, it's inevitable. I'm sorry, but there's little more to be done." He scribbled a note, left the bottle on the table, and departed without another glance.

For a moment, no one moved. Then Grandmama said crisply, "Arrogant nincompoop. He hasn't the wit to diagnose a head cold."

Bron slumped into a nearby chair. "He's treated her for years."

Lena's heart ached for him. "Maybe it's time he didn't," she said softly. She glanced toward the door to be sure no servants lingered, then lowered her voice. "Let's think about this. She was better in Torquay. For weeks, she was stronger than you'd seen her in months. You said so yourself. That wasn't merely sea air. Something here, in London, is making her worse."

Bron opened his eyes and stared at his aunt, tears falling down his face. "What are you saying?"

"I'm not certain," she said. "But it's more than fatigue. The doctor's too blind—or too comfortable—to see it. We need another opinion."

Grandmama's cane struck the floor with a firm tap. "I know just the man. Charles Howard of St. Thomas's. No society peacock, but a physician with sense."

Bron nodded. "Please send for him. I'd be grateful."

Lena looked back at Eleanor, watching the fragile rise and fall of her chest—the faint rhythm of life refusing to yield. *Lord, give us wisdom to find what's wrong, and strength to make it right.*

Outside, people celebrated one woman's long reign, but within the quiet house on Cavendish Square, they needed God's healing hand for another woman, just as cherished.

⁕

The new physician arrived late that evening—the advantage to having a dowager countess on the premises.

Dr. Howard was a lean, gray-haired man with keen blue eyes and a brisk manner. He wasted no time in examining Eleanor, questioning Bron as he did. Bron hovered close by, arms folded, watching as the man worked. Howard spoke little, but his gaze was sharp, his movements deliberate.

When he uncorked the tonic bottle resting on the bedside table and held it to the light, the air shifted.

"How long has she been taking this?" the doctor asked.

"Several months," Bron answered. "Prescribed by her regular physician, Dr. Marchand."

"Do you know who prepares it?"

"The apothecary on Brook Street, I believe."

Howard's brows drew together. He replaced the cork and set the bottle aside. "Her pulse is weak, but not failing. What did Dr. Marchand say?"

"He's been calling it chronic gastric inflammation," Bron replied. "But today, he declared her heart was failing."

"Has she been complaining of nausea, vomiting?"

Bron nodded. "Nausea, yes, and extreme fatigue."

Howard covered Eleanor back up with her blanket. "She's fighting something slow. I'll have this mixture tested at the hospital. If I'm right, it's not gastric inflammation at all, Mr. Jeffers. The problem is that I believe something is being added to her medicine, maybe even her food." He looked up and narrowed his eyes. "Deliberately."

Bron's throat tightened. "You think she's being poisoned?"

"I think it's likely. Arsenic, most probably—administered in small, steady doses. Weeks, perhaps longer."

Lena gasped softly.

Augusta's cane fell to the floor. "Heaven preserve us."

Howard pointed to the bottle. "Remove every bottle, every vial, every powder she's been given. Let no one give her anything to consume without your supervision. I'll let you know as soon as I have the results from the laboratory."

Once the doctor had gone, Bron paced the bedroom, while Lena and Augusta spoke in hushed tones.

"Who would do such a thing?" Lena asked, her voice tight.

"Someone close," Augusta said grimly. "Someone with access to her medicine."

"Or her meals," Lena added. "It might not be confined to the tonic."

Bron gave a low, humorless laugh. "That narrows it to everyone under this roof."

He moved to the mantel, gripping it until his knuckles turned white. "Cook prepares her tray. The butler carries it upstairs. The apothecary delivers the tonics. Marchand prescribes but never mixes the ingredients himself."

"Do you think any of them capable?" Lena asked.

Bron closed his eyes and pinched the bridge of his nose. He couldn't think of anyone who would hold a grudge against his sweet aunt. Unless ...

"There's one," Bron said after a pause. "A maid—Nora, I think her name was. My aunt dismissed her in the spring for theft."

"What did she steal?"

"A diamond necklace and matching bracelet. Eleanor didn't even call the police." He raked a hand through his hair. "Said the girl reminded her of herself at that age—too proud for her own good."

Lena's brow furrowed. "If she's been gone since spring, could she still be involved?"

"She's a beautiful young woman, if I remember correctly," Augusta said, "I'm sure she could convince some lovesick man who prepares or delivers Eleanor's tonic to add poison to the bottle."

Bron swallowed hard. "Then she'll wish she hadn't."

The words hung in the air like smoke.

Augusta's voice softened. "Bronley, you can't carry this alone. Let Scotland Yard handle it."

"I'll alert them first thing tomorrow. But tonight, I'll start questioning the staff. And I'm hiring a guard to stand outside her door whenever I'm not here."

Augusta gave a curt nod of approval.

He turned toward the bed again, his chest tight. "I've spent my life believing the world could be made right if one only worked hard enough—if laws were strong enough, arguments sound enough to hold back evil. But this—" His voice cracked. "This I can't reason with."

Lena stepped closer. "Then you'll have to trust the One who knows the answer."

He looked up at her, managing the faintest wry smile. "I should have guessed that would be your answer."

"It's the only one that's ever worked for me."

For a long moment, he said nothing, watching the candlelight flicker over Lena's face. Then, very quietly, "I wouldn't know where to start."

"Anywhere," she said. "Start with what's true. You love her. You want to help her. God will work with your prayers."

Her words lingered. Something inside him—some iron certainty he'd built his life upon—gave way. He wasn't sure he liked the feeling, but it was honest.

"I'll try," he said hoarsely.

Augusta rose from the settee, bracing on her cane. "You'll do more than try. You'll fight, same as she would for you."

Bron nodded, throat thick. He moved to the window, stirring the curtain aside. Beyond the glass, the city glowed through a misty haze. Somewhere, a carriage rattled by and laughter spilled into the street—cruelly out of place in this house of sickness and fear.

When he turned back, Lena's head was bowed, hands

clasped. At first, he thought she was merely exhausted. But, no, she was praying—silently, fervently.

She lifted her head and met his gaze.

Bron had always imagined himself as everyone's rock. Dependable. Strength under pressure. But he had nothing on Lena.

He realized in that moment that he wanted more than to just court this woman.

He loved her.

And once this mess was fixed, he wanted to spend the rest of his life with her.

TWENTY-FOUR

For the first time since Dr. Howard delivered his diagnosis, Bron felt the stillness press in, like the pause before a verdict.

They'd spoken with every servant who worked in Eleanor's employ. Most were retainers she'd had for at least fifteen years. The housekeeper had been with her since Bron was a boy.

Much to his chagrin, most of the interviews produced nothing of value—only a chain of polite answers with the undercurrent of fear of losing employment. The only deviation from the pattern came from a young footman whose heart had clearly been left behind when the beautiful, but thieving, maid was dismissed.

Bron questioned him gently at first, then firmly, but the lad's gaze slid away each time. The only confession he offered was of sentiment, not guilt.

"She weren't a thief. Not really, sir," he'd muttered, cheeks coloring. "She'd been desperate. You can think what you like, but she didn't hate Lady Langston for what happened. She were glad she weren't arrested and thrown in prison."

When the last servant had retreated down the corridor,

Augusta gave her verdict. "Call me naive, but I believe every-one's story. They all love Eleanor too much to hurt her. And they appreciate the more than fair wages and treatment they receive at Langston House."

Bron pinched the bridge of his nose. "Are we certain about the young footman? Is he hiding something?"

"I don't think so," Lena said from her chair near the window. She'd been silent through most of the questioning, taking notes in her neat, deliberate hand. Now she looked up, the lamplight turning her hair to copper. "You're too close to this, Bron. You've done what you can. Let Scotland Yard handle the rest."

Every instinct bristled. Letting go felt like negligence.

Lena rose and put a hand on his forearm. "You don't have to do everything."

He wanted to argue—wanted to remind her that failing to act, trusting Eleanor's doctor, had cost them all—but the gentleness in her expression stopped him.

Augusta tapped her cane once against the parquet floor. "Sound advice, and in the meantime, she will not sleep in this house."

Bron glanced toward the stairwell. "She's finally resting. We'll wake her with the move."

"We'll wake her now in order that she not wake up dead," Augusta said crisply. "We don't know *who's* trying to kill her, so until we do, she'll stay at Akethorpe House." She waved an imperious hand. "Lena, pack a small case. Bron, summon a carriage."

Bron's mouth curved despite himself. "Have we voted on this?"

"In this case, sense wins out over democracy," Augusta replied, turning toward the door.

Lena rose and smoothed her skirt. "She's right. Eleanor

will be better off, and we'll all rest easier knowing she's out of this house."

Bron exhaled, conceding.

Lena went off to do Augusta's bidding, and he made sure the Langston carriage was ready and waiting.

They roused Eleanor gently. She woke disoriented but compliant. Within minutes, they were on their way to the Akethorpe townhouse, hooves striking a steady rhythm as the horses moved through Mayfair.

Bron watched Eleanor's eyelids flutter and he turned to Lena. "I pressed that footman too hard. It did nothing but make him dig in."

"I think you were perfect," she said. "I honestly believe he doesn't know anything."

The carriage rattled along Grosvenor Street.

Lena placed a hand, warm and reassuring, on his. "You could pray, you know. I have been. It helps."

His stomach clenched, and he glanced out the window at the fading light. "I've tried. I can't find the right words." He gave a snort of derision. "Isn't that strange? The Merry Barrister at a loss for words."

"Just say what's in your heart. It doesn't have to be eloquent," Augusta said from the opposite seat without opening her eyes. "It works for me."

Lena startled. "I didn't know you prayed, Grandmama."

"Of course I do, dear. I'd have never made it to the other side of my marriage without it."

Bron found himself half smiling. He didn't intend to pray after that, but the thought formed anyway. *Lord, if I'm missing something, please show me. Make it plain. I can't figure this out on my own.*

The rest of the ride passed in near silence. When they reached Akethorpe House, the footmen assembled, offering quiet assistance. Within a quarter hour, Eleanor was settled in a cool upstairs room that faced the park.

Only when the door closed on her calm breathing did Bron let the tension in his shoulders ease. He joined the others in the drawing room below, where Augusta had gathered the household as if convening a council of war.

Her family wore that mixture of concern and helplessness that often accompanies a crisis. Lena explained everything in detail, missing nothing.

She would have made an excellent barrister.

He'd no doubt she'd make an excellent wife.

✦

Lena watched Bron pace back and forth by the window. She'd never seen him so taut with frustration, the restless energy of his mind most likely turning over all the possibilities for why his aunt lay sick in a bedroom on the floor above. The lines at his temples, faint before, seemed to have deepened in the past day, and an ache stirred inside her.

The desire to comfort him was nearly unbearable, yet one she could not indulge.

Papa and Myra, side by side on a settee, conversed in hushed tones while Grandmama left the room to check on Eleanor and Alix.

Alix, who adored Eleanor—and still wasn't speaking to Lena—kept vigil by Eleanor's bed.

Tris tried several times to get everyone to eat the food that Cook had prepared for them, but no one wanted to eat, least of all Lena. Her stomach felt queasy at the thought of someone wanting Eleanor dead.

They all jumped when Grandmama strode into the room.

"Eleanor is comfortable," she informed the group. "I've

sent word to Dr. Howard that we've moved her here. I'm sure he'll contact us when he has definitive answers on the contents of that tonic."

"Thank you," Bron said as he turned from the window. "I—"

His words were cut short when Wilkins appeared in the doorway.

"Lord and Lady Haverleigh."

Grandmama's brow lifted. "Show them in."

"Wait!" Bron moved from the window and spoke to Grandmama in a low tone. "Let's not tell them about what Dr. Howard said. The fewer people who know, the better."

Although Bron's suggestion was surprising, Lena agreed. Until they knew for certain what was going on, they couldn't take the chance that the Redgraves might inadvertently warn the culprit.

Cedric entered first, concern etched into his features, followed by his wife, gorgeous in a visiting toilette of pale lilac.

"We went by Langston House and were directed to you," Cedric said, bowing slightly to Grandmama.

Grandmama's expression didn't flicker. "Lady Langston is resting comfortably." She gestured to the one vacant settee in the room. "Please, have a seat."

"What did the staff tell you?" Bron took the chair closest to Cedric's side of the settee.

Cedric shrugged. "Only that Eleanor had taken a turn for the worse. I don't understand why you moved her here."

"I can't watch her every moment," Bron said as he ran a hand through his already disheveled hair. "But I don't trust the staff to do so either." He tipped his head to Grandmama. "Lady Akethorpe and her family have kindly offered to keep vigil."

"Is it that bad?" Cecilia asked, her hand flying to her throat.

"We don't know," Bron answered. "We're getting a second opinion."

Cedric fell back against the settee cushions. "How horrible!"

Lena wanted to applaud Bron's performance. Cedric and his wife appeared quite convinced.

"It's very distressing. Hopefully, another doctor will know how to help her," Cedric said, then placed a hand on his wife's arm. "Are you all right, Cecilia? You've grown very pale."

She pressed a hand to her temple. "Forgive me. I feel a dreadful headache coming on."

Cecilia's distress appeared genuine—yet something in her voice rang hollow. Practiced. Perhaps Lena had become too suspicious, but after all that had unfolded, even politeness felt suspect.

Cedric cleared his throat. "We'll leave you all now. You must be exhausted." He turned to Bron. "You'll, of course, keep us informed?"

"Of course," Bron said.

"Please give Eleanor our warmest wishes for recovery," Cecelia said in a soft voice.

Wilkins showed the Redgraves out, and Lena let out a breath she hadn't realized she was holding. A faint scent of Cecilia's lilac perfume lingered in the air, cloying and artificial.

"Good riddance," Grandmama said with a thump of her cane.

Tris tilted her head. "You don't like them, Grandmama?"

"Just her. I don't know what Cedric sees in that woman," Grandmama answered. "Oh, she's beautiful, to be sure. As beautiful as an ice queen and spending Cedric's money like it's water."

Lena didn't know anything about Lady Haverleigh's spending habits, but she agreed with Grandmama. The woman was as cold as ice. And a superb actress.

TWENTY-FIVE

The next morning, Lena rose early, as did everyone else in the house.

Each had taken turns staying with Eleanor, who slept soundly through the night.

When Bron said he was headed to Scotland Yard, Papa offered to go with him, saying that two witnesses were more official than one.

"Quite right," Grandmama added. "Best to have it all recorded properly."

Myra gazed at Papa, worry on her brow. "James, what about breakfast? You should eat something."

Papa pecked her on the cheek. "We won't be long, dear. The sooner we alert the police, the better."

"Take my phaeton," Grandmama instructed Bron. "It's smaller and will get you there faster."

Bron clapped his hands on his legs and rose. "Thank you, Augusta."

Myra gave Papa a watery smile. "Be careful."

Once the men had departed, Grandmama insisted that everyone remaining should eat something. When no one moved to the tea tray, she poured the tea herself. "Here, drink up," she said as she passed Myra a cup. "Don't worry so. It wrinkles the brow." She smiled for the first time all day. "Try faith instead—it's far more flattering."

From the window, Lena caught a glimpse of Bron standing on the walk beside Papa, heads bent in earnest conversation. A shiver of admiration—and fear—passed through her. *Lord, heal Eleanor back to her former self. And help Bron find whoever is behind this, before something else happens.*

The minutes ticked by, turning into an hour, then two.

Lena paced in front of the drawing room window, wearing the carpet thin in the same spot Bron had the night before. Evidently, they both thought more clearly while moving than sitting still.

Tris sat near the window, stitching a hopelessly uneven vine on an embroidery pattern Grandmama had insisted she try. Their grandmother didn't know Tris well enough—she wasn't the homemaker type. Myra sat beside her with a romance novel open on her lap, pretending to read. At the writing desk, Grandmama attended to overdue correspondence, her pen scratching steadily in defiance of the worry that shadowed them all.

Lena's hands itched for occupation, but every attempt at reading came to nothing. The words blurred. She'd finally set the book aside and had returned to the window.

"They've been gone almost three hours," Myra said, breaking the silence. "Surely it doesn't take that long to file a report."

"They probably insisted on speaking to the senior officer and then waited for him to find the time," Grandmama replied. "I'm certain they'll be back any moment."

Her reassurance might have worked—had the door not

opened that very instant. A pale-faced Wilkins entered, hesitating only long enough to find Grandmama.

"Beg your pardon, my lady. We've received word there's been an accident."

The world contracted to that single sentence. Grandmama rose from her chair like a woman of thirty. "Who?"

"Mr. Jeffers, Mr. Dennison, and Clark, who drove them. A carriage accident on Adam's Row. They've been taken to a doctor's office on Davies Street." He glanced at Myra. "I know nothing more."

For a moment, the room froze. Then Myra began to cry in a ragged, gulping way.

Grandmama took a deep breath. "If everyone would kindly avoid fainting until we reach the doctor's," she announced, "I'd be most obliged."

She turned to Wilkins. "Have my carriage brought round," she ordered.

Lena's heart thudded as the room seemed to spin. *Lord, let them be alright.* She swiftly exited the room and marched into the hall, collecting gloves, hat, and reticule. Her pulse beat against her temples, a furious rhythm of fear and prayer intertwined. She had known worry before, but this was different—sharper—lodged beneath her ribs where reason couldn't reach.

Alix appeared at the front door when she heard the commotion, and they all piled into the carriage, Augusta instructing Wilkins to watch after Eleanor and not leave her side.

By the time they reached the doctor's office, Myra was wailing about being too young to bury yet another husband until Augusta promised to bury her first if she didn't quiet down. The threat worked.

Tris and Alix sat beside Lena, both pale and quiet. Myra

whispered a psalm under her breath, mangling the order of the verses, but every word held a note of supplication.

The streets were crowded with carriages at this time of day, and when they reached Davies Street, Lena almost jumped out and ran the rest of the way. Shopkeepers poked their heads out of their doors at the sight of the Akethorpe crest on the carriage door, stopping outside a local doctor's office.

Lena alighted first, not waiting for help from the carriage driver. She opened the office door, and the smell of antiseptic hit her nose. Her eyes searched the empty front room. A nurse emerged from the back.

"I'm James Dennison's daughter," Lena told her.

"Ah, yes. Come with me."

She led Lena back to a large room occupied by three patients.

Papa's arm was cradled in a sling, and the driver had bandages on both hands. Bron, seated near the window, sported a white bandage around his head.

From behind Lena, Myra gasped.

Bron looked up at the sound, eyes clearer than Lena expected, though the skin around them was gray. "Before you scold," he said hoarsely, "we're all alive."

That was all it took. Lena's knees softened, and she had to grip the back of a chair to keep them from buckling.

"My dear sirs," Augusta said, sweeping forward. "When I told you to take the phaeton, I didn't mean it as an invitation to test its stability."

Papa managed a crooked smile. "It seems we've proven it remarkably sound. On the way back from Scotland Yard, a cat darted across the street. Our horse startled and bolted. The driver managed to keep us upright—by some miracle—but the ride was rough for a few minutes."

"It was by the grace of God that we survived," the driver interjected. "Begging your pardon, my lady, but it weren't me at all. Reins snapped clean through. Naught kept us from the paving but Providence itself."

Lena looked from one face to another, the words *grace of God* reverberating in her mind. She moved toward Bron without thinking. "You're hurt," she said quietly.

"It looks worse than it is," he assured her, though the drying blood along his temple said otherwise. "The doctor insisted on stitches. *I* almost insisted he wait until Augusta could critique his technique."

Augusta sniffed. "I've no interest in a man's needlework."

"They're fortunate," the nurse said, addressing the room. "Mr. Clark escaped with burns to his hands from the reins. Mr. Jeffers had a deep gash to the forehead—and received six stitches, and Mr. Dennison's dislocated shoulder was reset cleanly."

Myra's hand flew to her mouth. "Dislocated? Oh, James!"

He grinned. "It sounds far worse than it felt."

Bron's brow lifted. "Liar."

Papa shrugged.

The brief exchange broke the tension, and Lena allowed herself a breath of relief. She stood quietly at Bron's side, her gaze tracing the line of the wound. "You could have been killed," she whispered.

"I wasn't driving, obviously," he said slowly. "And I wasn't in control, no matter what I told myself. The horse ran mad, and all we could do was hold on." He paused, his right hand touching his bandage. "I prayed—if only for a moment—and then everything stilled. The wheel caught, but the carriage stayed upright. I've seen men die from less. This—this was mercy undeserved."

Lena's throat tightened. She ached to put her arms around him. "Mercy isn't about deserving," she said softly.

He looked at her then, really looked, as if the words brushed something raw. "No," he said at last. "It isn't."

The nurse cleared her throat. "If the ladies will excuse us, the doctor wants to look at them once more before allowing them to go home. It won't be but a minute."

Grandmama nodded once. "Do what you must."

Myra followed her to the front room, with Tris, Alix, and Lena close behind.

Unable to sit still, Lena leaned against a wall. She could hear the low murmur of Bron's voice answering questions, the occasional hiss of breath when the doctor must have touched a sore spot. Through the window came the distant clatter of carriage wheels, the cry of a street hawker, and a church bell striking the hour.

Alix, who'd been quiet, moved to Lena's side and leaned close. "Papa is fine," she whispered.

"Yes, I know."

"But this isn't just about Papa, is it? The worry about Bron almost brought you to your knees."

Lena couldn't answer.

Alix gave a small, knowing smile. "Then, for what it's worth, you have my blessing. Court him, love him—whatever you mean to do."

Lena felt something inside her settle. "Thank you for that. I'm sorry you had to find out about my feelings the way you did."

Alix looped her arm through Lena's. "I'll get over it. I'm a grown woman now."

Yes, she was.

The driver's words echoed in Lena's mind. *By the grace of God.*

She didn't doubt it for a second.

Twenty-Six

The lamps at Akethorpe House burned low, their glow soft and steady against the carved paneling. The rest of the household slept or pretended to. Bron had tried to sleep—he'd stretched across the vast bed, stared at the ceiling, counted the minutes until dawn—but his thoughts refused to still.

He left the room and wandered the corridors until the light spilling from the library door pulled him in.

Inside, Lena sat curled in one of Augusta's reading chairs, a book open in her lap. The lamplight caught her hair like a flame subdued behind glass.

She looked up at once. "Is Eleanor all right?"

"I'm sorry. I didn't mean to alarm you. I couldn't sleep and saw the light from the library." He leaned a shoulder against the doorframe, weary in body, restless in mind.

"It's fine." The corners of her mouth softened. "You're worried about Eleanor. Is that why you couldn't sleep?"

He nodded. "Much like you, I suspect." He crossed to the window and stood staring at the moon. "Scotland Yard was a disappointment. The inspector said they'd make inquiries 'when possible.' Translation, never."

He turned, pacing a few steps. "If Eleanor returns to her home—which she'll insist upon doing as soon as she's able—and she falls so ill she never recovers, they'll call it misfortune and move on. I won't wait around for that to happen." He raked a hand through his hair. "I'm going to find whoever's behind this myself."

Lena closed her book. "You sound very sure that you can."

"I have to be. It's my responsibility." His tone came out sharper than he meant. "I won't sit idle while someone wants her dead."

Her gaze held his, calm but unyielding. "You're a barrister, Bron, not a detective. You can't do this alone." She stood, setting the book aside. "You said yourself whoever did this is patient and clever. Don't be proud—be practical. Call Harry tomorrow. I imagine he's good at sorting through details and people. And my family will help. We should all put our heads together."

He studied her, the quiet authority in her tone. "You make it sound like a council of war."

"Maybe it is," she said. "Regardless, you shouldn't fight this by yourself."

He sighed and rubbed a hand along the back of his neck. "I don't like involving others when the threat is mine."

"When it involves someone we love—and each of us loves Eleanor—it's a threat to us all."

Bron nodded and met her eyes, and for a moment neither of them looked away. There was so much to say—so much bottled inside him that he feared he might burst and ruin the moment.

Instead, he cleared his throat. "I've spent my life trying to prove I had control over it. That I didn't need anyone telling me what to do or when to do it." He chuckled. "Comes from having an overbearing ..." He shouldn't blame his faults on his parent.

Lena tilted her head, her eyes steady on his face. "Go on," she said quietly.

He moved closer and stretched out his hand to take hers. It amazed him how small and delicate it felt. "I'm trying to loosen that grip. Bear with me."

With her free hand, Lena traced his scraped knuckles. "It's not me you need to ask this of."

Deep in his soul, he knew she was right.

"So, let me get this straight. Prayer before action. Gratitude in everything."

She smiled faintly. "You're getting the hang of it."

"At gratitude?"

"At faith."

He studied her, the gentle conviction in her tone. "I keep trying to reason my way to answers. It doesn't seem to work that way."

"It doesn't," she said softly. "Faith is built on surrender."

He let that settle. Surrender had never been his talent. But perhaps it was time to learn.

A gust rattled the windowpanes, carrying the scent of impending rain. Funny, he hadn't noticed storm clouds earlier in the day.

How easily life itself could tilt—how close they had come to losing Eleanor.

Augusta's clock chimed somewhere down the corridor.

Lena blinked and dropped his hand. She stepped back as if just realizing how close they stood.

A shame, that, because he was on the verge of leaning in and tasting her lips.

Bron sighed, crossed to the sideboard, and poured two small sifters of brandy, bringing one to her. "To calm the nerves," he said.

"Yours or mine?"

"Both."

Lena accepted the glass, fingers brushing his. The touch was small, accidental, but the warmth of it lingered.

She went to the window and stared out at the night. The moon bathed her in a soft light, and the breath caught in his chest. At that moment, she was the most beautiful woman he'd ever seen. Both inside and out.

He moved to stand beside her. "I told myself I'd never broach this subject again, but I have to, or I'll never forgive myself." Bron turned toward her so that he could see her reaction. "Is there any chance you can stay in England longer?" He paused, but before she could reply in the negative, he added, "I know my life is in upheaval right now, but I believe it will right itself soon, Lord willing." He let out a small chuckle. "If you don't stay, you may find me on your doorstep in Philadelphia."

She turned from the window but stared at the glass in her hands instead of looking at him. "I think Alix and I are on the mend." She inhaled a deep breath. "I'd like to see where this ... thing between us could lead, if that's what you're saying you want." When she looked up, her eyes roamed his face.

"Yes, that's what I want. More than anything." His voice was steady. He'd never felt more sure of anything in his life.

A tentative smile touched her lips. "I think I'll stay in England a while longer. If nothing else, then to help you solve this problem with Eleanor. I doubt Grandmama will object."

He placed his glass on the windowsill and brought a hand to her face, brushing the back of it across her cheekbone. "I'm looking forward to moving past this whole affair with Eleanor, seeing her better, and spending the rest of the time focused solely on you."

Turning her head slightly, she kissed his hand, the touch as light as a feather.

"You realize Augusta would forbid this entire conversation if she heard it," he whispered.

"She's asleep," Lena said. "And for once, so is Myra. We have the house to ourselves."

Bron tilted his head, the corner of his mouth lifting. "Dangerous words."

"Perhaps," she said, rising to her toes and placing a brief—much too brief—kiss on his lips. "But after today, I think we can risk a little danger."

He could have argued—should have—but she was closer now, close enough that he could smell the faint trace of rose water from her hair. Her gaze held his, calm and unwavering.

Their lips came together, and a rush of emotion washed over him, unlike anything he'd ever experienced before. Not in a courtroom. Not even in a motorcar race.

Much too soon, she pulled away and stepped back. "I'd better go."

Thank goodness one of them had a level head.

He nodded but put a hand on her arm before she could turn away. "Thank you," he said quietly.

"For what?"

"For praying for me."

For a long moment, neither spoke. The silence wasn't empty. It was full—of relief, of gratitude, of unspoken understanding.

At last, she squeezed his fingers gently. "You should rest, Bron."

"I will," he said, not moving. "Eventually."

When she finally slipped from the room, he moved to the chair she'd sat in earlier. The sweet scent of rose water lingered. Staring at the window, he said a prayer of gratitude.

Lost in thoughts of what his future might hold, he remained in the library until the first light of dawn kissed the horizon.

The scent of tea and freshly baked pastries hung in the air as Lena entered the Akethorpe dining room—Grandmama's so-called *war room*. The lower curtains were drawn, but midday light filtered through the high windows, striking dust motes into motion above the polished table.

After a brief discussion that morning, Grandmama had agreed with Lena's plan to work with Bron on catching Eleanor's would-be killer and was not at all surprised that Scotland Yard hadn't deemed the matter urgent.

Seated at the head of the table, Grandmama presided like a general, every inch of her posture declaring authority. Bron, Papa, Myra, Tris, and Alix sat arrayed before her, the stillness in the room like the pause before a storm. Lena took her seat beside Bron, feeling the tension crackle beneath the quiet.

It was odd how quickly their lives had shifted—from afternoon teas and garden parties to whispered suspicions and poison. She'd grown up reading novels filled with danger, but living through it was far less romantic.

The clock struck twelve as Wilkins appeared in the doorway. "Lord Henry Tisdale, my lady."

Harry swept off his hat and handed it to Wilkins, who quietly retreated, closing the door behind him.

"I received your message, Lady Akethorpe. It sounded intriguing to say the least."

"Thanks for coming," Bron said, rising to shake Harry's hand. His eyes swept the room. "I think you know everyone here but James Dennison and his second youngest daughter, Beatrice." He tipped his head. "James and Tris, this is Lord Henry Tisdale. Harry to friends."

Papa stood and shook Harry's hand.

"Nice to meet you," Tris said, already reaching for her

notebook. No deferential treatment for his title—just brisk acknowledgment.

Lena hid a smile. She'd heard Tris say more than once since her arrival in London, "I'm an American. I don't have to curtsy to anyone and certainly don't have to call them *my lord.*"

So she didn't.

Harry grinned and took the seat beside Alix. "All right, then. Tell me what I've walked into."

Bron explained quickly—Eleanor's sudden collapse, the tonic, the doctor's confirmation. Harry listened, brow furrowing deeper with each detail.

"How is Lady Langston now?" he asked.

"Recovering," Augusta said. "Slowly."

"And Scotland Yard?"

"They're too busy keeping the streets safe during the Jubilee to be of use," Bron said.

"Then I'll ask something else." Harry leaned forward, forearms on the table. "Have you considered that this might be connected to the motorcar sabotage?"

The room fell silent.

"What motorcar sabotage?" Lena asked, looking sharply at Bron.

His expression darkened. "I had my car examined after the accident with Max. The steering had been tampered with. I thought it might be a competitor."

"I think it was the first attempt." Harry's tone was gentle but grave.

Lena's pulse skipped. "An attempt on your life?" The words felt strange on her tongue, like something out of an adventure novel.

"It's possible," Bron admitted.

"You're still entered in that race next week?" She was afraid she already knew the answer.

"I am."

Her chair scraped against marble flooring as she shifted. "You can't take that risk—not now." She tried to keep her voice steady, but fear coiled beneath every word.

Augusta cleared her throat. "Let's keep to the facts. Lord Henry?"

"We're looking for someone with access and motive. That brings us to Cedric Redgrave."

"Cedric?" Bron's jaw tightened, and he shook his head emphatically. "No! He's like a brother!"

Lena's heart sank. Harry and Cedric were his closest friends. To suspect one of them would wound him deeply.

"If Lady Langston *and you* were gone," Harry continued, undeterred, "Cedric inherits the Suffolk estate tied to the barony—land, income, and title intact. His own finances are, by all accounts, precarious."

"Then he's capable of hiring someone. Or bribing an apothecary," Papa said, his hand flexing on the table.

"A new bottle of tonic arrives each week," Augusta said.

"Meaning," Myra said slowly, "it could be the courier—or anyone trusted to handle the delivery."

Lena tried to steady her breathing. The logic fit too neatly. But when she pictured Cedric's easy smile, she couldn't reconcile it with malice.

"Cedric might not be capable of it," she said, "but his wife could be."

Alix gasped. "Lady Haverleigh? She's so beautiful! And so attentive to Eleanor."

Lena nodded. "She's also clever, ambitious, and always at Eleanor's side. When I took their photograph that afternoon at Langston House, she looked at me as though she'd seen a ghost. I didn't realize it then, but she was frightened I'd noticed something."

Bron turned toward her. "You're certain?"

"As certain as I can be without proof. It wasn't irritation I saw—it was fear."

Harry tapped his pencil. "Lady Haverleigh could have arranged everything—and she's here often enough to slip the poison in the tonic herself."

"If her husband's fortune is collapsing," Augusta said, her eyes narrowing, "she would do whatever it takes to secure their position."

"Eleanor first," Bron said, voice low. "Then me."

The calm way he said it made Lena's heart lurch.

Papa nodded grimly. "Then we must catch her before she tries again."

"Not through the Yard," Bron said. "If we warn them, she'll vanish behind her husband's title before they even lift a pen."

Harry's gaze sharpened. "Then we set a trap—something to make her move again, but on our terms."

They didn't need just courage. They needed cunning. "What if word spreads that the doctor says Eleanor is fading fast?" Lena suggested quietly. "If Lady Haverleigh believes she's nearly dead, she'll shift focus to Bron."

Augusta's eyes gleamed. "Good thinking. We'll use her impatience against her."

"And the motorcar," Bron said. "If she thinks I'm distracted—too concerned about Eleanor to guard it—she may try to sabotage it again. It would be the easiest way to eliminate me."

Harry nodded. "Let's make sure everyone knows your racing car is currently at your coach house, giving her an excellent opportunity to do just that."

Tris lifted her pencil. "I want to help."

"Excellent, we'll take all the help we can get," Bron said. "And we need the news of both Eleanor's failing health and my upcoming race to spread quickly."

Myra brightened. "Leave the gossip to me. I'll tell Mrs. Chalmers next door that poor Lady Langston won't survive the week and that Mr. Jeffers is self-absorbed enough to take his machine out anyway. The story will spread faster than influenza."

"You've found your vocation, Myra," Augusta smirked.

"I suppose," Myra said, smiling. "If it's for a righteous cause."

Papa glanced at Harry. "We'll arrange shifts to watch your motorcar. Two men at all times."

Lena looked up, startled. "You mean to catch them in the act?"

"Exactly," Harry said. "We could also use photographic evidence. Your camera would help. We'll set it near a window facing the coach house. If the saboteur thinks they're unseen, they'll act more boldly."

"I can adjust the exposure," Lena said. "Cover the flash with red paper so it won't give us away."

Augusta looked pleased. "Then the pieces are in place. The house will look preoccupied—Bron at the motorcar, Eleanor *dying* upstairs, servants in disarray. Our serpent will think the garden safe to cross."

The plan settled over them, as fragile as spun glass.

Settling back in his chair, Bron exhaled slowly. "I'll be the bait, then."

Unease flickered behind his steady tone. He was trying to sound practical, but Lena could see the tension in his jaw.

"You don't have to pretend this doesn't worry you," she said softly.

"I'm not pretending," he replied. "I'm simply trying to make peace with it. Learning to not do everything on my own." He gave her a faint smile. "As per your instruction."

She tried to smile back. "You're improving at this, you know."

"At obedience?"

"At trust."

That earned her a long, quiet look that said more than either dared.

Augusta's voice broke in from the doorway. "If you two have finished mooning, the rest of us would like to save a life or two."

Lena pulled back, cheeks burning. "Yes, Grandmama."

The dowager swept away, satisfied.

As the others filed out—Myra already plotting her rumor, Papa discussing patrols with Harry—Lena lingered beside Bron.

"Promise me you'll be careful," she urged.

"I'll try."

"Try harder."

He gave a soft laugh, though his eyes didn't leave hers. "Yes, Miss Dennison."

A mixture of fear and resolve settled in her chest.

Tomorrow, if God willed it, they would see justice done.

TWENTY-SEVEN

Maybe they'd miscalculated.

Bron ran a hand through his hair in frustration.

Maybe the would-be murderer wouldn't try to get to him through his motor car, like they had before.

Awake since dawn, he'd gone down to the coach house at the back of his Kensington home and waited.

It was all he could do at this point.

The Jeffers Motorworks prototype gleamed in the center of the coach house, every polished bolt and brass fitting catching the light from the high windows. It looked ready to race. Ready to kill him if someone tampered just right.

He paced the narrow aisle between the workbenches, hands shoved in his pockets, trying not to imagine what the next twelve hours might bring. The trap was set. Word of his race to test the new vehicle had made its rounds through Mayfair. Myra's talent for gossip had ensured that everyone who mattered—and quite a few who didn't—knew that Bron Jeffers meant to drive, despite his aunt's "declining health."

All they needed now was for the saboteur to take the bait.

Harry had divided them like chess pieces across the property. He and James were stationed in the gardener's shed with a view of the coach house doors. Tris had commandeered a guest room, her notebook and spyglass in hand, scribbling timestamps each time someone passed through the yard.

Lena watched from the window of Bron's study, camera set and ready, turned just so. She had an eye for angles, she'd said, and he trusted her instincts more than any calculation he could make.

That was new for him.

Bron rolled his shoulders as he stood in the shadows inside the coach house. Once the saboteur snuck in—and they'd decided they would allow him to—Bron would be the closest, and the one most likely to bring the culprit down.

He checked the clock on the wall. He'd never been good at waiting. Yet here he was, forced to sit still while the minutes crawled, and danger refused to show its face.

Outside, sunlight spilled over the courtyard, bright and merciless. He could hear the distant rattle of a cart, the whinny of a horse, the faint call of church bells. Ordinary sounds, all of them, which somehow made the waiting worse.

He stared at the car. How easily something beautiful could become a weapon in the wrong hands.

The side door creaked open behind him, and Harry slipped in, closing it quietly.

"Any movement?" Bron whispered.

"None," Harry whispered back. "Either our quarry is patient, or our rumor hasn't reached the right ears."

"It reached all of London," Bron said dryly. "Give it time."

"You're wound tight." Harry crossed his arms, studying him.

"I prefer to think of it as alert."

"That's one word for it." Harry slowly shook his head. "You'll need to rest at some point."

"I'll rest when this is over."

Harry sighed, and before Bron could respond, a faint rustle—like fabric brushing against wood—sounded from outside. Harry's gaze shot toward the window. "There."

A shadow moved along the side of the building.

"Signal James," Bron whispered, and his pulse quickened.

Harry nodded once and slipped away.

Bron moved to the narrow gap between the workbench and wall, his breath shallow, the old instincts stirring—those same instincts that had always guided him when the world blurred past at thirty miles an hour. Everything narrowed to sound and motion. The creak of the outer door, the quiet movement of someone who wanted to remain unnoticed.

A hooded figure moved to stand beside the motorcar, moving with the hesitance of guilt.

Bron stayed perfectly still.

The intruder crouched beside the car, pulling something from a coat pocket. The faint glint of metal caught the light.

A spark of anger flared in Bron's chest. *Not again.*

He took one step forward, then another, as silent as he could.

The saboteur unscrewed a bolt on the steering linkage—exactly where the first "accident" had originated, but by a different method.

Bron moved and caught the man's arm before the wrench could strike again. "That's enough," he said firmly.

The intruder gasped, jerking back, almost pulling Bron's arm out of its socket—but Bron's grip was iron. The hood slipped, revealing a narrow face Bron didn't recognize.

The man struggled, eyes wide with terror. "I—let me go—"

"Not a chance." Bron forced him upright. "Who sent you?"

The man's mouth opened and closed.

Harry and James burst through the door, and the man stilled, sagging in defeat.

Bron shook the man's limp form. "Answer me! It will go better for you if you do."

"Lady Haverleigh," the saboteur ground out. "She hired me."

Bron wanted to punch the man. Instead, he asked in a low voice, "Did you try to poison my aunt?"

"I'm not saying anything more."

"Well, you can think about that while we wait for Scotland Yard." Bron pushed him into the tack room and locked the door.

After Harry and James left to hail a policeman, Bron leaned against the workbench, rubbing the ache from his shoulder. His pulse was still thudding, though the danger had passed.

A door creaked overhead, followed by the rush of footsteps on the stairs. Lena and Tris burst through the door.

"Did you get him?"

He nodded. "He said he was hired by Cecelia. She'll deny it, naturally, but I'm sure Scotland Yard will be able to convince him to tell them every incriminating detail."

The knot in his chest began to unwind.

"It's over. You did it." Lena placed her hand on his arm.

He looked down at her, and the words—simple as they were—struck him harder than he expected. "By God's grace, we did it."

He took her hand, and together they stepped into the sunlight.

The lamps in Bron's study burned low, their light washing the room in amber. He stood at the window, a glass of brandy untouched on the table behind him. The streetlights flickered across the wet cobblestones below.

He should have felt triumphant. Instead, he felt hollowed out, as though victory had taken the last of his strength.

"Lord Haverleigh, sir," Prichard said from the doorway.

Cedric stepped inside. His friend looked ten years older than when Bron had last seen him—clothes rumpled, eyes red-rimmed, the swagger gone from his gait.

"Bron," Cedric began, voice low. "They've taken her."

"I know." Bron turned slowly to face his cousin.

"She told me nothing. God help me, I didn't know."

Bron studied him for a long moment. The anger that had burned so fiercely a few days ago was gone, replaced by weary compassion. "You should sit."

Cedric obeyed, sinking into the chair opposite the fire. "I didn't see it—the desperation, the desire for more than I could give her. That I was nothing more than a means to an end. I was too proud to admit there was something wrong, with both my estate and my marriage."

Bron ran a hand around the back of his stiff neck. "You weren't the first man blinded by pride. Or love."

"You believe me, then? That I had no part in it?"

"I do," Bron said simply. "I've seen the kind of man who kills for gain, Cedric. You're not one of them."

Cedric's shoulders sagged with relief. "Thank you."

Bron poured another brandy and handed it over. "Drink. Then tell me what you plan to do."

"I don't know," Cedric admitted as he stared at the floor. "Sell what's left of the estate, perhaps. Settle my debts. Leave England for a time."

Bron nodded. "I'll help you arrange it. We'll clear your creditors quietly before the scandal spreads too wide."

Cedric's head jerked up. "After all this? You'd still help me?"

"You're family." Bron's voice softened. "You were my friend well before either of us even knew what debt was, or that a woman could make a fool of a man. You'll have a chance to rebuild, but only if you take it."

Cedric's Adam's apple bobbed. "I don't deserve it."

"Neither do I deserve the grace I've been given," Bron said. "We all fall short."

The words surprised even him, but they rang true.

"Thank you, Bron." Cedric stood, gripping Bron's hand tightly.

When Cedric left, the silence returned. Bron turned back to the window, watching the rain roll down the pane.

Another knock followed. This time, the visitor wasn't announced.

Father.

Aubron Jeffers looked as composed as ever—silver hair neat, expression inscrutable—but there was a hesitation in his manner Bron had never seen before.

"I heard about Lady Haverleigh," his father said. "A sordid affair."

"Justice, at least, has been served," Bron replied.

His father's gaze drifted toward the window. "And your aunt?"

"Recovering. Stronger each day."

"Good." The earl nodded, then cleared his throat. "I read Scotland Yard's report. It mentioned Lady Haverleigh even tried to use your motorcar against you."

Bron braced himself for Father's disapproval.

"I never understood your fascination with the thing." Father stepped closer. "I thought it reckless—a distraction from a respectable career. But today I wondered if perhaps it's the only thing you've truly believed in that was entirely your own."

Bron was momentarily at a loss for words. "That may be the kindest thing you've ever said about it."

His father's mouth twitched, and he moved to the window, hands behind his back. "I used to have ideals. Wanted to make sure that every man had proper representation. Then I married your mother, God rest her soul, and her fortune gave me more than I could have ever dreamed of. I thought I needed to earn the right to it. Represent our peers to the best of my ability." He turned and faced Bron once more. "But watching you— you've reminded me that decency is its own form of ambition."

Bron blinked, momentarily unmoored. "I wasn't expecting approval."

"Don't mistake it for that," his father said dryly. Then, more quietly, "Only recognition."

They stood in companionable silence, the patter of the rain on the window the only sound in the room.

Finally, Father said, "What will you do now?"

"I've accepted the offer to work with the Legal Aid group, even though I know you're against it. And I'll teach a few law classes in the evening for working students. They deserve the chance Oxford never gave them."

"Both are noble pursuits." His father nodded slowly and then cleared his throat. "I apologize for my earlier reaction at the Garden Party. Somewhere along the way, I'd forgotten why I entered law."

Bron nodded. He wouldn't give his father too much grief over his earlier anger. But while the man was in a capitulating mood, he might as well lay out all his plans. "I still intend to build my motorcar business. There's a future in it—manufacturing, not racing. The next generation will travel farther and faster than we ever dreamed."

His father chuckled softly. "And what of you? Will you still chase speed?"

"No." Bron looked out the window. "I've finally learned the difference between moving fast and moving forward."

His father studied him for a long moment, then said quietly, "Your mother would have liked Miss Dennison."

Bron's head lifted in surprise.

"Eleanor told me about her, and I've watched her since you've been escorting her family around London. Saw her at Buckingham Palace. She seems sensible, intelligent. You've chosen well."

"You're getting ahead of yourself," Bron said, though his voice betrayed him.

"You'll marry her," his father said gently. "You just haven't told her yet."

TWENTY-EIGHT

The sun had begun its slow descent, painting the gardens in honey and rose. The air smelled faintly of damp earth and wisteria, the sweetness of renewal after two days of rain. Lena stood at the terrace balustrade, both hands resting on the cool stone, Alix and Tris beside her.

Tomorrow, Papa, Myra, and Alix would be returning to Philadelphia.

"I'll miss you both terribly," Alix said with tears in her voice.

"I'll be back home before Thanksgiving," Tris reminded her. "And you'll be the toast of Philadelphia society. You'll never notice I'm gone."

Alix sighed. "After everything that's happened here, being the belle of the ball doesn't feel quite so important anymore."

Tris snorted. "Don't tell Myra that."

Lena put an arm around Alix's waist and gave her a light squeeze. "What do you have in mind to keep you busy, then?"

Alix shrugged. "I don't know. I'll figure it out."

"Maybe you could be the second Dennison daughter to attend college," Tris said in a teasing tone.

Hands on her hips, Alix glared at Tris. "Maybe I will!"

College might be good for Alix. It surprised Lena that she hadn't considered that before.

Behind her, the door opened. She didn't have to turn. Bron's step had a rhythm she could now recognize anywhere —purposeful, even when he meant to tread lightly.

"I thought I'd find you all here," he said. His voice held that teasing quality she'd despised when she first met him, but now adored.

She turned and smiled. "Are we that predictable, Mr. Jeffers? How boring for you."

"I prefer *reliably consistent*. And I find it very exciting."

Tris cleared her throat. "Let's go have some tea, Alix."

"But I don't want ..." Alix glanced at Lena.

Lena just shrugged.

Alix laughed and turned to Tris. "How thoughtful of you. I'd love some tea." She turned from the balustrade and moved inside.

Tris didn't follow right away but put a hand on Lena's arm and leaned in close. "Your job as surrogate mother is done," she whispered. "And we all thank you for it from the bottom of our hearts. Now it's time to live your life."

"Thank you," Lena breathed, her heart clenching at the words.

Tris gave Bron a wink and went back inside.

He leaned against the stone railing, hands tucked into his pockets, his hair a little tousled. He looked more himself than she had ever seen him—free of the strain that had shadowed him since their arrival in London.

"Eleanor told me you had a productive conversation with your father," she said.

"That's one word for it." He exhaled, his gaze drifting toward the horizon. "We actually managed to speak without raising our voices. I think that's a first since I was sixteen."

"And?"

"And he admitted he's proud of me." He looked almost incredulous as he said it, then shook his head, smiling. "It only took an attempted murder to get there."

She laughed softly. "Small price to pay."

He studied her, and something in his eyes gentled. "I also spoke with Cedric. He's contrite—genuinely. I told him I'd help manage his estate until he can climb out of debt. He's agreed to work with a steward Eleanor recommended."

"That was kind of you," she said.

"Perhaps. Or perhaps it was the first sensible thing I've done in months."

"I think you've done several sensible things lately."

His lips curved. "Then I'd better be careful. People might start calling me responsible."

"I'll make sure of it," she said, matching his tone.

They fell quiet for a while, watching the last of the light scatter over the manicured hedges. Somewhere beyond the garden, a bird trilled once, twice, then fell silent.

"I wanted to tell you something," Bron said at last. "A decision, actually."

Lena turned to face him fully. "Should I brace myself for a collision?"

"Not this time." He rested his elbows on the railing, shoulders brushing hers. "I've accepted a position with the Legal Aid group. They defend people who can't afford barristers. It's not glamorous work, but it feels right."

Her chest warmed. "That sounds exactly like you."

"Does it?" he asked, sounding almost surprised.

She nodded.

He smiled faintly, touched. "I've also agreed to lecture a few nights a week. Law for those who can't pay Oxford's tuition but still have the mind for it." He paused and shuffled his feet. "And the motorcar business—"

"Oh no," she said with mock alarm.

"—is staying," he finished, amused. "But I'm done with racing. If I'm going to build a future worth keeping, I can't spend it trying to outrun death. I want to design something lasting."

Lena's throat caught at the quiet conviction in his tone. "You have everything mapped out, it would seem."

"I do." He paused. "With you by my side."

Her pulse stumbled. She looked away to hide the smile tugging at her lips. "You're remarkably certain for someone who hasn't even proposed."

Laughing softly, he turned and took her hand. "Miss Helena Dennison, will you do me the honor of being my wife?"

"I think," she said quietly, "that's the most reckless thing you've ever done. We haven't even properly courted yet. What if we don't suit?"

"We suit just fine," he said and bent to kiss the tip of her nose. "But you didn't answer me."

She loved the intoxicating power of making the calm and collected Merry Barrister squirm. "Mr. Jeffers, I'd love to be your wife."

The air between them shimmered, and the garden below swayed gently in the evening breeze, the scent of roses rising on the air.

Lena lifted his hand to her lips and kissed his palm. "If you're going to give up racing," she said, her voice soft but playful, "you'll need a new kind of thrill."

He raised an eyebrow. "And what do you suggest?"

"Children. Lots of them. I want to be a *real* mother. Is that alright with you?"

His thumb brushed across her lips in a slow, deliberate touch that made her heart flutter like a thousand butterflies had taken up residence. "It sounds like fun."

And in that moment—under the first stars of a London evening, with Bron beside her—Lena realized her future would never be dull.

Epilogue

Three months later
Akethorpe Hall, Suffolk, England

Augusta stood at the edge of the great hall with her cane tucked lightly beneath her hand, more out of habit than necessity. Light from hundreds of candles shimmered off the marble floors, and the sweeping garlands of hot-house roses strung between the galleries emitted a heady fragrance. Music swelled, warm and elegant, as Lena and Bron glided past in their first dance as husband and wife.

Lena looked radiant. Not in the ostentatious way London society prized, but with a quiet, settled joy that reminded Augusta achingly of Lena's mother.

"That girl of ours," Myra murmured at Augusta's elbow. "Isn't she beautiful?"

Ours. The word warmed Augusta enough to forget she ought to remain aloof.

"She is," Augusta said. "And quite self-possessed for a bride. I consider that a good omen for the marriage. Hysteria is highly overrated."

Myra laughed softly, her eyes shining. The woman glowed tonight—motherly pride wrapped up in emerald silk. "She was so calm this morning, I wondered if she felt anything at all. Then I saw her step into the church and look at Bron, and—" Myra pressed a hand to her chest. "It nearly undid me."

Augusta allowed herself a small smile. "Bronley Jeffers has that effect on women. Even on our cautious Helena."

"Especially on Helena," Myra replied with a knowing tilt of her head.

Across the floor, Bron drew his wife into a graceful turn. His face was unguarded, brighter than Augusta had ever seen it. For a young man who once hid behind charm and mischief, he now danced like someone who had finally found the place he fit best.

"That boy has rooted himself," Augusta murmured. "I wondered if he ever would."

Myra followed her gaze, her expression softening. "She steadies him. They're so well-matched, aren't they?"

Augusta did not often praise aloud, but tonight was a night for sentiment. "Yes. Better than you and I even imagined." She winked, and Myra blinked, then laughed with delight.

The waltz came to an end, guests applauding. Bron brushed a kiss against Lena's cheek. Lena flushed prettily and whispered something that made Bron look as though the floor itself had turned to clouds.

Augusta's chest tightened—pleasure, memory, and the sting of time all entwined together.

She shifted her cane and looked beyond the couple to the wide terrace, where guests strolled out for a breath of autumn air. "The Walravens seem to be enjoying themselves," she observed. "I must admit, I find them quite agreeable. Uncomplicated. Sincere."

"I'm so glad they were able to come," Myra said, pleased.

"Laura insisted they wouldn't have missed this for the world. Caroline nearly cried when Lena asked her to be a maid of honor."

"Walravens cry?" Augusta arched a brow. "I must mark this historic day."

Myra swatted her lightly with her fan, laughing.

A sudden burst of animated chatter drew their attention. Beatrice was waltzing past with Harry Tisdale, their steps quick and spirited. The two were locked in a heated exchange, neither giving an inch. Tris jabbed a finger at his chest. Harry replied with an affronted hand to his heart. If not for the smiles tugging at both their mouths, one might think murder hovered in the air rather than friendship.

"Oh dear," Myra said. "Should we intervene?"

Augusta shook her head. "Certainly not. Nothing bonds two people faster than a lively quarrel. Besides, I suspect Harry enjoys being contradicted."

Myra eyed them skeptically. "And Tris enjoys contradicting."

"Yes." Augusta's lips curled. "They'll do nicely."

Through the open terrace doors, Alexandra drifted in with the young Ned Walraven at her side, chattering excitedly. Time had softened what once had been the sharp edges of infatuation and disappointment. Augusta made a mental note to commend the girl later. Healing from youthful heartbreak was no small accomplishment.

Myra followed Augusta's gaze. "Alix has grown so much this year."

"She has." Augusta exhaled. It was wonderful to have all her grandchildren at Akethorpe Hall. Well, all but Louise, who was in her fifth month of pregnancy and not well enough to travel. Maybe next year.

The musicians struck up another waltz, couples moving to the floor. Bron offered Lena his arm again, and this time she leaned into him with a reliance Augusta had seldom seen from the girl before.

Myra clasped her hands. "They look so happy."

"They are," Augusta said quietly. "Truly."

And with that, a settling peace slipped into her bones, as though the very air affirmed what her heart already knew. Lena—steady, dutiful, self-sacrificing—had finally laid down the weight she'd carried since childhood. She was allowed to be cherished now. Allowed to begin her new life.

Myra touched her arm. "What do you hope for them? Bron and Lena?"

Augusta watched as Bron whispered something into his wife's ear—something that made her laugh, her head tipping back in an unmistakably unguarded way.

"For them," Augusta said, her voice steady and sure, "I hope for a life marked by courage. Love requires it. Faith requires it. And they have both."

Myra nodded, thoughtful. "And for yourself?"

Augusta hesitated. She had not considered that question in years—even decades. But tonight, with her house full of life and love, she allowed herself the self-reflection in which she so seldom indulged.

"For myself," she said slowly, "I hope to see what becomes of all of them. These young people ... they've revived something in me." She let her gaze sweep the hall. "I should like to see it bloom."

Myra's hand pressed warmly over hers. "You will."

The orchestra eased into a final, lilting refrain. On the dance floor, Bron gathered Lena close, her head resting briefly against his shoulder. The sight of them—complete, anchored, beginning their new life—brought a quiet ache to Augusta's heart.

Her daughter would have been proud.

The music faded into applause as the pair slipped toward

the terrace, Bron's hand at the small of Lena's back in a gesture so natural it seemed ordained.

Augusta stood straighter, her cane tapping lightly against the floor. "Come, Myra. Let's have some champagne. We have many reasons to celebrate tonight."

Myra beamed. "Yes. We certainly do."

Perfect, Series Book 1 - After being jilted by his fiancée and denied a promotion, William Walraven must open Denwall Department Store's first New York emporium before Christmas—or lose his chance at leading the family empire. He can't afford distractions ... until he saves Ivy King from being run over by a beer wagon and finds himself drawn to the determined bookseller whose shop his new store may destroy.

Ivy is fighting to keep her family bookshop alive. Falling for a charming department store heir is the last thing she needs—especially when a mysterious attack on Will's brother pulls her into a dangerous investigation and into Will's world.

Unexpected, Series Book 2 - Zella Capp has built her life on independence and a carefully guarded secret. When she's tapped to lead Denwall Department Stores' new fashion publication—a role that could launch her dream career—she's thrust into Philadelphia high society, where every whispered rumor carries weight.

Bert Walraven prefers accounting ledgers to society events, but he can't ignore the unexpected pull he feels toward the vivacious Zella. When anonymous threats and sabotage endanger the magazine, Zella and Bert are drawn into a dangerous game that threatens her career, his heart, and the truth she's terrified to reveal.

Schooled in Love, Series Book 4 - Rule-breaking American heiress Beatrice Dennison discovers a rare book in her uncle's library, and promptly enlists buttoned-up Cambridge academic Lord Henry Tisdale to help translate it. But the centuries-old text holds more than history—it draws them into long days in the library, whispered discoveries, and a partnership neither expected.

As they work side by side, Tris and Harry must face meddling family, academic rivals, and an attraction that threatens everything they've built on opposite sides of the Atlantic. When the truth about the manuscript forces a choice, they must decide whether to cling to their carefully ordered lives—or risk everything for a once-in-a-lifetime love.

Worth Keeping, Series Book 5 - **Coming August 2026!**

ALSO BY KIMBERLY KEAGAN

Heart of Hope (Hearts of the West multi-author series)

Visit www.KimberlyKeagan.com for a free download of her latest novelette.

A Note From Kimberly

Thank you for reading Lena and Bron's story. Your support means the world to me! If you enjoyed the book—and I hope you did—please take a quick minute to leave a review. It doesn't have to be long—just a sentence or two telling what you liked about the story.

This book wouldn't exist without the support of so many wonderful people. I'm especially grateful to my family and friends—your love and support keep me going; to my talented editor, Lynne Pearson; and to my incredible critique partners, Christina, Denise, and Marie. Most of all, I give thanks and glory to my Lord and Savior, Jesus Christ.

Let's stay in touch, lovely reader! A great place to connect is through my *Puddings & Pages* email newsletter. As a thank-you, new subscribers receive a complimentary e-book. You can sign up at KimberlyKeagan.com.

A Free Novelette

Go to KimberlyKeagan.com and download a free novelette with a subscription to Kimberly's email list.

Or scan the QR Code to subscribe.

ABOUT THE AUTHOR

Kimberly Keagan's love of romance novels started at the age of thirteen. Whenever she could get away with it, she ignored her chores in favor of a story she couldn't put down.

By God's grace, she married her own handsome hero, and together they raised two wonderful children. She earned a degree in accounting and enjoyed a career in investor relations, writing financial reports and press releases. Terrific jobs, but not very romantic.

Now, she's following her dream of writing her own historical romance stories with strong heroines, swoon-worthy heroes, and quirky secondary characters.

When not reading or writing, Kimberly likes to bake, garden, watch sports, and research her family tree.

Connect with Kimberly at: www.kimberlykeagan.com.

Risky Business

Copyright © 2026 by Kimberly Keagan

KimberlyKeagan.com

Published by Ventana Publishing, LLC

All rights reserved. No part of this book may be reproduced in any form or by any electronic or mechanical means, including information storage and retrieval systems, without written permission from the author, except for the use of brief quotations in a book review.

This is a work of fiction. Names, characters, businesses, places, events, locales, and incidents are either the products of the author's imagination or used in a fictitious manner. Any resemblance to actual persons, living or dead, is coincidental.

All scripture quotations are taken from the King James Version of the Bible.

All hymn lyrics as found in the public domain.

Cover design by Ventana Publishing LLC

Paperback ISBN: 979-8-9925731-4-5

www.ingramcontent.com/pod-product-compliance
Lightning Source LLC
Chambersburg PA
CBHW051316130726
47987CB00004B/1825